## Lords of Disgrace

*Bachelors for life!*

Friends since school, brothers in arms, bachelors for life!

At least that's what *The Four Disgraces*—Alex Tempest, Grant Rivers, Cris de Feaux and Gabriel Stone—believe. But when they meet four feisty women who are more than a match for their wild ways these Lords are tempted to renounce bachelordom for good.

Don't miss this dazzling new quartet by

**Louise Allen**

Read Alex Tempest's story in
*His Housekeeper's Christmas Wish*
Already available

And Grant Rivers's story in
*His Christmas Countess*
Out now!

Look out for Cris's and Gabriel's stories, coming soon!

## Author Note

I have been exploring the world of four quite disgraceful lords who are each going to meet their match in the very unexpected love of their life.

This time it is the turn of Grant Rivers, a man with dark secrets he keeps close to his heart. He is a man in a hurry, for very pressing reasons, but even he can't abandon someone in even more of a hurry than he is—a young woman giving birth in a ruined bothy on the wild Scottish Borders on Christmas Eve. Grant finds himself with more than he bargained for as a result of helping Kate Harding, and I hope you enjoy finding out as much as I did what happens when two people with secrets find themselves forced to learn to trust and rely on each other.

You can meet Grant before his encounter with Kate in *His Housekeeper's Christmas Wish*, the story of the first Lord of Disgrace, Alex Tempest. The next two—Cris de Feaux and Gabriel Stone—are yet to come.

# HIS CHRISTMAS COUNTESS

Louise Allen

First published in Great Britain 2015
By Mills & Boon, an imprint of HarperCollins*Publishers*
1 London Bridge Street, London, SE1 9GF

Large Print edition 2016

© 2015 Melanie Hilton

ISBN: 978-0-263-26287-2

Our policy is to use papers that are natural, renewable and recyclable
products and made from wood grown in sustainable forests.
The logging and manufacturing processes conform to the legal
environmental regulations of the country of origin.

Printed and bound in Great Britain
by CPI Antony Rowe, Chippenham, Wiltshire

**Louise Allen** loves immersing herself in history. She finds landscapes and places evoke the past powerfully. Venice, Burgundy and the Greek islands are favourite destinations. Louise lives on the Norfolk coast and spends her spare time gardening, researching family history or travelling in search of inspiration. Visit her at louiseallenregency.co.uk, @LouiseRegency and janeaustenslondon.com.

## Books by Louise Allen

## Mills & Boon Historical Romance

### *Lords of Disgrace*

*His Housekeeper's Christmas Wish*
*His Christmas Countess*

### *Brides of Waterloo*

*A Rose for Major Flint*

### *Danger & Desire*

*Ravished by the Rake*
*Seduced by the Scoundrel*
*Married to a Stranger*

### **Stand-Alone Novels**

*From Ruin to Riches*
*Unlacing Lady Thea*
*Scandal's Virgin*
*Beguiled by Her Betrayer*

### *Silk & Scandal*

*The Lord and the Wayward Lady*
*The Officer and the Proper Lady*

### **M&B special release**

*Regency Rumours*

## Mills & Boon Historical *Undone!* eBooks

*Disrobed and Dishonoured*
*Auctioned Virgin to Seduced Bride*

Visit the Author Profile page
at millsandboon.co.uk for more titles.

# Chapter One

*December 24, 1819—the Scottish Borders*

Becoming pregnant had been so easy, so catastrophically simple. An unaccustomed glass of champagne, a little unfamiliar flattery, a night made for romance, a careless, innocent tumble from virtue to ruin.

Somehow that ease increased the shock of discovering just how hard giving birth to the baby was. *It is because I'm alone, I'm cold, I'm frightened,* Kate told herself. *In a moment, when these pains stop, I will feel stronger, I'll get up and light the fire. If I can get there, if there is any dry kindling, if I can strike a spark.*

'Stop it.' She spoke aloud, her voice echoing in the chill space of the half-ruined bothy. 'I *will* do it because I have to, because I must, for the baby.' It was her fault her child would be born in a tumbledown cottage on a winter's day, her miscalculation in leaving it so late to run away, her lack of attention that had allowed the pickpocket to slip her purse from her reticule in the inn yard, leaving her penniless. She should have gone to the workhouse rather than think she could walk on, hoping for some miracle and safe shelter at the end of the rough, muddy road.

Her mind seemed to have turned to mush these past few days. Only one message had been clear: *get away before Henry can take my baby from me.* And she would do anything, anything at all, for this child, to keep him or her safe from her brother's clutches. Now was the time to move, while there was still some light left in the lowering sky. She tried to stand up from the heap of musty straw, but found she could not. 'Pull yourself together, Catherine Harding. Women give birth every day and in far worse conditions than this.' Beyond caring that she was reduced to a lumbering, clumsy creature, she managed to get on to her hands and knees and began to crawl towards the hearth and the broken remains of the fire grate.

The weakness caught her before she could move more than a few feet. It must be because she had eaten so little in the past day and night. Shaking, she dug her fingers into the dirt floor and hung on. She would gather a little strength in a moment, then she could crawl nearer to the cold hearth. Surely giving birth could not take much longer? Learning some basic facts of life would be far more useful to young women than the art of watercolours and playing the harp. Learning the wiles of hardened rakes and the consequences of a moonlit dalliance would be even more valuable. Most of all, learning that one could not trust anyone, not even your closest kin, was a lesson Kate had learned too late.

If the mother she could not remember had survived Henry's birth… *No.* She caught herself up before the wishful thinking could weaken her, before the haunting fear of what her own fate might be overwhelmed her. She was still in the middle of the floor. How much time had passed since she had thought to light the fire? Hours? Only minutes, from the unchanging light. Kate inched closer to the hearth.

Something struck a stone outside, then the sound of footsteps muffled by the wet turf, the snort of a horse and a man's voice.

'This will have to do. You're lame, I'm lost, it is going to snow and this is the first roof I've seen for the past ten miles.' English, educated. Not an old man, not a youth. *Hide.*

She backed towards the heap of straw, animal instinct urging her to ungainly speed. A plank table had collapsed, two legs eaten through by rats or damp, and she burrowed behind it, her breath sobbing out of her lungs. Kate stuffed her clenched fist into her mouth and bit down.

'At least water's the one thing we're not short of.' Grant Rivers dug a broken-handled bucket from the rubbish heap outside the tumbledown cottage and scooped it into the small burn that rushed and chattered at the side of the track. His new horse, bought in Edinburgh, twitched an ear, apparently unused to forming part of a one-sided conversation.

Grant carried the bucket inside the part of the building that had once been a byre. The place was technically a but and ben, he supposed, one half for the beasts, one half for the family, the steaming animals helping them keep warm through the long Border winters. There was enough of the heather thatch to provide some shelter for the horse and the dwelling section had only a few holes in the roof, although the window and door had long gone. At least the solid wall turned its back on the prevailing wind. He could keep warm, rest up. He was enough of a doctor to know he should not ignore the headache and the occasional dizziness, the legacy of that near-fatal accident a week ago.

He lifted off the saddle, took off the bridle, used the reins as a tether and tipped the bag of oats from his saddlebag on to a dry patch of ground. 'Don't eat it all at once,' he advised the chestnut gelding. 'It's all you are getting until we reach civilisation and I've half a mind to steal it to make myself porridge.'

There was sufficient light to see by to clean out the big hooves and find the angular stone that had wedged itself into the off-hind. It looked sore. He gave an apologetic rub to the soft muzzle that nudged at him. His fault for pressing on so hard even though he suspected he would be too late for his grandfather. At least he had been able to send a letter saying the things in his heart to the man who had brought him up, letting the old man know that only dire necessity kept him from his side at the end.

He must also get back to Abbeywell for Charlie's sake. It was the last place he wanted to be, but the boy needed his father. And Grant needed his son, for that matter. Christmas was always going to be grim this year with his grandfather's health failing, but he had not expected it to be this bad—him bedridden in Edinburgh with his head cracked open and Charlie left with his dying great-grandfather. Grant had planned to leave the city on the seventeenth, but that was the day a labourer, careless with a scaffolding plank in the New Town, had almost killed him. As soon as he had regained consciousness and realised he was incapable of walking across the room, let alone travelling, Grant had written the letter. The reply had arrived from the steward two days ago. His grandfather was not expected to last the night.

Grant had hoped to be with his son for Christmas Day. Now he might make it by that evening if the gelding was sound and the weather held. 'We'll rest up, let the bruising ease, stay the night if I can get a fire going.' Talking to a horse might be a sign of concussion, but at least it made something to listen to beyond the wind whistling up this treeless Borders valley. Unless the direction of that wind changed, the makeshift stable was fairly sheltered and the horse was used to Scottish weather.

And for him the familiar cold of a Northumberland winter was no different from this. There was enough rubbish lying about the place to burn. He'd make a fire, pass the night with the food in his saddlebags and allow himself a dram from his brandy flask, or the illicit whisky James Whittaker had handed him as they'd parted yesterday in Edinburgh's New Town.

*Something in the air...* Grant straightened, arms full of dry scraps of wood, nostrils flaring to catch that faint rumour of scent. Blood? Blood and fear. He knew the smell of both from those weeks in the summer of '15. The killing days when he and his friends had volunteered to join the fight to see Napoleon finally defeated. The memory of them had saved his neck in more than a few dark alleyways before now.

A low moan made the horse shift uneasily. The wind or an animal? No, there had been something human in that faint wisp of sound. He did not believe in ghosts and that left someone hurt or in distress. Or a trap. The cottage would make a handy refuge for footpads. 'Eat your oats,' he said as he eased the knife from his left boot and tossed the armful of wood away.

He moved fast as the wood clattered into the far corner, then eased around the splintered jamb of the inner door to scan the single living room. It was shadowed and empty—a glance showed a broken chair, a scattered pile of mouldy straw, an over-turned table, cobwebs and shadows. There was that soft, desperate sound again and the scent of fear was stronger here. Caution discarded, he took three strides across the earth floor and pulled away the table, the only hiding place.

It did not take several years of medical training to tell him that he was looking at a woman in labour and a desperate one at that. Of all the medical emergencies he might have confronted, this was the one from his nightmares. Literally. Her gaze flickered from his face to the knife in his hand as she scrabbled back into the straw.

'Go away.' Her voice was thready, defiant, and there was blood around her mouth and on the back of the hand resting protectively on the mound of her belly. She had bitten her fist in an attempt to muffle her cries. His stomach lurched at the sight. 'One step more and I'll—'

'Deposit a baby on my boots?' He slid the knife back into its sheath, made himself smile and saw her relax infinitesimally at his light tone. When he tossed his low-crowned hat on to the chair, exposing the rakish bandage across his forehead, she tensed again.

'Don't be ridiculous.' Her voice was English, educated, out of place in this hovel. She closed her eyes for a moment and when she opened them again the effort to stay focused and alert was palpable. 'This baby is *never* coming out.'

'First one?' Grant knelt beside her. 'I'm a doctor, it is going to be all right, trust me.' *There's two lies to begin with—how many more will I need? I'm not qualified, I've never delivered a baby and I have no idea whether* anything *is going to be all right.* He had, however, delivered any number of foals. Between theoretical knowledge, practical experience of female anatomy and years of managing a breeding stables, he would be better than nothing. But this child had better hurry up and get born, because he was trapped here until it was.

He was big, he was male, he seemed to fill the space and the bandage made him look like a brigand, despite the well-made clothes. But his quiet confidence and deep, calm voice seeped through Kate's cramped body like a dose of laudanum. *A doctor.* The answer to her incoherent prayers. There were miracles after all.

'Yes, this is my first child.' *And my last. No amount of pleasure is worth this.*

'Then let's get this place warm.' He shrugged

out of his greatcoat and laid it over her. It smelt of horse, leather and man, all strangely soothing. 'We'll make you more comfortable when the fire's lit.'

'Dr...?'

'Grantham Rivers, at your service. Call me Grant.' He poked at the grate, went into the stable and came back with wood. His voice was pleasant, his expression, what she could see of it, unruffled, but she could sense he was not happy about this situation. For all the easy movement, the calm voice, he was on edge.

'Grantham?' Incredible the effect of a little warmth and a lot of reassurance, even if she was all too aware that her rescuer wished he was somewhere else entirely.

'I was conceived there, apparently, in the course of a passionate wedding night at the Bull Inn.' He was striking a flint on a steel cupped in his palm and surrounded by some sort of tinder. It flared up and he eased it into the wood, nursing the flame with steady, competent hands. 'It could have been worse. It might have been Biggleswade.'

She had never imagined laughing again, ever, at anything. Her snort of amusement turned into a moan as the contraction hit her.

'Breathe,' he said, still tending the fire. 'Breathe and relax.'

'Relax? Are you mad?' Kate lay back, panting. Breathing was hard enough.

'No, just male and therefore designed to be unsatisfactory at times like this.' His mouth curved into a smile that she could have sworn was bitter, but it had gone too fast to be certain. 'What is your name?'

Caution resurfaced. She was at his mercy now. If he were not the good man he appeared to be, then there was nothing she could do about it. Her instincts, sharpened by the desperate need to protect her baby, told her to gamble and trust him. But with her life, not with her secrets. Should she lie about her name? But that would serve no purpose. 'Catherine Harding. Miss,' she added as an afterthought. Might as well be clear about that. 'My friends call me Kate.'

Dr Rivers began to break the legs off the table and heap the pieces by the fire. Either it was very rotten or he was very strong. She studied the broad shoulders flexing as he worked and decided it was the latter.

'Where's the baby's father?' He did not seem too shocked by her situation, but doctors must be used to maintaining a neutral front, whatever their patients' embarrassing predicaments.

'Dead.' That *was* a lie and it came without the need for thought. Then, hard on the heels of the single word, the wariness resurfaced. This man seemed kind and promised to help her, but he could still betray her if he knew who she was. And, almost certainly, if he knew what she had been part of. He was a gentleman from his voice, his clothes, his manner. And gentlemen not only helped ladies in distress—or she hoped they did—but they also stuck together, protected each other against criminal conspiracies.

'I'm sorry about that.' Grant Rivers laid the tabletop on the earth floor, heaping up the drier straw on it. He was asking her something. She jerked her mind back to dealing with the present. 'Have you any linen with you? Shifts, petticoats?'

'In my portmanteau. There isn't much.' It had been all she could carry.

He dug into it, efficiently sorting through. A nightgown went on one side, then he began to spread linen over the straw, rolling her two gowns into a pillow.

'Dr—'

'Grant.'

'You are very efficient.' A contraction passed, easier than before. He was making her relax, just as he had said.

'I had a short spell in the army. Even with a batman, one learns to shift for oneself. Now, then.' He eyed her and she felt herself tense again. 'Let's get you into something more comfortable and on to this luxurious bed.' It was getting darker and she could not read his expression. 'Kate, I'm sorry I'm a man, I'm sorry I'm a complete stranger, but we have got to get you into a nightgown and I have got to examine you.' He was brisk, verging on the impatient. 'You're a patient and just now you can't afford to be shy or modest.'

*Think of the baby,* she told herself. *Think of Grant Rivers as a guardian angel. A Christmas angel, sexless, dispassionate. I have no choice but to trust him.* 'Very well.'

He undressed her like a man who knew his way around the fastenings of women's clothing. *Not sexless, then.* She was out of her stained, crumpled gown and underclothing before she had time to be embarrassed. He'd placed the nightgown so it had caught a little warmth from the fire and soon she was into that and on to the bed, sighing with relief at the simple comfort of it, before she had the chance to realise her nightgown was up around her waist.

'There, we just place this so.' Grant swung the greatcoat over her. 'Now a light, something hot to drink. Lie back, concentrate on getting warm.'

Kate watched from between slitted eyes as he built up the fire, brought in a bucket of water and set it by the hearth. He lit a small lantern, then dipped water into a mug, adding something from a flask balanced on a brick by the flames, and washed his hands in the bucket. His actions were rapid, yet smooth. *Efficient* was probably the word. A man who wanted to get things done and who wouldn't waste time. A man who was forced to wait on this baby's schedule. Both his efficiency and, strangely, his impatience were reassuring. She was seeing the essence of this man.

'Where did the lantern come from?'

'I carry one in my saddlebags. I'll just find something else for water. We'll need a fair bit before we're done. Luckily the last occupants were fairly untidy and there's a promising rubbish heap outside.'

He ought to seem less than masculine, coping so handily with domestic tasks, but he merely appeared practical. Kate studied the broad shoul-

ders and narrow hips, the easy movement, the tight buckskin breeches. She never expected to feel the slightest flutter of sensual need for a man again as long as she lived, but if she did, purely theoretically, of course, Grant Rivers was more than equipped to provoke it. He was definitely very—
'*Ooh!*'

'Hang on, I'll be with you in a minute.' He came back in carrying an assortment of pots, water sloshing out on to the floor. He held out his hands to the fire. 'My fingers are cold again.'

*What has that got to do with...?* Kate sucked in an outraged breath as, lantern in hand, he knelt at her feet and dived under the greatcoat tented over her knees.

'It is remarkable how one can adapt to circumstances,' she managed after five somewhat stressful minutes. Incredibly she sounded quite rational and not, as she felt, mildly hysterical.

Grant emerged, tousled but composed, and sat back on his heels, shaking thick, dark brown hair back out of his eyes. He smiled, transforming a face she had thought pattern-book handsome into something approaching charming. 'Childbirth tends to result in some unavoidable intimacies,' he said. 'But everything seems to be proceeding as it should.'

The smile vanished as he took a pocket watch from his waistcoat and studied it.

'How much longer?' She tried not to make it sound like a demand, but feared it had.

'Hours, I should think. First babies tend to be slow.' He was at the fire, washing his hands in yet another container of water, then pouring something from a flask into a battered kettle with no handle.

*'Hours?'*

'Drink this.' He offered the brew in a horn beaker, another of the seemingly inexhaustible contents of his saddlebags. 'I'll get some food in a minute. When did you last eat?'

That needed some thought. 'Yesterday. I had breakfast at an inn.'

Grant made no reply, but when he brought her bread and cheese made into a rough sandwich, she noticed he ate nothing. 'What are you going to eat? This is all the food you have with you, isn't it?'

He shrugged and took a mouthful of the liquid in the horn beaker. 'You need the energy. I can live on my fat.'

He rested his head against the rough stone wall behind him and closed his eyes. *What fat?* With a less straightforward man she might have suspected he was fishing for compliments, but it did not seem to be Grant Rivers's style.

What was he doing as a doctor? She puzzled over him, beginning to slip into a doze now the food was warm in her stomach. He was educated, he had been in the army. There was no wedding ring on his finger—not that there was anything to be deduced from that—and there was an engraved signet on his left hand. His clothes were good. And yet he was riding over the Marches without a servant and prepared for a night of rough living.

A piece of wood slipped into the fire with a crackle, jerking her fully awake again. 'How did you hurt your head?' Was he fleeing from something?

'A stupid accident in Edinburgh. I'd been staying with a friend in the New Town and the place is covered in building sites. Some fool of a labourer dropped a plank on me. I was out cold for a couple of days and in no state to move much after that, but there's nothing broken.'

He closed his eyes and she did the same. She let herself drift off, reassured. She was safe while he was there.

## *Chapter Two*

The night passed with intervals of sleep interrupted by increasing waves of contractions. At some point Kate was conscious of simply abandoning herself to Grant Rivers, to the competent hands, the confident, reassuring voice, the strength of the man. There was no choice now, but her instincts told her this was a good man, and if she was mistaken, there was nothing she could do about it. As time passed, on leaden feet, her trust grew.

She held on to his fingers, squeezing until she felt his bones shift under her grip, but he never complained. He was going to deliver her baby, he was going to save her so she could hold her child in her arms. He was her miracle. She was tired beyond anything she had ever experienced, this was more difficult than she could have imagined and she seemed to have been in this place for years. But it would be all right. Grant Rivers would make it all right.

It was taking too long. Kate was exhausted, the light was dreadful and he had no instruments. He knew full well that if there were complications, he did not have the knowledge to deal with them.

As dawn light filtered through the cobwebbed windows, Grant took a gulp of the neat whisky, scrubbed his hands over his face and faced down the fear. She was *not* going to die, nor was the baby. This time, at this crisis, he could save both mother and child. There was no decision to be made about it, no choice. He had only to hold his nerve, use his brain, and he would cheat death. This time. He stretched, went out to check on the horse, then saw the tree growing at the back of the bothy and smiled.

'Talk to me, Kate. Where do you come from, why are you here, alone on Christmas morning?'

'Not alone.' She opened her eyes. 'You're here, too. Is it really Christmas?'

'Yes. The season's greetings to you.' He showed her the little bunch of berried holly he had plucked from the stunted tree and was rewarded with a smile. *Hell, but she looks dreadful.* Her face was white and lined with strain, her hair was lank and tangled, her eyes bloodshot. She was too thin and had been for some time, he suspected, but she was a fighter.

'How old are you?'

'Twenty-three.'

'Talk to me,' he repeated. 'Where are you from? I live just over the Border in Northumberland.'

'I'm from—' She grimaced and clutched at his bruised hand. 'Suffolk. My brother is a…a country squire. My mother died when he was born, my father was killed in a hunting accident a few years ago. He was a real countryman and didn't care for London. Henry's different, but he's not important or rich or well connected, although he wishes he was. He wanted me to marry well.'

A gentlewoman, then, as he had thought. 'You're of age.' Grant wiped her face with a damp cloth and gave her some more of the warm watered brandy to sip. It should be hot sweet tea, but this was all he had.

She was silent and he guessed she was deciding how much to tell him, how much she trusted him. 'He controls all my money until I marry with his blessing. I fell in love and I was reckless. Naive. I suppose I had a very quiet, sheltered country life until I met Jonathan.' She gave a twisted shrug. 'Jonathan's…dead. Henry said that until I had the baby I must stay at the lodge near Edinburgh that he inherited from an uncle, and then he would… He *said* he would find a good home. But I don't trust him. He'll leave my child at a workhouse or give her to some family who won't love her…' Her voice trailed away. 'I don't trust him.'

It wasn't the entire story. Kate, he was certain, was editing it as she went along. He couldn't blame her. This probably happened all the time, well-bred young women finding themselves in a difficult situation and the family stepping in to deal with the embarrassment, hoping they could find her an unsuspecting husband to take her off their hands later. It was a pity in this case, because Kate, with her fierce determination, would make a good mother, he was sure of that.

He settled back against the wall, her hand in his so he would know when another contraction came, even if he drifted off. He was tired enough to sleep without even the usual nightmares waking him, but Kate's fierce grip would rouse him. How much time was this going to add to his journey? Charlie knew he was coming and he was a sensible boy for his age, but he'd been through too much and he needed his father. *He needs a mother, too.*

There was nothing he could do to hasten things now. He shifted, trying to find a smooth place on the craggy wall, and prodded at the other weight on his conscience, the one he could do nothing about now. Grant had disappointed his grandfather. Not in himself, but in his reluctance to remarry. Over and over again as he grew frailer the old man had repeated his desire to see Grant married. *The boy's a fine lad,* he'd say. *But he needs brothers, he needs a mother... You need a wife.*

Time and time again Grant had repeated the same weary excuses. He needed more time, he had to find the right woman, to get it right this time. He just needed *time*. To do what? Somehow learn to read the character of the pretty young things paraded on the marriage mart? Discover insights he hadn't possessed before, so he didn't make another disastrous mistake? His own happiness didn't matter, not any more, but he couldn't risk Charlie. *I promise,* he had said the last time he parted from his grandfather. *I promise I will find someone.* And he had left for the Continent, yet again.

He neither needed nor wanted a wife, not for himself, but Abbeywell needed a chatelaine and Charlie needed a woman's care.

'What will you do when the baby is born?' he asked, focusing on the exhausted woman beside him.

'Do next? I don't know,' she said. 'I can't think beyond this. There is no one. But I'll manage… somehow.'

*She's not a conventional beauty, but she's got courage, she's maternal.* Time seemed to have collapsed, the past and the present ran together. Two women in childbed, one infant he could not help, one perhaps he would save. But even if he did, nothing would prevent this child being born illegitimate, with all the penalties that imposed.

The germ of an idea stirred. Kate needed shelter, security for her child. Would she make a good governess for Charlie? He pursued the idea around. Charlie had a tutor, he did not need someone with the ability or knowledge to teach him academic studies. But he did need the softer things. Grant remembered his own mother, who had died, along with his father, of a summer fever when he had not been much older than his own son was now. She had instilled ideas about kindliness and beauty, she had been there with a swift hug and a kiss when male discipline and bracing advice was just that bit too harsh.

A mother's touch, a mother's instinct. Kate was not a mother yet, but he sensed that nurturing disposition in her. Charlie didn't need a governess, he needed a mother. Logic said...*marry her.*

What was he thinking? *I'm too tired to think straight, my brain's still scrambled.*

In the stable the gelding snorted, gave a piercing whinny. Grant got to his feet, went to the outer door and peered through the faint mist the drizzle had left behind it. A couple of men, agricultural workers by the looks of them, were plodding along the track beside a donkey cart. He went back inside and Kate looked up at him. Her smile was faint, but it was there. *Brave girl. Are you wishing for the impossible? Because I think it is walking towards us now.*

'We're still in Scotland,' he said, realising that his mad idea was possible to achieve. *Am I insane? Or are those strangers out there, appearing right on the heels of that wild thought, some kind of sign?* 'There are two men, farmers, coming along the track.' *Witnesses.* 'Kate—marry me.'

\* \* \*

*'Marry you?'*

It was hard to concentrate on anything except what was happening to her, anything beyond the life inside that was struggling to be free. Kate dragged her mind back from its desperate focus on breathing, on the baby, on keeping them both alive. She remembered the mix of truth and lies she had told him and stared at Grant.

In the gloom of early-morning light he did not appear to have lost his mind, despite the blow to the head. He still looked as much like a respectable, handsome English gentleman as might be expected after a sleepless night in a hovel tending to a woman in childbed.

'I am not married, I am not promised to another. I can support a wife, I can support the baby. And if you marry me before the child is born, then it will be legitimate.' His voice was urgent, his expression in the morning light intent. He smiled, as though to reassure her, but the warmth did not reach his eyes.

'Legitimate.' *Legitimate.* Her child would have a name, a future, respectability. They would both be safe and Grant could protect her from the results of Henry's scheming. Probably. Kate rode out another contraction, tried to think beyond the moment, re-call *why* she couldn't simply solve this problem by marrying a complete stranger. He could certainly hide her, even if unwittingly. She would have a new name, a new home, and that was all that mattered for the baby.

She was so very tired now, nothing else except her child seemed important. Grant was a doctor liv-ing in the wilds of Northumberland, hundreds of miles from London. That should be safe enough. But why would he? Why would he want her and her baby, another man's child? *Legitimate. We would be hidden.* The tempting words swirled through her tired brain, caution fighting desperation and instinct. 'But there's no time.'

'This is Scotland,' Grant said. 'All we have to do is to declare ourselves married before witnesses— and two are heading this way. Say *yes*, Kate, and I'll fetch them and it will be done.'

'Yes.' He was gone before she could call the words back. She heard his voice raised to hail someone. *Yes, I will do it. Another miracle to go with my good angel of a doctor. A Christmas miracle. He never need find out the truth, so it can't hurt him. What is the term? An accessory after the fact. But if he doesn't know...*

'Aye, we'll help you and gladly, at that. I'm Tam Johnson of the Red House up yonder and this is my eldest son, Willie.' The accent was broad Border Scots. 'You're lucky to catch us. We're only going this way to do a favour for a neighbour.'

There was the sound of shuffling feet outside and Grant ducked back in. 'May they come through now?' Kate nodded and he stood aside for two short, burly, black-haired men to enter.

They seemed to fill the space and brought with them the smell of wet sheep and heather and peat smoke. 'Good morning to you, mistress.' The elder stood there, stolid and placid. Perhaps he attended marriages in tumbledown cottages every day of the week. Beside him the younger one twisted his cap in his hands, less at ease than the man who was obviously his father.

'Good day,' she managed, beyond embarrassment or social awkwardness now.

Grant produced a notebook, presumably from his capacious saddlebags. She wondered vaguely if he had a packhorse out there. 'I assume we need a written record that you can sign?'

'Aye, that'll be best. You'll be English, then? All you both need to do is declare yourselves married.

To each other, that is.' The older Mr Johnson gave a snort of amusement at his own wit.

'Right.' Grant crossed the small distance and knelt beside her, took her hand in his. 'I, Grantham Phillip Hale Rivers, declare before these witnesses that I take you, Catherine—'

'Jane Penelope Harding,' she whispered. He was only a doctor. They did not put announcements of their marriages in London newspapers.

'Catherine Jane Penelope Harding, as my wife.'

Another contraction was coming. She gritted her teeth and managed, 'Before these witnesses, I, Catherine Jane Penelope Harding, declare that I take you, Grantham Phillip...Hale Rivers, to be my husband.'

'We'll write the record outside, I think.'

She was vaguely conscious of Grant standing, moving the Johnsons out of the room, then her awareness shrank to the pain and the effort. Something was happening, something different...

Where was Grant? She listened and heard him, still in the stable.

'Thank you, gentlemen.' There was the chink of coins. 'I hope you'll drink to our health. You'll bring the donkey cart back down here after noon?'

'Aye, we will, no trouble at all.' That was the

older man, Tam Johnson. 'You'll not find it far to Jedburgh now the rain's stopped. You'll be there by nightfall. Thank you kindly, sir, and blessings on your wife and bairn.'

*'Grant!'*

He ducked under the low lintel and back into the inner room. 'I'm here.'

'Something's happening.'

'I should hope so.' He took up the lamp. 'Let's see what this child of ours is doing.'


Grant made her feel secure, Kate thought hazily. Even in those last hectic minutes she had felt safe and when the first indignant wails rent the air he had known just what to do.

'Here she is,' he'd said, laying the squirming, slippery, red-faced baby on her stomach. 'The most beautiful little girl in the world at this minute and very cross with the pair of us by the sound of her.'

Time had passed, the world had gone by somewhere outside the bubble that contained her and the child in her arms. She was conscious of Grant moving purposefully about. At some point he took the baby and washed her and wrapped her up in one of his clean shirts, then washed Kate and helped her into a clean nightgown and wrapped them both up in his coat.

There was something hot to drink, porridge to eat. Perhaps the Johnsons had left food or had come back. She neither knew nor cared. When Grant had spoken to her, asked her if she could bear to travel, she had nodded. He had sounded urgent, so she made herself agree, told herself that he would take care of them and all she had to do was hold her baby safe at her breast.

It was bumpy at first, and her nose, about all that was exposed, was cold, but that was all right because Grant was there. Then they were in his arms again and there was noise and people talking, women's voices, warmth and a soft bed. They must have stopped at an inn to rest.

Kate looked up at him standing over her, looking dishevelled and very tired. And…*sad*? This was the man she had married. It seemed unreal. 'Thank you.'

'My pleasure.' He sounded almost convincing. 'What are we going to call her?'

'Anna, after my mother.' She'd decided that in the course of the bumpy journey. *Anna Rivers. And I am Mrs Rivers now. We are safe and all at the cost of a few lies.* Not little, not white, but she would be a good wife to him, be happy in her modest home. He would never know.

'Anna Rosalind, then, for my mother.' When she looked up, surprised by the possessive note in Grant's voice, he shrugged. 'She's an important small person, she needs at least two names. I've found you a nursemaid. She's used to newborns.' A cheerful freckled face appeared at his side. 'This is Jeannie Tranter and she's happy to adventure into England with us. It isn't far now, only across the border into Northumberland.'

'Oh, good.'

*I wonder whereabouts in Northumberland Grant lives...but it doesn't matter, we're safe now, both of us, hundreds of miles away from Henry, hundreds of miles away from a vengeful earl and the law. We can go anywhere and no one will take her away from me because she belongs to Grant now.* That was all that mattered. *We both belong to him.*

The thought drifted in and she frowned. Her baby had a father, but she had a husband. A man she did not know, a man who had total control over her life, her future.

Something touched her hair and she opened her eyes. Grant was still looking down at them.

She remembered to smile at him, then turned her attention back to the baby.

'I'll take a bath, then I'll be in the parlour if you need me,' Grant said to Jeannie Tranter.

The girl nodded briskly, her attention on the woman and baby in the bed. 'Aye, sir, I'm sure we won't need to disturb you.'

*And that's put me in my place as an unnecessary male.* It had been the same the last time. *Don't think about the last time.* The bathwater in front of the fire was still hot, the pleasure of scrubbing away the grime of the past twenty-four hours or so blissful. He soaped his hair, ducked under and came up streaming, then found he had no inclination to get out. Baths were good places to think.

Grant had dozed a little, then woke without any sensible thinking done at all to find the water cool. He splashed out to dry off and find something from his depleted wardrobe to change into. A childbirth used up an inordinate amount of clean linen.

By the time he was in the private parlour pouring a glass of wine, his legs stretched out on the hearthrug, his brain had woken up. Just what had he done? A good deed? Perhaps, although tying a woman, a complete stranger, to him for life was a risky act of charity. Or was it an entirely selfish act, a gesture to his guilty conscience, as though he could somehow appease his grandfather's shade by doing what the old man had so wanted and thus fulfilling his promise? The uncomfortable notion intruded that he had found himself a wife and a stepmother for Charlie without any effort at court-ship, without any agonising about choices.

*The easy way out? Too late to worry about motives, I've done it now. And the child's a girl, so no need to worry about the inheritance, should it ever arise, God forbid.* He'd married a plain woman of genteel birth with a social-climbing brother who was going to be very pleased indeed when he discovered who his new brother-in-law was. That could be a problem if he wasn't careful. Grant rolled the wine around his mouth as he thought it all through.

Pushing doubts aside, he had someone to look after the household, someone who appeared to be bright enough not to be a dead bore on the occasions when he was at home. And Kate had courage and determination, that was obvious enough. He had a wife and only time would tell if it had been a wise decision or a reckless gamble.

There were fifty miles to cover tomorrow, over moorland and open country. If the roads were good and the weather held, they'd do it in the day and he would be only one day later than he had hoped. The inn had a decent chaise for hire, the stables held some strong horses by the looks of them— and they'd be needed, because there wouldn't be a change to be had until they were over the border. The gelding was sound now, it had only been a bruised hoof.

The rhyme 'For Want of a Nail' ran through his head. In that old poem the loss of the nail meant the loss of the shoe, the loss of the horse and its rider and, eventually, the loss of the battle and a kingdom. Because of his own haste his horse had been lamed, he'd had to stop and he'd gained a wife and child. Grant got up and rang for his supper and another bottle. He was maundering, comparing a disaster to—what? What crazy optimism made him think this marriage between two desperate strangers could be anything *but* a disaster?

# Chapter Three

'Mr Rivers is a very good rider, is he not, ma'am?'

'Hmm?' From her position lying full length Kate couldn't see more than the occasional treetop passing by. 'Is he?'

Jeannie, the nursemaid, stared at her. 'But surely you've seen him riding, ma'am?'

'Yes. Yes, of course. I don't know what is the matter with me.'

'Not to worry, Mrs Rivers. My nana, who taught me all about looking after mothers and babies, she always said that the mother's mind is off with the fairies for days after the birth.'

*My mind is certainly somewhere and I wish it would come back, because I need to think.* Anna was sleeping soundly in the nurse's arms and Jeannie seemed exceedingly competent. The chaise had an extension at the front so that when the wall section below the front window was removed it could be placed in front of the seat to make a bed where a passenger could stretch out almost full length. Kate had slept heavily and although she felt weak and shaky she was, surely, in a fit state to take responsibility for herself. She should be thinking about what she had done and what the consequences would be.

*I have married the man, for goodness' sake! A complete stranger. What is his family going to say?* Grant was persuasive enough, but surely he couldn't convince them that he was the legitimate father of this child by a mother they'd heard nothing about before?

'I want to sit up.' Lying like this made her feel feeble and dependent. Besides, she wanted to see what Mr Rivers—what her husband—looked like on a horse.

Jeannie handed her Anna and helped her sit up. That was better. Two days of being flat on her back like a stranded turtle probably accounted for her disorientation. Kate studied the view from the chaise window. It consisted of miles of sodden moorland, four horses with two postilions and one husband cantering alongside.

Jeannie was a good judge of horsemanship. Grant Rivers was relaxed in the saddle, displaying an impressive length of leg, a straight back and a steady gaze on the road ahead. His profile was austere and, she thought, very English. Brown hair was visible below his hat brim. What colour were his eyes? Surely she should have noticed them? Hazel, or perhaps green. For some reason she had a lingering memory of sadness. But then she'd hardly been in a fit state to notice anything. Or anyone.

But she had better start noticing now. This was her husband. Husbands were for life and she had begun this marriage with a few critical untruths. But they could do Grant no harm, she told herself as she lay down again and let Jeannie tuck her in. There was this one day to regain some strength and get some sleep, then there would be a family to face and Anna to look after in the midst of strangers. But by then she would have her story quite clear in her head and she would be safe in the rustic isolation of the far north of England.

They stopped at three inns—small, isolated, primitive. Jeannie helped her out to the privy, encouraged her to eat and drink, cradled the baby between feeds. Her new husband came to look at her, took her pulse, frowned. Looked at Anna, frowned. Swung back on to his horse, frowned as he urged the postilions to greater speed. What was so urgent? Anyone would think it was life and death.

\* \* \*

'I think we must be here, ma'am.' The post-chaise rocked to a halt. Kate struggled up into a sitting position and looked around. Darkness had fallen, but the house was lit and lanterns hung by the front door. Away from the light, the building seemed to loom in the darkness. Surely this was bigger than the modest home a country gentleman-doctor might aspire to?

She looked for Grant, but he was already out of the saddle, the reins trailing on the ground as he strode up the front steps. The doors opened, more light flooded out, she heard the sound of voices. She dropped the window and heard him say, 'When?' sharply and another voice replied, 'In the morning, the day before yesterday.'

Grant came back down the steps. 'In you come.'

'Where are we?' But he was already lifting her out, carrying her in his arms across to the steps. 'Anna—'

'I have her, Mrs Rivers. I'm right behind you, ma'am.'

'This is Abbeywell Grange, your new home.'

There was a tall, lean man, all in black, who bowed as Grant swept her in through the front door. A butler, she supposed, fleetingly conscious of a well-lit hall, a scurry of footmen. The smell of burning applewood, a trace of dried rose petals, beeswax polish, leather. There were evergreen wreaths on the newel posts of the stairs, the glow of red berries in a jug. She remembered Grant's offering of the holly sprig and smiled. This was an old, loved home, its aura sending messages of reassurance. She wanted to relax and dared not.

'Welcome home, my lord. We are all very relieved to see you. The staff join me in expressing our deepest condolences.'

*Condolences? On a marriage?* Then the whole sentence hit her. 'My lord? Grant, he called you *my lord*. Who are you?'

But the butler was already striding ahead towards the end of the hall, Grant on his heels. 'Master Charles... Lord Brooke, I should say, will be happy to see you, my lord. It has been quite impossible to get him to go to bed.'

'Who is Lord Brooke?' she asked in a whisper as the butler opened the door into a drawing room. A fire crackled in the grate, an aged pointer dog rose creakily to its feet, tail waving, and, on the sofa, a small boy sat up, rubbing his eyes.

'Papa!'

'Charlie, why aren't you in bed? You're keeping Rambler up.' Grant snapped his fingers at the dog. It was obviously an old joke. The boy grinned, then his eyes widened as he saw what his father was carrying.

Grant settled Kate in a deep armchair by the hearthside and Jeannie, with Anna in her arms, effaced herself somewhere in the shadows.

'Charlie.' There was deep affection in Grant's voice as he crouched down and the boy hurled himself into his arms. So, this was why he had been so impatient to get back, this was what the discovery of a woman in labour had been keeping him from. *He has a son. He was married? A lord?* This was a disaster and she had no inkling how to deal with it.

'You got my letter explaining about the accident?' The boy nodded, pushed back Grant's hair and touched the bandage with tentative fingers. She saw his eyes were reddened and heavy. The child had been crying. 'It's all right now, but I'm sorry I wasn't here when you needed me. Then on my way from Edinburgh my horse picked up a stone and was lamed with a bruised hoof, so I lost a day and a night.'

'Great-Grandpapa died on Christmas Eve,' Charlie said. His lower lip trembled. 'And you didn't come and I thought perhaps you'd... Your head... That they'd been lying to me and you were going to...'

'I'm here.' Grant pulled the boy into a fierce hug, then stood him back so he could look him squarely in the face. 'I'm a bit battered and there were a couple of days when I was unconscious, which is why I couldn't travel, but we've hard heads, we Rivers men, haven't we?'

The lip stopped trembling. 'Like rocks,' the boy said stoutly. 'I'm glad you're home, though. It was a pretty rotten Christmas.' His gaze left his father's face, slid round to Kate. 'Papa?'

Grant got up from his knees, one hand on his son's shoulder, and turned towards her, but Kate had already started to rise. She walked forward and stopped beside Grant.

'My dear, allow me to introduce Charles Francis Ellmont Rivers, Lord Brooke. My son.'

Kate retrieved a smile from somewhere. 'I... Good evening, Charles. I am very pleased to meet you.'

He bowed, a very creditable effort for a lad of— what? Six? 'Madam.' He tugged at Grant's hand.

'Papa, you haven't said who this lady is, so I cannot greet her properly.'

'This is Catherine Rivers, my wife. Your stepmama.'

Kate felt the smile congeal on her lips. Of course, if Charles was Grant's son, then she was his…

'Stepmama?' The boy had turned pale. 'You didn't say that you were going to get married again, Papa.'

'No. I am allowed some secrets.' Grant apparently agreed with the Duke of Wellington's approach: never explain, never apologise. 'You have a new half-sister as well, Charlie.' He beckoned to Jeannie and she came forward and placed Anna in his arms. 'Come and meet her, she is just two days old.'

The boy peered at the little bundle. 'She's very small and her face is all screwed up and red.'

'So was yours when you were born, I expect,' Kate said with a glare for Grant over Charlie's head. 'Why didn't you tell me?' she mouthed. *The boy isn't a love child. He's the product of a first marriage. I married a widower. And a nobleman.* She wrestled with the implications of Charlie having a title. It meant Grant was an earl, at least. Which meant that Anna was Lady Anna, and she was—what?

Earls put marriage announcements in newspapers. Earls had wide social circles and sat in the House of Lords. In London.

'There never seemed to be a good time.' Grant gave a half shrug that suddenly made her furious. He should have warned her, explained. She would never have agreed to marry him.

'What is her name?' Charlie asked, oblivious to the byplay. Anna woke up and waved a fist at him and he took it, very carefully.

'Anna Rosalind.' One starfish hand had closed on Charlie's finger. His face was a mixture of panic and delight. 'Would you like to hold her?'

'Yes, please.'

Grant placed her in Charlie's arms.

'Very carefully,' Kate said, trying not to panic. 'Firm but gentle, and don't let her head flop. That's it—you are obviously a natural as a big brother.' She was rewarded by a huge grin. She could only admire Grant's tactics. The surprise of a new baby sister had apparently driven Charlie's doubts about a stepmama right out of his head.

'Grant,' she said, soft-voiced, urgent, as Jeannie helped the boy to sit securely on the sofa and held back the inquisitive hound. 'Who *are* you?'

'The fourth Earl of Allundale. As of two days ago.'

'I suppose that was something else that there was no time to mention?' Again that shrug, the taut line of his lips that warned her against discussing this now.

Her husband was an earl. But he was also a doctor, and heirs to earldoms did not become doctors, she knew that. It was a conundrum she was too weary to try to understand now. All she could grasp was that she had married far above her wildest expectations, into a role she had no idea how to fill, into a position that was dangerously exposed and public. Even in her home village the social pages in the newspapers were studied and gossiped about, the business of the aristocracy known about, from the gowns worn at drawing rooms to the latest scandals. How could the wife of an earl hide away? But Grant had no need to fear she would make a scene in front of his son: unless they were thrown out into the dark, she found she was beyond caring about anything but warmth, shelter and Anna's safety this night.

'You are worn out. Charlie, give your sister back to her nurse and off you go to bed. I'll come and see you are asleep later.' Grant reached for the bell pull and the butler appeared so rapidly that he must have been standing right outside the door. 'Grimswade, can you dispatch Master Charles to his tutor? And you will have prepared my wife's rooms by now, I've no doubt.'

Grimswade stood aside as Charlie made a very correct bow to Kate, then ducked through the open door. 'Certainly, my lord. His late lordship had some renovation work done. In anticipation,' he added.

Grant stilled with his hand on the bell pull. 'Not the old suite?' His voice was sharp.

'No, my lord, not the old suite. The one on the other side of your own chambers. The doors have been changed. One blocked up, another cut through. His late lordship anticipated that you would wish to retain your old rooms even after he had…gone.'

Kate wondered if she would have to stand there all night while they discussed the interior layout of the house. She didn't care where she slept as long as it had a bed, somewhere for Anna, and the roof was not actually leaking.

'Very well. Have you made arrangements for the child and her nurse?'

'Yes, my lord.' Without any change in voice or expression Grimswade managed to express mild affront at the suggestion that he was in any way unprepared. 'My lady, if you would care to follow me.'

*That is me. I am—what? A countess?*

'I'll carry you.' Grant was halfway across the room.

'Thank you, no. Do stay here.' Something, Kate was not sure what, revolted at the thought of being carried. Grant Rivers's arms—her *husband's* arms—were temptingly strong, but she was tired of being helpless and he was altogether too inclined to take charge. She had to start thinking for herself again and being held so easily against that broad chest seemed to knock rational thought out of her brain.

In a daze she managed the stairs, the long corridor, then the shock of the sitting room, elegant and feminine, all for her.

'I will have a light supper served, my lady. The men are filling your bath in the bathing chamber next to the dressing room through there.' Grimswade gestured towards the double doors that opened on to a bedchamber, one larger than she had ever slept in. 'And this is Wilson, your maid.'

'Luxury,' Kate murmured to Jeannie as the butler bowed himself out and the maid, a thin, middle-aged woman, advanced purposefully across the room. 'Too much. This is not real.' Fortunately the sofa was directly behind her as she sank back on to it, her legs refusing to hold her up any longer.

'You're just worn out, ma'am—my lady—that's all.' Jeannie's soft brogue was comforting. With a sigh Kate allowed herself to be comforted. 'It will all come back to you.'

The next hour was a blur that slowly, slowly came back into focus. Firm hands undressing her, supportive arms to help her to the bathing room, the bliss of hot water and being completely clean. The same hands drying and dressing her as though she was as helpless as little Anna. A table with food, apparently appearing from thin air. The effort to eat.

And then, as she lay back on the piled pillows of a soft bed, there was Anna in her arms, grizzling a little because she was hungry, and Kate found she was awake, feeling stronger and, for the first time in days, more like herself.

'We might be confused and out of place,' Kate said as she handed the baby back to Jeannie after the feed, 'but Anna seems perfectly content.'

'You've not stayed here before, then, my lady?'

'No. I'm a stranger to this house.' *And to my husband.* 'Where are you to sleep, Jeannie?'

'They've set up a bed for me in the dressing room, my lady, just for tonight. It's bigger than the whole of the upstairs of our cottage,' she confided with glee. 'And there's a proper cradle for Lady Anna.'

'Then you take yourself off and get some rest now. I expect she'll be waking you up again soon enough.'

The canopy over the bed was lined with pleated sea-green silk, the curtains around the bed and at the windows were a deeper shade, the walls, paler. The furniture was light and, to Kate's admittedly inexperienced eye, modern and fashionable. The paintings and the pieces of china arranged around the room seemed very new, too. Strange, in such an old house. The drawing room, the hallway and stairs had an antique air, of generations of careful choices of quality pieces and then attentive house-keeping to deepen the polished patina.

Kate threw back the covers and slid out of bed. Deep-pile carpet underfoot, the colours fresh and springlike in the candlelight. Grant had reacted sharply when her chambers were mentioned. Interior decoration seemed a strange thing to be concerned about, given the circumstances—surely a new wife who was a stranger, another man's baby carrying his own name, a bereavement and a son to comfort must be enough to worry about. *Another puzzle.*

She moved on unsteady legs about the room, admiring it, absorbing the warmth and luxury as she had with the food earlier, feeling the weariness steal over her again. In a moment she would return to the big bed and be able to sleep. Tomorrow she would think. There was a murmur of voices, just audible. Idly curious, Kate followed the sound until she reached a jib door, papered and trimmed so it looked at first glance like part of the wall it was cut into.

The handle moved easily, soundlessly, under the pressure of her hand, and it swung inwards to show her a segment of another bedchamber. Masculine, deep-red hangings, old panelling polished to a glow, the glint of gilded picture frames. Grant's bedchamber. For the first time the words *husband* and *bed* came together in her mind and her breathing hitched.

On the table beside the door was a small pile of packages wrapped in silver paper. She glanced down and read the label on the top one. *Papa, all my love for Christmas. Charlie.* It was obviously his very best handwriting. Her vision blurred.

Grant's voice jerked her back. He must be speaking to his valet. She began to ease the door closed. 'Thank you for coming by. Tomorrow I'd be grateful if you'd take a look at my wife and the baby. They both seem well to my eye, especially given the circumstances—Kate must be very tired—but I won't be easy until a doctor has confirmed it.'

*Another doctor?* Kate left the door an inch ajar. There was a chuckle, amused, masculine, with an edge of teasing to it. 'It seems to me that you did very well, given that you've never been trained for a childbirth. Or were you, in the year you left Edinburgh?'

'I observed one. I had, thank Asclepius and any other gods that look after inept medical students, studied the relevant sections of the textbooks before I did so and some of it must have stuck. I'd just about reached the limits of my book learning, though, and after the last time—'

The other man made some comment, his voice low and reassuring, but Kate did not register the words. *Grant is not qualified? He is not a doctor.* The embossed metal of the door handle bit into her fingers. *He lied to me.* The irony of her indignation at the deception struck her, which did nothing for her temper.

'I thought perhaps so much experience with

brood mares might have helped, but I can tell you, it didn't,' Grant confessed.

*Brood mares. He thought he could deliver my baby as though she were a foal.*

She heard Grant say goodnight to his visitor as she set foot in his bedchamber. He turned from closing the door and saw her. 'Kate, what's wrong? Can't you sleep?'

'You are not a doctor.' He came towards her and it took only two steps to be close enough to jab an accusing finger into his chest. 'You delivered my baby, you told me not to worry. You fraud!'

## Chapter Four

Grant stepped back sharply, the concern wiped from his expression. 'I have two years of medical training, which is more than anyone else within reach had. There *was* no one else to deliver your baby.'

'You might have told me.' She sat down abruptly on the nearest chair. 'You thought you could treat me like a brood mare.'

'Ah, you heard that. Damn. Look, Kate, you were frightened, in pain, and you hadn't the first idea what to do. You needed to be calm, to conserve your strength. If I had told you I had never delivered a baby before, would that have helped you relax? Would that have helped you be calm?'

She glared at him, furious that he was being perfectly reasonable, when something inside her, the same something that had latched on to those words, *husband* and *bed*, wanted nothing more than to panic and make a fuss. And run away.

Grant stood there, patient—and yet impatient, just as he had been in the bothy. He was good at self-control, she realised. If he wasn't so distracted by grief for his grandfather and worry for his son, she would not be allowed a glimpse of that edginess. And he was right, perfectly right. He had some knowledge and that was better than none. He had kept her calm and safe. Alive. Anna was healthy. Kate swallowed. 'I am sorry. You are quite correct, of course. I am just...'

'Embarrassed, very tired and somewhat emotional.'

'Yes,' she agreed. *And confused. Damn him for being so logical and practical and right, when I just want to hit out at something. Someone.* 'You did not tell me you are an earl.' She had wanted to hide, go to ground. Now she was in the sort of marriage that appeared in society pages, was the stuff of gossip.

Grant ran his hand through his hair. He was tired, she realised. Very tired. How much sleep had he had since he had walked into that hovel and found her? Little, she supposed, and he was travelling with a recent head injury. 'I didn't think it relevant and you weren't in any fit state for conversation.' His mouth twisted. 'My grandfather was dying, or had just died. I was not there and I did not want to talk about it. Or think about it. All I wanted was to get back to Charlie.'

'Were you too late to see your grandfather because of me?'

Grant shook his head and sat down opposite her. It was more of a controlled collapse than anything, long legs sprawled out, his head tipped back, eyes closed. The bandage gave him a rakish air, the look of a pirate after a battle. 'No, I wouldn't have reached him in time, not after the accident in Edinburgh. But even so, there was no choice but to stay with you—he would have expected it himself.'

No, she supposed there hadn't been a decision to make. No one could walk away from someone in the situation she had been in. No decent person, at any rate. She had married a decent man. Her agitation calmed as she looked at him, studied his face properly for the first time. She was thinking only of herself and Anna, but she owed him a debt. The least she could do was to think about his needs. 'I'm sorry. Go to bed. You are worn out.'

Grant shook his head and opened his eyes. They were green, she realised with a jolt, seeing the man and not simply her rescuer. But a warm green verging on hazel, not the clear green of a gemstone under water... 'Soon. I need to look in on Charlie.'

She was not going to exhaust him more by complaining about the fact he had not told her he had been married, that he had a son as well as a title. That could keep until the morning. She was certainly not going to look for any more resemblances to Jonathan. 'I will go back to bed, then. Goodnight.'

There was silence until she was through the jib door. She wondered if he had fallen asleep after all. Then, 'Goodnight, Kate.' She closed the door softly behind her.

'Goodnight, Kate. Goodnight, *wife*,' Grant added in a whisper as the door closed. Perhaps he should have kissed her. Poor creature, she looked dreadful. Pale, with dark shadows under bloodshot eyes, her hair pulled back into a mousy tail, her face pinched with exhaustion and a confusion of embarrassment and uncertainty. He could only hope that when she was recovered and suitably dressed she would at least look like a lady, if not a countess.

He hauled himself to his feet and stripped off his clothes with a grimace of relief. He felt as if he'd spent the past year in them. Naked, he stood and washed rapidly, then rummaged in the clothes press and pulled out loose trousers, a shirt and a robe, dressing without conscious thought. Comfort, something he could catnap in if Charlie needed him to stay and chase away nightmares, these would do. His eye caught the glint of silver paper and he went to investigate. Christmas presents. He picked them up, torn between grief and pleasure.

When he slid quietly into Charlie's room the mounded covers on the bed heaved and a mop of dark blond hair emerged. 'Papa!'

'I had hoped you were asleep by now.' Grant sat on the edge of the bed and indulged himself with a hug that threatened to strangle him. 'Urgh! You're too strong for me.'

Charlie chuckled, a six-year-old's naughty laugh, and let go. He looked up at Grant from under his lashes. 'I'm glad you're home.'

'So am I. I'm sorry I was not here when Great-Grandpapa died.'

'Dr Meldreth took me in to see him. He was very sleepy and he told me that he was very old, so he was all worn out and he wanted to go and be with

Great-Grandmama, so I mustn't be sad when he left. But I am.'

'I know, Charlie, so am I. And we will be for a while, then we'll remember all the good times we had, and all the things we used to talk about and do, and you won't feel so bad. What did you do on Christmas Day?'

'We went for a walk and to church, and then I opened my presents because Great-Grandpapa said I must do so.' He sniffed. 'He gave me his watch. I...I blubbed a bit, but it made me really proud, so I'm glad. And thank you very much for the model soldiers and the castle and the new boots. Then we had Christmas dinner and Mr Gough showed me how to make a toast. So I toasted *absent friends*, for both you and Great-Grandpapa.'

'It sounds to me as if the household was in very good hands with you in charge, Charlie.' Grant managed to get his voice under control, somehow. 'I found my presents—shall I open them now?'

Grant went to retrieve the gifts and they opened them together. His grandfather had given him a miniature of his parents, newly painted, he realised, from the large individual portraits that hung in the Long Gallery. He read the note that accompanied it, blew his nose without any attempt to conceal his emotion and turned to Charlie's gift, which he had set aside.

'This is excellent!' It was a large, enthusiastic and almost recognisable portrait of Rambler, his old pointer dog, framed in a somewhat lopsided, and obviously home-made, frame. 'I will hang it in my study next to the desk. Thank you, Charlie. You go to sleep now. Do you want me to spend the night here?'

'I'm all right now you are home, Papa. And Mr Gough let me talk to him all I wanted. He thought it would be better after the funeral when we can say goodbye again.'

The tutor had proved as sensitive as he had hoped when he hired him. 'You know where I am if you want to come along in the night.' Grant tucked his son in, bent down and gave him a kiss that, for once, didn't have his son squirming away in embarrassment. He seemed to understand and to be taking it well, but he was so young. Grant felt a pang of anxiety through the haze of weariness that was closing in like fog. Perhaps he would sleep without nightmares if he was this tired.

'I didn't know you were going to get married again, Papa.' The voice from under the blankets was already drowsy.

*Neither did I.* 'Go to sleep, Charlie. I'll explain in the morning.' *Somehow. And I hope to heaven that you take to your new mother and sister, and she takes to you, because if not I've created the most damnable mess.*

'She's being a little angel, my lady.' Jeannie tucked the sleeping baby back into the crib she had brought into the sitting room while Kate was feeding Anna. Fed, clean and cuddled, she truly was sleeping like a small, rather red-faced cherub.

Kate, fresh from Wilson's best, and exhausting, efforts to turn her into something approaching a respectable lady, retreated to the sanctuary of the sofa next to the crib. Wilson was handicapped by an absence of any gowns to dress her in, to say nothing of Kate's figure, which, it was obvious, was not going to spring back instantly into what had been before. A drab, ill-fitting gown that was seriously the worse for wear was not helped by a headful of fine mousy hair that was in dire need of the attentions of a hairdresser.

She looked a frump, and an unhealthy one at that, she knew. Her husband, once rested and with a view of her in a good light, was going to be bitterly rueing his impetuous, gallant gesture.

His knock came on the thought and Kate twitched at the shawl Wilson had found in an effort to drape her body as flatteringly as possible. A harassed glance at her reflection in the glass over the fireplace confirmed that the wrap's shades of green and brown did nothing to help her complexion.

'Good morning. May I come in? Did you sleep well?' The dark smudges were stark under Grant's eyes and the strong-boned face seemed fined down to its essentials. The rakish bandage had gone, leaving the half-healed cut and angry bruising plain across his forehead.

'Good morning. Yes, of course.'

She was not going to huddle on the sofa, trying to hide. She might look a fright, but she had her pride. Kate swung her feet down to the floor, pushed her shoulders back, lifted her chin and curved the corners of her mouth up. That felt very strange, as though she had not smiled properly in months. Perhaps she had not, except at Anna.

'Dr Meldreth is here, Kate. I think it would be a good idea if he checked you and Anna over.'

'He studied with you in Edinburgh, I gather?' He nodded. 'But unlike you is actually qualified?' That was a sharp retort—she could have bitten her tongue. If it were not for Grant's time at the university, he would have been far less capable of helping her bring Anna safely into the world.

'Exceedingly well qualified,' Grant said before she had a chance to soften her words. He kept any annoyance out of his voice, but his expression hardened. He must think he had married a shrew. 'I'll show him in, shall I?'

He didn't wait for her nod, but ushered in a short, freckled, cheerful man about his age. 'My dear, Dr Meldreth. Meldreth—Lady Allundale. I'll leave you together and I'll be in my study when you've finished, Meldreth.'

Kate summoned her two female supporters and managed to produce a calm, friendly smile for the doctor. He examined Anna and then, swiftly and tactfully, Kate, maintaining a steady flow of conversation while he did so. *Excellent bedside manner,* Kate decided. She felt confident in having him as their doctor.

'You are both in excellent health and the little one is just as she should be,' he assured her when she rejoined him in the sitting room. 'But you need to rest, Lady Allundale. Rivers told me what a rough time you've had of it and I don't think you have been eating very well, have you? Not for quite a while.'

'Probably not, Doctor.'

He closed his bag and straightened his cuffs with a glance at Wilson and Jeannie. It seemed he wanted privacy. Kate nodded to the other women. 'Thank you, I will ring when I need you.' When they were alone she made herself look him in the eye. 'There was something you wished to say to me?'

'I will be frank. I am aware that your marriage only just preceded little Anna's birth. I am also aware that Grant will fudge the issue, making it seem that yours was a long-standing relationship and that the marriage took place some time ago, but was kept quiet. Probably his grandfather's ill health can be made to account for that.'

'I assume that, as a doctor, you will exercise professional discretion.'

'Certainly.' He did not appear surprised by the chill in her voice. 'I simply wished to make the point that—' He broke off and cursed softly under his breath. 'This is more difficult than I thought it would be. I wanted to assure you that I will give you all the support I can. I also wonder just how much of Grant's past history you are aware of.'

She could freeze him out, look down her nose and assume the air of a thoroughly affronted countess or she could take the hand of friendship he appeared to be offering her. She needed a friend.

'I know nothing. I was not even aware that he was the heir to an earldom when I married him. Nor that he was a widower with a child.'

'He will tell you himself, I am sure. But he was close to the old earl—Grant's parents died when he was not much older than Charlie is now. His grandfather brought him up and did a good job of it, for all that he probably leaned too much on the side of tradition and duty. Grant married a suitable young lady, to please his grandfather and do what it seemed was his duty, and talked himself into believing that was how marriage should be.' He pushed his hand through his sandy hair. 'I am saying too much, but you have to know this—Madeleine was a disaster. Possibly the only thing that could have made the situation worse was the way she died.'

'What happened?' Somehow Kate made herself sit quietly attentive for the answer. She had thought she was coming to some safe, comfortable home. A doctor's household, decent and respectable. Modestly prosperous. Instead she found herself married to an earl, with his unburied predecessor somewhere in the house. Her husband had married tragically, she had a stepson—and a new baby. And she had the overwhelming feeling that she could not cope with any of this. But she had to. Grant had thrown her a lifeline and she had a duty to repay him by being a proper wife, a good stepmother to Charlie—and, somehow, a passable countess.

'There was a fire. Rivers was…injured, but he managed to get Charlie out. They couldn't save Madeleine.'

'When?'

'Four years ago. We do not think Charlie remembers any of it, thank God.'

'That is a blessing.' *Poor little boy.* 'Thank you. Forewarned, at least I can try not to blunder into sensitive areas.'

'Some blundering might be a good thing, frankly.' Dr Meldreth stood up. 'Rivers took it too well, too stoically, for the child's sake. I am not sure he ever really put it behind him. And now he is bone-weary, he's exerted himself sooner than he should after a blow to the head and he's feeling as guilty as hell because he didn't get back in time to see his grandfather before he died.'

'I will try to make him rest and hope he feels able to talk to me.' Kate rose and held out her hand to the doctor. 'Thank you. It is good to know he has a friend close by.'

'I'll be back in a couple of days, unless you send for me earlier.' Meldreth shook hands briskly. 'I wasn't sure whether to mention anything, but Rivers said you've got courage, so...' He shrugged. 'I'll see myself down to the study. Good day, Lady Allundale.'

After that it was hard to sit with any composure. So, the situation was such that the good doctor would not have said anything unless he thought she had courage. That was hardly reassuring.

But perhaps it was time she started drawing on that courage, assuming she did actually possess any. If only she did not feel so ignorant. She had experienced the upbringing of any country gentlewoman, with the neighbouring wives doing their best to support a motherless girl. But, although her manners would not disgrace her, she had no experience of the kind of social life Grant would be used to. Now she was presumably expected to know how to greet a duke, curtsy to a queen, organise a reception and look after scores of tenants and staff.

Well, there was no time like the present to begin. Kate rang for Wilson. 'I do not know when the funeral will be, but I must have respectable mourning clothes.' If they were going to have to improvise and dye something with black ink, then the sooner they started, the better.

'It is tomorrow, my lady. His lordship said not to disturb you about it. There'll just be gentlemen there, no ladies, so you can stay in your rooms.'

Her little burst of energy deflected, Kate sat down again and gazed out at the grey skies, trying to make sense of the world she found herself in and her place in it, and failing miserably. Luncheon was brought up. Grimswade delivered a pile of novels, journals and newspapers. She fed Anna and cuddled her, dozed a little, tried to pay attention when Wilson suggested they make a list of all the essentials she needed to buy. Dinner arrived, a succession of perfect, luxurious little courses. Kate refused the red wine, but found she had the appetite to demolish virtually everything else that was put in front of her. The doctor had been correct. She had been neglecting herself out of worry.

Grimswade appeared as the footman was carrying out the dishes. 'Is there anything else you require, my lady?' Butlers, she knew, cultivated a bland serenity under all circumstances, but she thought he looked strained. The whole household seemed to be holding its breath.

Was there anything she could do? *Nothing,* Kate concluded as the door closed behind the butler. Just keep out of the way. Charlie was with his father and a stranger's clumsy sympathy would be no help to them. She should have asked Grimswade when the rest of the family would arrive. At least they could take some of the burden off Grant's shoulders. How lonely this felt, to be in the middle of so many people and yet completely cut off from their fears, their hopes.

She gave herself a brisk mental shake for the self-pity. She and her child were safe, protected and, at least for a few days, hidden. They had a future, even if it was shrouded in a fog of unknowns. Grant and Charlie were mourning the loss of someone dear to them and the best thing she could do was to intrude as little as possible. Grant had made it clear he did not want her involved or he would have confided in her, wouldn't he?

## Chapter Five

She had slept well, Kate realised as she woke to the sound of curtain rings being pulled back. In the intervals when Jeannie had brought her Anna to feed she had listened for sounds from Grant's bedchamber, but none had reached her.

The light was different. She sat up and saw the heavy snow blanketing the formal gardens under a clear, pale grey sky. 'What a heavy fall there must have been in the night, Wilson. Is the house cut off?'

The maid turned and Kate saw her eyes were rimmed with red. She had been crying. *Of course, the funeral.* She felt helpless.

'Very heavy, but the turnpike road is open, my lady, and the men have cleared the path to the church.' Wilson brought a small tray with a cup of chocolate and set it on the bedside table, then went to make up the fire. 'I'll be back with your bath-water in half an hour, my lady.'

The luxury, the unobtrusive, smooth service, suddenly unnerved her. She was a countess now, yet she was the daughter of an obscure baronet, a girl who had never had a Season, who had been to London only three times in her life, who was the mother of a child conceived out of wedlock and the sister of a man who had embroiled her in unscrupulous criminality. *I can't do this...*

The door opened as she took an incautious gulp of hot chocolate and burned the inside of her mouth. 'Wilson?'

'It is us. Good morning.' The deep voice held grief and weariness under the conventional greeting. 'I came to tell you that we will be leaving for the church at ten o'clock. The procession will go past the window, if you wish to watch.' Grant stood just inside the room, one hand resting on Charlie's shoulder, the boy pulled close to his side. Charlie's eyes were red and he leaned in tight to his father, but his chin was set and his head high. Grant looked beyond exhausted, although he was clean-shaven, his dark clothes and black neckcloth immaculate.

'I am so very sorry.' The cup clattered in the saucer as Kate set it down and Grant winced. She threw back the covers, slid out of bed and then just stood there in her nightgown. What could she do, what right had she to think she could even find the comforting words? Her instinct was to put her arms around the pair of them, hug them tight, try to take some of the pain and the weariness from them, but she was a stranger. They would not want her.

'There will be local gentlemen in church, those who can make it through the snow. And the staff, tenants and so on. There will be a small group returning for luncheon, but the staff have that well in hand and you should not be disturbed.' He might as well be speaking to some stray guest who deserved consideration, but was, essentially, an interloper. 'There will be no relatives, no one to stay. We only have cousins in the West Country, too far to attend in this weather, and a great-aunt in London, who likewise could not travel.'

Kate sat down on the edge of the bed. 'I am so sorry,' she repeated. 'Is there anything I can do? Letters to write, perhaps? You will want to spend your time with Charlie.'

'Thank you. My grandfather's… *My* secretary, Andrew Bolton, will handle all the correspondence. There is nothing for you to do.' Grant looked down at the boy as they turned towards the door. 'Ready? We should go down to the hallway now.'

'I'm ready.' Charlie's straight back, the determined tilt of his head, were the image of his father's. He paused and looked back at Kate. 'Good morning, Stepmama.'

Kate watched the procession from her window. The black-draped coffin was carried on the shoulders of six sturdy men, cushions resting on it with decorations and orders glittering in the pale sunlight. Grant walked behind, his hand on Charlie's shoulder, the two of them rigidly composed and dignified. Behind paced a crocodile of gentlemen in mourning clothes followed by tenants in Sunday best and a contingent of the male staff.

She found a prayer book on a shelf in the sitting room and sat to read the burial service through quietly.

By the time luncheon had been cleared away Kate decided that she was going to have to do something. She had cracked the jib door into Grant's bedchamber open a fraction so that she would know if he had come up to rest, and by four o'clock he had not. She handed a fed, gurgling Anna to Jeannie, cast a despairing glance in the mirror at her appearance and set off downstairs.

'Have the guests left?' she asked the first footman she encountered. He was wearing a black armband, she noticed with an inward wince for her own lack of mourning.

'Yes, my lady.'

'And where is my husband?'

'In his study, my lady.'

'Will you show me the way, please?'

He paused at the end of the hallway outside a dark oak door. 'Shall I knock, my lady?'

It looked very much closed. Forbiddingly so. 'No, I will. Thank you…'

'Giles, my lady.'

She tapped and entered without waiting for a response. The room was warm, the fire flickering in the grate, the curtains closed against the winter chill. There were two pools of light, one over a battered old leather armchair where Charlie slept, curled into a ball like a tired puppy, the other illuminating the papers spread on the desk.

It lit the hands of the man behind the desk, but left his face in shadow. 'Grant, will you not come to bed?' she asked, keeping her voice low.

There was a chuckle, a trifle rusty. 'My dear, that is a most direct suggestion.'

Kate felt her cheeks flame. 'I was not trying to flirt, my lord.' *I would not know how and certainly not with you.* 'Surely you need to rest, spend a few hours lying down. You must be exhausted.' She moved closer, narrowing her eyes against the light of the green-shaded reading lamp. The quill pen was lying on its side on top of the standish, the ink dry and matte on the nib. Grant had run out of energy, she realised, and was simply sitting there, too tired to move.

'Perhaps I am.' Grant sounded surprised, as though he had not realised why his body had given up. He made no attempt to stand.

'Why did you marry me, if you will not allow me to help you?' Kate sat down opposite him, her eyes on the long-fingered, bruised hands lying lax on the litter of papers. They flexed, then were still. Beautiful hands, capable and clever. She had put those discoloured patches on the left one. She had a sudden vision of them on her skin, gently caressing. Not a doctor's hands any longer, but a lover's, a husband's. Could he see her blush? She hated the way she coloured up so easily, was always consumed with envy for those porcelain-fair damsels who could hide their emotions with ease.

'You felt sorry for me, I can see that. It was a very generous act of mercy, for me and my child,' she went on, thinking aloud when he did not answer. 'And, for some reason, your grandfather was anxious to see you married again and you would do anything to make him happy.' Still silence. Perhaps he had fallen asleep. 'But I cannot sit upstairs in my suite for the rest of my days.'

'Not for ever, no. But for now you are still a new mother. You also require rest. Is there anything you need?' he asked.

At least he was not sleeping where he sat. Kate did not wish to bother him with trivial matters, but he was talking to her, maybe she could distract him enough to consider sleep... 'I have no clothes.' His expressive fingers moved, curled across a virgin sheet of paper. 'Other than two gowns in a sad state and a few changes of linen,' she added repressively. 'I need mourning.'

'It can wait.' The words dropped like small stones into the silence, not expecting an answer.

At least he was not sleeping where he sat. If she could rouse him enough, she might persuade him to get up and go to his bed. 'Not for much longer.

I cannot appear like this, even if it is only in front of the servants.'

He focused on her problem with a visible effort. 'The turnpike is clear. Tomorrow, if the snow holds off, Wilson can go into Hexham and purchase enough to tide you over until you are strong enough for a trip into Newcastle.'

'Thank you.' Kate folded her own hands in her lap and settled back in the chair. If he thought he could send her back to her room with that, he was mistaken. The silence dragged on, filled with the child's breathing, the soft collapse of a log into ash, her own pulse.

'Are you going to sit there for the rest of the afternoon and evening?' Grant enquired evenly when another log fell into the heart of the fire.

'Yes, if you will not go and rest.' She kept her tone as reasonable as his. 'You will be no good to Charlie if you make yourself ill with exhaustion.'

'So wise a parent after so few days?' There was an edge there now.

'One needs no expertise, only to be a human being, to know that the boy will need your attention, your presence, while he grieves. You are in no fit state for anything now, after so many days without proper rest. And you cannot deal with your own grief by drugging yourself with tiredness.'

'How very astringent you are, my dear.' Grant moved suddenly, sat up in his chair and gathered together the papers in front of him. 'No soft feminine wiles to lure me upstairs, no soft words, only common-sense advice?'

'If you wanted the sort of wife who deals with a crisis by feminine fluttering, who feels it necessary to coax and wheedle, then you have married the wrong woman, my lord.' She kept her voice low, conscious of Charlie so close. But she could not rein in the anger entirely and she knew it showed. 'I do not know what your first wife was like, although I am sure she was raised to be a far more satisfactory countess than I will be, I am afraid. But I will try to enact little scenes of wifely devotion for you from time to time, as you obviously seem to expect them.' *His first wife was a disaster, Dr Meldreth said. I will be one, too, although a very different kind of disaster.*

'Demonstrations of wifely devotion would certainly be a novelty. However, if you can refrain from enacting scenes of any kind, I would be most grateful.' Grant pushed back his chair, went to lift

Charlie in his arms and murmured, 'If I could trouble you for the door?'

*I must make allowances for his exhaustion, for his bereavement,* Kate told herself as she followed the tall figure through the hallway and up the stairs. Giles the footman was lurking in the shadows and she beckoned him over. 'His lordship is going to rest. Please let the rest of the household know that he is not to be disturbed until he rings. It may well be that this disrupts mealtimes, so please pass my apologies to Cook if that is the case. Perhaps she can be ready to provide something light but sustaining at short notice?'

The footman's gaze flickered to Grant's unresponsive back. Kate waited, eyebrows raised as though she found it hard to understand his hesitation. She had never had to deal with superior domestic staff of this calibre and she suspected he knew it. The way she looked wouldn't help. But, like it or not, it seemed she was mistress of this household now and she must exert some authority or she would never regain it.

'My lady.'

'Thank you, Giles.' She nodded as though never doubting his obedience for a moment and climbed the stairs. By the time she reached the landing

Grant had turned off down a side passage. She followed him to the doorway of what must be the boy's bedchamber. A tall, fair-haired young man came out of an inner doorway and turned down the covers. Between them they got the child out of most of his clothes and into bed, exchanged a few words, and then Grant came out.

'That's his tutor, Gough. He'll sleep in the side chamber in case Charlie wakes.' Grant kept going into his own rooms. Without conscious thought Kate followed him. '*I* do not require tucking up in bed, Kate.'

'I do not know *what* you require, my lord.' She turned abruptly, in a way that should have sent her skirts whirling in a dramatic statement of just how strained her nerves felt. They flopped limply about her ankles, adding to her sense of drabness. 'Your son has both more sense and better manners, from what I can see.'

She reached the jib door to her room, pulled it open, and a hand caught the edge of it, pushed it back closed. Grant frowned down at her. 'What is wrong?'

'*Wrong?*' Would the man never give up and just lie down and sleep? Kate turned back, raised one hand and began to count off on her fingers. 'Let

me see. You do not tell me you had just inherited an earldom. You do not tell me you are a widower with a son. You drive yourself to the brink of collapse trying to do everything yourself. I find myself mistress of a great house, but the servants do not appear to expect me to give them orders…'
*I need to hide and I find myself a member of the aristocracy.*

'You have just given birth, you should be resting.' Grant pushed the hair out of his eyes with one hand, the other still splayed on the door. She rather suspected he was holding himself up.

'I am quite well and I have a personal maid and an excellent nursery maid. I do not expect to talk about all those things now, but I do expect my *husband* to go and rest so we can discuss them sensibly in the morning.'

'Very well.' He turned back through the door with all the focus of a man who was very, very drunk with lack of sleep. He walked to the bed. Kate followed him and watched as he sat down and just stared at his boots as though he was not certain what they were.

'Let me.' Without waiting she straddled his left leg with her back to him and drew off the boot. Then switched to the other leg. 'Now your coat.'

Grant's mouth twitched into the first sign she had seen of a smile for days. 'Undressing me, wife? I warn you, it is a waste of effort just now.'

*Is he flirting again? Impossible.* She caught a glimpse of herself in the mirror, a drab creature with a lumpy figure, a blotchy complexion and a frightful gown, next to Grant's elegant good looks. Mocking her was more likely. 'Stand up. I am not going to clamber about on the bed.'

He stood, meekly enough, while she reached up to push the coat from his shoulders. She was slightly above average height for a woman, but he was larger than she had realised, now she was standing so close. No wonder he had lifted her so easily. She found herself a little breathless. Fortunately the coat, like the boots, was comfortable country wear and did not require a shoehorn to lever off. The fine white linen of his shirt clung to his arms, defining the musculature. He had stripped off his coat in the bothy, she recalled vaguely. Doubtless the other things she had to focus on had stopped her noticing those muscles. Ridiculously she felt the heat of a rising blush. Kate unbuttoned his waistcoat, pushed that off, then reached for his neckcloth.

Grant's hand came up and covered her fingers

as she struggled with the knot. She looked up and met his gaze, heavy-lidded, intent. 'You have very lovely blue eyes,' he murmured. 'Why haven't I noticed before?'

He was, it seemed, awake. Or part of him was, a sensual, masculine part she was not ready to consider, although something fundamentally feminine in her was certainly paying attention.

*It is my imagination. He is beyond exhausted, too tired to be flirting. Certainly not flirting with* me. Kate shot another glance at the mirror and resisted the urge to retort that at least there was something about her that he approved of.

'I was quite right about you.'

'What?' she demanded ungrammatically as she tugged the neckcloth off with rather more force than necessary, pulling the shirt button free. The neck gaped open, revealing a vee of skin, a curl of dark hair. It looked…silky.

'You have courage and determination.'

Kate began to fold up the length of muslin with concentration. 'I am trying to get you to rest. What about that requires courage?'

'You don't know me.' He sat down. 'I might have a vicious temper. I might hit out at a wife who provoked me.'

'I think I am a reasonable judge of character.' She had wound the neckcloth into a tight knot around her own hand. Patiently, so she did not have to look at him, Kate began to unravel it. This close she could smell his skin, the herbal, astringent soap he used, the tang of ink on his hands, the faint musk that she recognised as *male*. But Grant smelt different, smelt of himself.

She walked to the dresser and placed the neckcloth on the top, distancing herself from the sudden, insane urge to step in close, lay her head on his chest, wrap her arms around the lean, weary body. *Why?* To comfort him perhaps, or because she wanted comfort herself, or perhaps a mixture of the two.

When she turned back Grant was lying down on top of the covers, still in shirt and breeches. He was deep, deep asleep. She stood looking down at him for a moment, studied the fine-drawn face relaxed into a vulnerability that took years off his age. How old was he? Not thirty-two or -three, as she had thought. Twenty-eight, perhaps. His hair flopped across his forehead, just as Charlie's did, but she resisted the temptation to brush it back from the bruised skin. The long body did not stir when she laid a light blanket over him, nor when she drew the curtains closed slowly to muffle the rattle of the rings, nor when she made up the fire and drew the guard around it.

*My husband is a disturbingly attractive man,* she thought as she closed the jib door carefully behind her. Anna was crying in the dressing room, she could hear Jeannie soothing her.

'Mama will be back soon, little one. Yes, she will, now don't you fret.'

A husband, a stepson, a baby. Her family. She had a *family* when just days before all she had was a scheming brother who had always seen her as wilful and difficult and the babe inside her, loved already, but unknown.

Anna, Charlie, Grant. When her husband woke, refreshed, he would see her differently, realise he had a partner he could rely on. She owed him that, she owed Anna the opportunity to grow up happily here. The anxiety and the exhaustion had made her nervy, angry, but she must try to learn this new life, learn to fit in. As the pain of the funeral eased, she would be there for them all. Charlie would learn to like her, perhaps one day to love her. And somehow she would learn how to be a countess. She shivered. How could a countess stay out of the public eye?

*When tomorrow comes, it will not seem so over-whelming, I'll think of something.* 'Is that a hungry little girl I can hear? Mama's coming.'

# Chapter Six

Hunger woke Grant. One minute he had been fathoms down, the next, awake, alert, conscious of an empty stomach and silence. Gradually the soft sounds of the household began to penetrate. The subdued crackle of the fire, someone trudging past in the snow, the distant sound of light, racing feet and the heavier tread of an adult in pursuit. Charlie exercising his long-suffering tutor, no doubt. Close at hand an infant began to cry, then stopped. *Anna. I have a daughter.* And a wife.

There was daylight between the gap in the curtains, falling in a bright snow-reflecting bar across the blanket someone had draped over his legs. Grant pushed the hair out of his eyes, winced and sat up, too relaxed to tug the bell pull and summon food and hot water.

Now, today, he must take up the reins of the earl-

dom. That was perhaps the least of the duties looming before him. He had known for nearly twenty
years, ever since his father died, that he would in-
herit. His grandfather had run a tight ship, but had
taught Grant, shared decisions as he grew older,
explained his thinking, given him increasing re-
sponsibilities. There were no mysteries to discover
about the estates, the investments or the tenants and
he had inherited an excellent bailiff and solicitor
along with the title.

Charlie was going to be all right, given time and
loving attention. Which left Kate. His new wife.
What had he been thinking of, to marry her out of
hand like that? She was certainly in deep trouble,
all alone with a new baby and no means of support,
but he could have found her a cottage somewhere
on one of the estates, settled some money on her.
Forgotten her.

His grandfather had been fretting himself into a
state over Grant's first marriage. Blaming himself
for ever introducing Grant to Madeleine Ellmont,
worrying that Grant was lonely, that Charlie had
no mother, that the future of the earldom relied on
a healthy quiverful of children. So much so that
Grant had come to hate the house that had always
been his home. But he could have lied to him, made

up a charming and eligible young woman whom he was about to propose to, settled the old man's worries that way.

What had prompted that impetuous proposal when he already knew his grandfather must be beyond caring about his marital state? Something about Kate had told him he could trust her, that she was somehow *right*. He had glimpsed it again yesterday when he had looked into her eyes and seen a spark there that had caught his breath for an instant.

A clock struck ten. Lord, he'd slept more than twelve hours. Grant leaned out of bed and yanked the bell pull. He had to somehow get everything right with Kate. She was unsettled to discover she was a countess with a stepson and that was understandable. He had an edgy feeling that he had disconcerted her when she was helping him to undress. He kept forgetting that while she might be a mother she seemed quite sheltered, not very experienced. What had he said? Nothing out of line, he hoped. For the first time he wondered about Anna's father and just what that love affair had been—a sudden moment of madness, a lengthy, illicit relationship, or…

'You rang, my lord?' said Giles the footman.

Grant frowned at him for a second. It took some

getting used to, being *my lord* now. 'Hot water, coffee. Ask Cook to send up some bacon, sausage… Everything. She'll know.'

When the water came he washed and then shaved himself while Giles found him clean linen and laid out plain, dark clothes. That was something else to add to the list, a valet.

When he tapped on the jib door and went through into Kate's suite he found her in the sitting room, the baby in the crib by her side, her hands full of a tangle of fine wool. She was muttering what sounded like curses under her breath.

'Good morning. Cat's cradles?'

'Oh!' She dropped the wool and two needles fell out of it. 'Mrs Havers, the housekeeper, brought me this wool and the knitting needles. She thought I might like to make a cot blanket, which was very thoughtful of her. I didn't like to tell her I haven't tried to knit since I was six.' She grimaced at the tangle. 'And *tried* was the correct word, even then. Did you need me, my lord?'

'Grant, please. I came to see how you are and to thank you for persuading me into bed yesterday. I had gone beyond being entirely rational on the subject.' There was colour up over her cheeks and he remembered making some insinuating comment about luring him into bed. *Damn.*

'I hope you feel better this morning.' She bent her head over the knitting once more, catching up the dropped stitches. 'Charlie was up and about quite early, testing the bounds of his tutor's patience. He seems a pleasant young man, Mr Gough.'

'He's the younger brother of a friend from university. I thought he would be a good choice as a first tutor—he has plenty of energy and Charlie seems to have taken to him.'

Kate picked up the wool and began to wind it back into a ball, her gaze fixed on her hands. 'You slept well?'

'Yes, excellently. How is Anna this morning?'

Grant sat down and retrieved a knitting needle from the floor as Kate answered. He might as well order the teapot to be brought and some fancy biscuits—this seemed like a morning call, complete with stilted, meaningless polite chat, achieving nothing.

'Tomorrow, I intend going down to London. I must present myself at the House of Lords, the College of Heralds and at Court.' He was escaping.

'Oh.' She set down the wool and sat up in the chair as though bracing herself. 'I am sorry, I had not realised we would be leaving so soon. I am not certain I feel up to the journey yet.'

Surely that was not panic he saw in her eyes? He shook his head and realised Kate had taken that as a refusal to listen to her objection.

'But…if we must, may we stop in Newcastle on the way? Then I can buy a respectable gown or two to tide me over.' She looked around, determined, it seemed, to obey his wishes. 'Where have Jeannie and Wilson got to? I am sure we can be ready in time.'

'There is no need for you to disturb yourself. I had no intention of dragging you away. I will take Charlie and Gough with me, I don't want to leave the boy without me yet. They can come back on the mail after a few weeks, once I am certain he is all right.' Kate closed her eyes for a moment and he felt a jab of conscience at not realising how exhausted she must be. 'When you feel up to it you will find Newcastle will serve for all your needs while you require only mourning clothes.'

'Very well. As you wish, my lord.' Kate picked up the wool and needles again with a polite smile that seemed to mask something deeper than relief. 'And you will send Charlie back, you say?'

'The moment I am certain he doesn't need me. In

the longer term I will be too occupied with business to give him the company he needs and the house and servants will be unfamiliar to him. He will be better here, where he feels secure. I will send for him again after a month or two—travelling long distances will be no hardship for him, he'll find it an adventure—but I want him based here.'

'Of course. As you think best. I can see that London might not be a good place for a small boy in the longer term if you cannot be with him most of the time.'

Grant told himself he should be pleased to have such a conformable wife, such an untemperamental, obliging one. Perversely, he felt decidedly put out. Through yesterday's fog of tiredness he seemed to recall the sparkle that temper had put in Kate's eyes, the flush on her cheeks, the stimulus of a clash of wills. Women were moody after childbirth, he knew that. This placidity was obviously Kate's natural character.

'Grant?' She was biting her lip now. 'Grant, will you put a notice about the marriage in the newspapers? Only, I wish you would not. I feel so awkward about things...'

Newspaper announcements had been the last thing on his mind, but he could see she was embarrassed. 'No, I won't. An announcement of the birth, yes, but it will give no indication of the date of the marriage. "To the Countess of Allundale, a daughter." All right?' Kate nodded and he hesitated, concerned at how pale she had gone. Then she smiled and he told himself he was imagining things. 'If you'll excuse me, my dear, I have a great deal to do.' She would no doubt be delighted to see the back of him—and why should it be otherwise?

*May 5, 1820*

*Home.* Warmth on his back, clean air in his lungs, the sun bathing the green slopes of the Tyne Valley spread out before him. Grant stood in his stirrups to stretch, relishing the ache of well-exercised muscles. However ambiguous his feelings about Abbeywell, he had been happy here once and perhaps he could be again, if only he could blank out his memories and find some sort of peace with his new wife.

His staff had obviously thought he was out of his mind to decide to ride from London to Northumberland instead of taking a post-chaise, but he knew exactly what had motivated him. This had been a holiday from responsibility, from meetings and parties, from political negotiating and social duty. And a buffer between the realities and reason of London and the ghosts that haunted this place.

If he was honest, it had also been a way of delaying his return to his new wife and facing up to exactly what his impulse on that cold Christmas Day had led to.

'I like her,' Charlie had pronounced on being questioned when he came on a month's visit to the London house in March. But he was too overexcited from his adventurous trip on the mail coach with Mr Gough to focus on things back in Northumberland. He wanted to talk to his papa, to go with him to the menagerie, to see the soldiers and the Tower. And Astley's again, and...

'You get on together all right?' Grant had prompted.

'Of course. She doesn't fuss and she lets me play with Anna, who is nice, although she's not much fun yet. May we go to Tatt's? Papa, please?'

*Doesn't fuss.* Well, that would seem to accord with Kate's letters. One a week, each precisely three pages long in a small, neat hand. Each contained a scrupulous report on Charlie's health and scholastic progress, a paragraph about Anna—she can hold her head up, she can copy sounds, she can throw her little knitted bunny—and a few facts about the house and estate. *Millie in the kitchen has broken her ankle, the stable cat caught the biggest rat anyone had seen and brought it into the kitchen on Sunday morning and Cook dropped the roast, it has rained for a week solidly...*

They were always signed *Your obedient wife, Catherine Rivers*, each almost as formalised and lacking in emotion as Gough's reports on Charlie or his bailiff's lengthy letters about estate business. And never once did she ask to come to London or reproach him for leaving her alone.

He replied, of course, sending a package north weekly, with a long letter for Charlie, a note for Gough, answers to Wilkinson's estate queries. And there would always be a letter one page long for Kate, with the kind of gossip that Madeleine, his first wife, had expected. What the royal family were doing, what the latest society scandal was— omitting the crim. con. cases, naturally—the latest fads in hem lengths and bonnets as observed in Hyde Park. Signed *Your affct. husband, Grantham Rivers.*

The parkland rolled before him like a welcome carpet and the road forked, the right hand to the house, the left to the rise crowned with the mausoleum his great-grandfather had built in the 1750s.

The chestnut gelding was trotting along the left-hand way before Grant was conscious of applying the reins. No rush, it was only just noon, no one was expecting him to arrive on any particular day.

The classical monument sat perfectly on its hillock, turning the view into a scene in an Arcadian painting. It was a Greek temple with its portico facing south, its basement full of the ancestors his great-grandfather had removed from the church vault, its inner walls made with niches for the future generations of Rivers. 'So we can admire the view,' the first earl had reportedly announced. 'I'm damned if I'm spending eternity in that damp vault with some dullard of a preacher sermonising on top of me.' The countess of the day had had mild hysterics at the sentiment and had been ignored and now she, too, shared the prospect.

Grant tied the gelding to a ring on the rear wall of the building and strolled round to the front. There were stone benches set under the portico and it would be good to rest there awhile and think about his grandfather.

The sound of laughter stopped him in mid-stride. He recognised Charlie's uninhibited shrieks, but there was a light, happy laugh he did not recognise at all. He walked on, his boots silent on the sheep-cropped turf, and stopped again at the corner.

A rug was spread out on the grassy flat area in front of the temple steps and a woman in a dark grey gown was sitting on it, her arms wrapped around her knees, her eyes shaded by a wide straw hat as she watched Charlie chasing a ball. An open parasol was lying by her side.

'Maman, look!' Charlie hurled the ball high, then flung himself full length to catch it.

The woman clapped, the enthusiasm of her applause tipping her hat back off her head to roll away down the slope. Long brown hair, the colour of milky coffee, glossy in the sunlight, tumbled free from the confining pins and she laughed. 'Catch my hat, Charlie!'

Maman? Grant started forward as Charlie caught the hat, turned and saw him. He rushed uphill shrieking, 'Papa! Papa! Look, Maman—Papa's home.'

The woman swung round on the rug as Charlie thudded into Grant, his hard little head butting into his stomach. He scooped him up, tucked him under his arm and strode down to her. She tilted her head back, sending the waves of hair slithering like unfolding silk and giving him an unimpeded view of an oval face, blue eyes, a decided chin and pink lips open in surprise.

'My...my lord, we did not expect to see you for another day at least.' Her face lost its colour, her relaxed body seemed to tighten in on itself.

*Kate? Of course it is Kate, but...* He did something about his own dropped jaw, gave himself a mental shake and managed to utter a coherent sentence. 'I made good time.' He set Charlie on his feet. 'Maman?'

'Stepmamas are in fairy stories and they are always wicked. So I asked Mr Gough for the words for *mama* in lots of languages and we looked them up and I chose *maman*. Maman likes it,' his son assured Grant earnestly. 'She said it was *elegant.*'

'Will you not sit down?' It was extraordinary how it was possible to sound quite calm outwardly when her insides were in a jumble of feelings, the overriding one of which was confusion. Kate gestured towards the open basket and managed what she hoped was a welcoming smile. 'Do have some luncheon. We have enough food to withstand a siege. Charlie, as always, assured Cook that we might be lost in the woods for days. We never are, but Cook does not like to take the risk.'

*When in doubt when dealing with a man, feed the beast,* her mother had always said with a chuckle. Kate kept her tone serious and was rewarded by the slight upward tilt of one corner of Grant's mouth. He had a sense of humour, then. It had not been possible to detect it in his dutiful letters, which had not been made any less dry by the fact they contained nothing but gossip. Presumably that was all wives were supposed to be interested in.

Wives, of course, were perfectly capable of reading the news-sheets and keeping informed that way, although that simple fact did not seem to occur to men. Her brother, Henry, had always been amazed when she revealed an opinion on anything from income tax to child labour and he firmly believed that thinking led to weakening of the feminine brain. Kate pushed away the resentment and watched her husband as he moved round to drop to the rug at her side and discovered Anna lying under the parasol, kicking her legs and chewing on a bone ring.

Grant reached over and tickled her and the resentment retreated some more. He was good with the children, she must remember that.

'She has grown and she looks to be thriving. As do you,' he added. 'I scarcely recognised you.'

From the way Grant shut his mouth with a snap

he realised that was a less than tactful remark. Instead of saying so Kate wrestled her hair into a twist and jammed the hat back on top. 'Babies tend to grow in the natural course of things. But she is very well, as am I.' She sent him a considering, sideways glance, making sure he saw it. 'You look much better than I remembered.'

That very forward remark obviously caught him by surprise. Grant tossed his low-crowned hat aside and shifted round to look directly at her, eyes narrowing. 'Thank you. I think.'

She had known him to be a good-looking man when she married him, but not this attractive, with a London gloss on his hair and clothes, his face tanned from his long ride north. 'In December you looked haggard, bruised and exhausted. You were recovering from a blow to the head and you were grieving,' Kate said with a slight shrug. His eyes moved down to her breasts as she moved and she caught her breath at the answering flare of heat in her belly. The fact that she had a figure obviously interested him. No doubt it was the transformation of her bosom; men could be very predictable.

It was nearly five months since Anna's birth now. She had passed through exhaustion to a conviction that when she felt stronger she never wanted a man to touch her again. After all, her first, and only, experience had not been so pleasurable as to have her yearning for more.

And that comfortable state had lasted for three months until the moment when she had looked up from the dinner table to see Grant's portrait hanging on the opposite wall, just as it had since the day she arrived. It had been part of the decoration of the house, hardly regarded, but that evening she had felt a startling stab of attraction as she met the direct green gaze. The feeling had been so visceral, so unashamedly physical, that she'd choked on her fish terrine and Mr Gough had rushed round the table to offer her water.

Since the arrival of Grant's letter announcing his return she had been in an unseemly state of confusion, alarm and anticipation. This was her husband—and husbands expected their *rights*.

# Chapter Seven

'After all, I was in the process of giving birth,' Kate continued calmly, hoping the frankness of her words accounted for the heat in her cheeks. The thought of Grant exercising his husbandly rights made her positively breathless. 'It is hardly surprising that we both now appear to be tolerably well looking in comparison. Of course, I could tell that you were a well-favoured man, even then, but it must be a relief for you to discover that I am not *quite* as bracket-faced as you feared.'

'It is difficult to know how to reply to that.' Grant was not used to being left at a loss for words, she could tell. Possibly he was slightly flattered, although he must be accustomed to being regarded as good-looking. Possibly also he was feeling a trifle awkward about letting her see what he had thought of her before.

'There is no need to say anything.' She was not a conventional beauty, she never had been, but she thought that these days she looked at least tolerable, and, if Grant now thought so, too, she was content with that.

'I have been away a long time, longer than I intended.' He had decided to get all the apologising over at once, it seemed. Kate wondered if the length of his absence had anything to do with his mental image of his new wife. Had he escaped to London and the arms of a beautiful mistress? As apologies went, it was not very effusive, more a statement of fact than of regret.

'We have managed very well and you were a most regular correspondent.' *Not that I understand you any better now than before you left. And you are a man, not a saint, so I must not feel jealous of a mistress—she is only to be expected. But if you take one up here, one that I know about, that will be a different matter.* The stab of jealousy was unexpected and she diverted it into a vicious cut at the pastry in front of her. 'Would you care for a slice of raised pie?' she enquired to cover the impulse to snap out a demand to know all about this theoretical other woman. 'It is chicken and ham.'

'Papa, are you home for long?' Charlie had been

sitting almost on his father's feet, obviously on the point of bursting with the effort to Be Good and not interrupt the adults.

'For the summer. Ough!' Grant fell back on the rug under the impact of Charlie's flying leap and hug. 'You are too big for jumping on your poor father. Big enough to come out with me and start learning about the estate, I think, provided you keep up your lessons to Mr Gough's satisfaction. Now, sit quietly and eat your picnic while I talk to your stepmama.' Grant settled the boy between them and against her side Kate could feel her husband's encircling arm and the child's skinny little body quivering with happiness like an overexcited puppy.

The arm was warm and it was tempting to lean into it, to feel the muscled strength braced to support her. Kate sat up straight and filled a plate for Grant from the picnic basket.

'Thank you. Have you heard from your brother yet?' he asked as he took the food from her.

'No. I have not written to him and I would, of course, have mentioned it in my letters if I had. I do not want him to know of this marriage. I do not want him to know where I am. To be perfectly frank, we were not close. We did not part on good

terms and it would be awkward…' She'd scoured
the newspapers daily, looking for the arrest or trial
of Sir Henry Harding, baronet, for blackmail. But
perhaps aristocrats had other ways of dealing with
the potentially explosive matter of extortion. She
shivered. But there had been no notice of Henry's
death, either.

'Awkward to have him asking questions about
our marriage?'

She nodded, grateful that he had jumped to the
wrong conclusion. She did not want Henry to know
about her marriage because, beside him embroiling
her any deeper in his schemes, she had no idea how
he would react. At best, he would attempt to borrow money from his new brother-in-law. At worst,
he could cause the most dreadful scandal and she
could not inflict that on Grant.

'I would be much happier if you did not make
contact with him.' *And find out who Anna's father
is and realise just how I came to lose my virginity
to the man and became an accomplice in blackmail.*
Grant was the kind of principled gentleman who
would never allow such dishonesty to go unpun-
ished, whatever the scandal. *Let sleeping dogs lie…*

Grant shrugged. 'We are going to have to deal
with him sooner or later. In the meantime, are you

opposed to entertaining a small house party? It had not occurred to me to propose it, but now I see you looking—'

'More the thing?' Kate suggested, swallowing the hurt. Had he really thought to shut her away up here, an unpaid housekeeper and guardian for his son, simply because he considered her plain and awkward? Now, it seemed, he did not fear she would embarrass him in front of his friends. The fact that she had welcomed the seclusion was neither here nor there.

'More rested,' Grant supplied smoothly. 'And from your letters it sounds as though you have the household well in hand.'

'Your staff are well chosen and well trained. Once they had accepted that I really was your wife, and not some stray you had picked up on the moors, they have proved most cooperative.' Not that she would have stood for any nonsense. She had been used to helping run a small household, so she knew the principles, and she was all too aware that if she did not secure the respect and loyalty of the staff of this much larger one right from the start, then she never would. It was another mark in Grant's favour, the loyalty and affection they showed for him.

'How small a house party?' she enquired, leaning away from him to give Anna a quick kiss and to hide the uncertainty that she could manage the sort of gathering an earl might hold. Provided it was here, on what had become her own turf, she was not too anxious.

'No more than three close friends of mine, potentially with partners. I've had enough formal socialising in London to last me several months. Charlie, do you remember Lord Weybourn?'

'Uncle Alex?'

'Yes. He was married in January. I thought to ask him and his wife to stay. And, if they are still in the country, Lord Avenmore and Lord Edenbridge. They are old friends,' he added for Kate's benefit. 'The two bachelors might bring their unmarried sisters, perhaps, to balance out the men.'

'That sounds delightful.' Kate took a bread roll from the basket, then sat with it in her hands, wondering why she had picked it up. The longer Grant sat beside her, the more her appetite deserted her. It was nerves, that was all. She was happy that he was back, for Charlie's sake if nothing else—only, there was a hollow feeling of anticipation, as though the air had been sucked out of her lungs. This was her husband and he was going to expect to begin a normal married life, with all that entailed. Part of that hollowness was apprehension, but a good part was excitement and she had been making herself face that ever since the arrival of the letter announcing his return.

She put the bread roll back untasted, handed Charlie an apple turnover and smiled as he ran off, mouth full, to retrieve his ball. Beside her Grant was silent and she sought for small talk to fill the void. 'It has been…quiet. I am glad you are back. The children are very absorbing, of course.'

'But they are not adults. You have been lonely.' When she murmured agreement he asked, 'Have none of our neighbours called?'

'Dr Meldreth and his wife and the vicar and his sister, that is all. Please, do not make too much of it. I am in mourning, after all, and in the country people do observe that very rigorously. I see them in church on Sunday, naturally, and I usually dine with Mr Gough.'

'Now I am back I will visit all our neighbours, let the ladies know we are not in strict mourning any longer. You should get any number of calls within days.'

Charlie's voice floated down from the portico of the mausoleum. '…and now Papa's back I will help him with the estate, just like he helped you, Great-

Grandpapa. You'll be proud of me when I do that, I expect, Mama.'

'What the devil?' Grant swung round, sending the lemonade jug rocking. 'Who is he talking to? My grandfather, his mother? Is the child delusional?'

'Of course not.' Kate grabbed his arm as he began to get to his feet. Grant shot her a frowning look, but settled back down beside her when she did not relax her grip. 'He missed his great-grandfather, so we started coming down here so that he could talk to him. And then he realised that his mama was here, too. He understands that we do not know what happens after death and he doesn't think he is talking to ghosts or anything unhealthy like that. But it comforts him, helps him to sort out his feelings. Rather like writing a diary, I suppose.' Kate came up on her knees beside Grant, her hand on the unyielding arm braced to push him to his feet. 'Did I do wrong? He is not at all morbid about it and this is a lovely place. A peaceful place, where he can remember happy times.'

'He cannot remember his mother, he never really knew her, she died when he was only just two.' Grant stayed where he was, but the tension radiated off him. Had he loved his first wife so much that he could not bear any mention of her? But that was not what Dr Meldreth had implied. The staff in the house acted and spoke as though Charlie's mother was a grief that could not be spoken about, becoming thin-lipped and awkward if Kate made any reference to her. There were no portraits, not even in Charlie's room.

'He says he remembers her scent and the fact that she always wore blue, but that is all. I have no idea whether it is accurate, but it helps him to have that faint image. He is certain that she was beautiful.'

'She was.' Grant's voice softened. 'Blonde and blue-eyed, which is why she favoured blue in her dress. She always wore jasmine scent and on a warm evening it lingered in the air like the ghost of incense...' Kate closed her eyes at the hint of pain beneath the reminiscent tone. 'Charlie would do well to forget she ever existed,' he said and turned so his back was to the little temple.

'Grant!' Kate stared at him, then scooped up Anna as the baby began to cry, as unsettled by his abruptly harsh tone as she was.

'She was a disaster as a mother.'

*And a disaster as a wife?* 'He need not know that,' Kate said fiercely.

'Of course not, what do you take me for?'

'I do not know. I do not know *you*. But he needs the confidence of knowing he had a mother who loved him, even if she was not very good at it in your eyes. What does it matter if *you* do not like it, if it is best for Charlie?'

'Damn it, Kate. You presume to lecture me on my own child?'

'Yes, of course I do.' She glared back at him over the top of Anna's bonneted head, aware that she was bristling like a stable cat defending her kittens. Then she saw the darkness in Grant's eyes, the memory of goodness knew what past miseries. 'I am sorry, but I am his stepmother and you left him with me to look after. He is still only a little boy, not ready for harsh truths.' She rocked the baby, trying to soothe her. 'What did she do that was so unforgivable?'

Grant got to his feet in one fast movement, a controlled release of pent-up tension. 'I am sorry, but I have no intention of raking over old history. Madeleine is in the past and there is nothing you need to know.' He bent to pick up his hat. 'If you will excuse me, Kate, I will ride on to the house and take Charlie with me. I assume a footman is coming out in the gig to collect you and bring the basket back?'

'Yes, I expect him very soon.' Kate was glad of Anna grizzling in her arms, demanding her attention. She did not want to look into those shadowed eyes and see his anger with her, or his pain over his beautiful, lost wife.

He called to Charlie and the boy came running to be hoisted up into the saddle in front of his father. Grant gave him the reins. 'Wave goodbye to your stepmama.'

When the sound of hooves died away and Charlie's excited chatter faded amongst the trees, Kate fed and changed Anna, packed away the baby things in one basket and the remains of the picnic in the other and got to her feet, too restless to wait for the footman and the gig.

She had to think about Grant, but not about what would happen that night. If she began to imagine that, then she would be in more of a state of nerves than a virgin on her wedding night. The virgin might have a little theoretical knowledge, but Kate knew exactly what would happen and the thought of being in Grant's bed made her mind dizzy and her body ache.

She had lain with Jonathan just once and she had believed herself in love with him, a delusion she now knew was born out of ignorance, a desperation to get away from home and the lures of an accomplished rake. And the experience had been a sadly disappointing one, even though she had not truly understood what to expect. But she hardly knew Grant, the man, at all, he had never so much as kissed her hand and she was most certainly not tipsy with moonlight and champagne. And yet, just the thought of him made her breath come short and an ache, somewhere between fear and anticipation, form low down. Goodness knew how she had managed a rational conversation with him appearing like that.

Kate tucked Anna more snugly into her little blanket, settled her into the folds of her shawl to make a sling and began to walk back to the house. It would take almost half an hour with her arms full of her wriggling, chubby baby. Time enough to think about something other than how long Grant's legs had looked, stretched out on the rug, how the ends of his hair had turned golden brown in the sunlight.

Time, in fact, to consider that locked door on the other side of Grant's suite of rooms in the light of what he had said about Madeleine, the beautiful wife who had been such a bad mother and who had died in a fire.

She had realised almost from the beginning that the forbidden suite must have been her predecessor's rooms. She could understand that the chambers would hold difficult memories for Grant, but even so, it was surely long past the time when they should have been opened up, aired, redecorated and put to use. What would happen when Charlie was old enough to be curious about the locked door? It was unhealthy to make a mystery out of his mother like that, and if he ever discovered that was where she had died, he might well have nightmares about it.

None of the keys on her chatelaine fitted the lock and all the servants denied having the right one, either. Eventually Grimswade told her that neither his late lordship nor his young lordship had wanted the rooms opened. 'The earl holds the only key, my lady,' he told her, his gaze fixed at a point over her head.

Since then Kate had tried hard not to allow the locked room to become a Bluebeard's chamber in her imagination, applying rigorous common sense to keep her own nightmares at bay. She had found her way around the house without looking at the door if she could help it, she had asked no further questions of the staff, but it refused to be forgotten. There were times when she seriously considered picking the lock with a bent hairpin, or seeing if a slender paperknife would trip the catch, then told herself to not even think about something so unseemly.

Now she wondered just what Madeleine's crimes had been. *A disaster as a mother.* That, somehow, did not make sense. Surely she could not have beaten the child—neither Grant nor his grandfather would have allowed her unsupervised access if they feared violence. And being a distant and cold mother was nothing unusual amongst the nobility, Kate knew. Many a child was raised almost entirely by servants without anyone accusing the parents of being a disaster.

The only explanation Kate could think of was that she was a failure as a wife and therefore morally unfit to be a mother. Had she taken a lover—had Grant found them together in her bedchamber? It was an explanation, but it was difficult to imagine Grant being cuckolded. In fact, her mind refused to produce an image of a more attractive alternative who might have tempted his wife to stray.

'Which is very shallow of me,' she admitted to Anna. The baby stared back at her with wide green eyes. 'Grant is intelligent, good-looking, and he was the heir to an earldom when she married him. But good looks and position are not everything. If Madeleine had found her soulmate…'

*Then she should have resisted temptation. Madeleine was married, she had made vows, she had a child. Which is easy enough for me to say. Despite being a well-brought-up, respectable young lady, I gave my virtue easily enough.* Of course, having a scheming brother who put her in the way of a man who could be trusted to yield to temptation when it was offered and who could not afford a scandal had helped her along the path to ruination. Her becoming pregnant was, as far as Henry was concerned, the perfect gilding on his plan to blackmail her lover. *What if Jonathan came back now, walked around that bend in the path ahead?*

Kate watched the bend approach. No one appeared around it, of course, least of all the rakish Lord Baybrook. And if he did, he would not be coming with protestations of undying love, with explanations of how she had entirely misunderstood his flat refusal to marry her when Henry had confronted him two months later, after she had been forced to confess her predicament.

Not that she had seen him then, of course. Henry, as befitted the male head of the household, had taken himself off to London to, as he put it, *deal with the matter*. Only, he had not dealt with it, not brought her a husband back. At the time it had struck her as strange that her brother had not been more angry, but she had decided that perhaps he had been relieved that he had not found himself facing the viscount at dawn on Hampstead Heath. Then she had found the letter in Henry's desk, the coldly furious response to blackmail, the counter-threats. But Lord Baybrook had not called Henry's bluff. He would pay, she thought, reading the letter. Pay—and then she was certain that one day he would find some way to make Henry pay and Kate, too, the woman Jonathan thought had deliberately set out to ensnare him.

Anna gurgled and Kate stopped, her feet sinking into the soft mulch of the path. There was nothing to be gained by brooding on it, fretting over the long arm of a vengeful aristocrat or wincing in shame at her own part in her brother's schemes. Most certainly, she was in no position to judge Grant's first wife on moral grounds. Equally certainly, if she had the choice between Grant Rivers, Lord Allundale, and Jonathan Arnold, Lord Baybrook, she had no doubt which man she would choose now.

# Chapter Eight

Grant sat up in the marble bath and considered the tricky, but eminently safe, subject of plumbing. His grandfather had installed baths with a cold-water supply and drains for the main bedchambers, but he had not risked the newfangled systems of boilers and piped hot water. Grant had agreed with him at the time, but lugging the cans of hot water upstairs and along endless corridors certainly made a great deal of work for the servants.

He lathered the long-handled brush and scrubbed his back while calculating the safe location for boilers and the length of pipework one would need. It was technical, complicated, and was entirely failing to stop him brooding on the subject of his wife. His second wife.

He had been deep in discussion with his secretary and the steward when he heard her voice in the hallway that afternoon. Six months ago Mr Rivers would have pushed aside the piles of paperwork and asked the men to wait while he went out to greet her. But the Earl of Allundale could not do anything as unfashionable and demonstrative as interrupting an important meeting in order to speak to his wife for no reason whatsoever. A few months in London society had reminded him forcefully of that.

Madeleine had always said he was far too casual, not sufficiently aware of his own consequence, or of hers. Now he was the earl he should behave like one, and, given the circumstances of their marriage, Kate was going to need all the consequence he could bring her, he was very conscious of that.

Now he put aside the brush and lay back to critically survey what he could see of his body as he stretched out under the water. Toes, kneecaps and a moderately hairy chest broke the surface. No stomach rising above the soap suds, thank goodness. The London Season was enough to put inches on anyone foolish enough to eat and drink all that was on offer during interminable dinner parties, suppers at balls, buffets at receptions. But with rigorous attendance at the boxing salons, sessions with the fencing master and long rides in the parks, at least the elegant new clothes he'd ordered when he'd first arrived still fitted him by the end.

Alex had laughed at him for having a fashionable crop, but he had hardly noticed the teasing—contemplating his old friend Alex Tempest married to the woman he had believed on first sight to be a nun was enough to distract any man.

Alex and Tess had seemed happy. Blissfully so and physically, too. Shockingly they hardly seemed able to keep their hands off each other—Lord and Lady Weybourn appeared to have no reservations about appearing unfashionably in love.

Grant reached out and pulled the plug out, then, when the bath emptied, he put it back and turned on the cold-water tap. He made himself lie still until it reached his shoulders. It had dawned on him when he reached London that he was a married man again. Which meant that he should be faithful to his wife. It was not something that had entered his head when he made that rash proposal, and sex had not been exactly at the forefront of his mind for at least a month before that, what with the anxiety about his grandfather and then so much travelling, culminating in his accident in Edinburgh.

Now he lay in the cold water and made himself calculate. This was May. It had been mid-November when he had ended that pleasant little dalliance with the Bulgarian attaché's wife in Vienna. Nearly six months. Despite the chill of the bath, blood was definitely heading downwards with the realisation of such prolonged celibacy. Damnation. He could hardly sling a towel round his hips and stride off to his wife's bedchamber to deal with the matter. That was not the way to approach one's first night in the marriage bed. And what were Kate's expectations of that marriage bed anyway?

Grant climbed from the bath and stood in front of the fire while he towelled himself dry. The logical way to discover her feelings and views on any subject was simply to ask her. On the other hand, he hardly knew the woman. Wife or not, he could not just sit down and have a frank and open discussion about sex. She would be shocked.

He had been away a devil of a long time and he had a guilty conscience about that, he realised as he towelled his back. He could expect to receive, at the very least, some wifely remonstrance on the subject before he was forgiven. Yet when they had met in front of the mausoleum Kate had simply not acknowledged that there had been anything wrong, so he could neither justify himself nor be forgiven. Maddening. The question was, did she realise how awkward that was and was she administering a particularly subtle punishment? Or did she care too little to be annoyed with him? Probably the latter.

The faint sound of splashing stopped him, the towel still stretched across his shoulder blades. Of course, when the suites had been changed around, the two new bathing rooms had been carved out of a small, little-used retiring room and the walls must be simply lath and plaster. He padded across and applied his ear to the panelling. Definite splashing and the sound of Kate's voice.

Grant stepped back with a grimace. The next thing, he would be peering through the keyhole at his own wife. The sounds were certainly exercising his imagination in a thoroughly arousing way, as though his body needed any more encouragement. He gave his back one sharp slap with the towel and went out to the dressing room, where Griffin, his smart new London valet, was laying out his smart new London clothes. If nothing else, his wife would not be confronted by the travel-worn, battered, weary, grief-stricken man she had married. He gave a grunt of satisfaction as he lowered his chin the half-inch to perfect the set of the waterfall knot in his neckcloth, nodded his thanks to

Griffin and headed for the drawing room and the start of his new marriage.

Kate paused at the head of the stairs for one last calming breath, twitched her black silk skirts into order and descended the staircase in a manner befitting a countess. She had waited nearly four and a half months for this evening and the unexpected encounter with Grant that morning had done nothing to make this any easier. The exhausted, kind, patient stranger she had married was now an alert, attractive, impatient, secretive stranger. Nothing had changed for him, it seemed, except for the fact that he'd had nearly four and a half months' worth of town bronze, the status of an earl and an endless amount of time to regret marrying her. She had her looks back, her confidence as the mistress of a large country house and an inconvenient attack of physical attraction for the aforesaid stranger.

*I want a proper marriage, not simply make-believe for the rest of our lives. But what does he want?* She smiled at Giles as the footman opened the door for her and then checked on the threshold as Grant turned from the contemplation of a landscape painting she had placed over the hearth, a replacement for one of the old earl's more blood-thirsty hunting scenes.

'A definite improvement.'

For a moment she thought he meant her appearance, then he gestured to the painting. *At least he is smiling.* 'I am glad you think so.' Kate went to her usual armchair by the fireplace. The distance across the room had never felt so long, nor her limbs so clumsy. Grant moved as though he would intercept her, touch her, but she sat down before he could reach her side. With a feeling of relief that she recognised as sheer nerves she picked up her embroidery frame from the basket beside the chair. She wanted this man, but she had no idea how to cope with him.

'Naturally, I would not remove any portraits, but I found that sitting here every evening under the glazed eyes of a slaughtered stag was somewhat dampening to the spirits,' she said as she found the needle, then dropped her thimble.

Grant stooped to retrieve it and handed it to her. He moved back, but remained opposite her, one elbow on the end of the mantelpiece. In any other man she would have supposed the pose was intended to draw attention to his clothes or his figure, and it certainly did that, but Grant's attention seemed to be all on her.

'That is a charming gown. Have you been sending to London for the latest fashions?'

She had been pleased with it, although a trifle nervous of the low neckline, which the dressmaker assured her was high by London standards. 'No, merely for the latest fashionable journals. I have discovered a most accomplished dressmaker in Newcastle and an excellent fabrics warehouse.'

'In that case you might wish to accompany me into the city next week and choose something for half mourning. I imagine you are weary of unrelieved black and grey and the six months isn't too far away. I hardly feel the need to apply the strictest rules, do you?'

'We are mourning *your* grandfather, it is for you to decide, but I must confess that some colour would be welcome.' It would be a delight, to be truthful, even if it was only shades of lavender and lilac. She placed a careful row of French knots. 'Were your friends very surprised at the news of your marriage?'

Grant's eyebrows rose at the abrupt change of subject and it seemed to Kate that in moving to take the chair opposite her he was taking the time to compose his reply with care. 'My three closest friends know something of the truth.' He shrugged. 'I could hardly deceive them that our relationship was of long-standing, they know my movements too well. But I would trust them with my life and you may rely on their absolute discretion. As far as acquaintances in town are concerned, I confided in a few incorrigible gossips that Grandfather had not approved of the match, hence a secret Scottish wedding and no announcement. They were titillated enough by the disapproval not to question the date and one or two were obviously on the verge of remarking that it was convenient that his death precluded an uncomfortable confession to him following the birth of our child.'

'How…distasteful.'

'Society can be like that, I find. The prospect of gossip and scandal sharpens even the most respectable tongue.' He shrugged. 'But it plays into our hands. They'll spread the tale and provided no one has the effrontery to demand to know the date of the wedding it will soon become of no matter, and even if some conclude that we anticipated the wedding, no one will hold that against you. It will soon be old history.'

'They won't hold it against me because too many

of them have done the same, no doubt.' His lips twitched at the tartness of her tone. 'Did you tell people who I am?' she asked, trying not to sound as worried as she was. 'And what is supposed to be the reason for your grandfather's disapproval?'

'I mentioned that you were from a respectable minor gentry family in Suffolk.' She managed not to let out a long sigh of relief. 'The fact that your father was merely a country squire without connections or an established place in society was sufficient explanation for Grandfather to oppose the match. The old man was a product of his generation—nothing less than the daughter of an earl, and one bringing a substantial dowry and influence with her into the bargain, was good enough for the Earl of Allundale.'

'I see.' Kate unpicked the knot she had just set, which had become unaccountably tangled. *So presumably Madeleine had been Lady Madeleine, even though she was married to a mere Mr Rivers.*

'That was his view,' Grant said. 'I do not share it. Having married a lady with just those qualifications as my first wife, I know all too well they are no guarantee of anything. However, it makes a perfectly plausible reason.'

'Of course,' she agreed. *And the old earl was*

*quite correct—what do I bring to this marriage? We could have a good marriage, as long as I can keep my secrets, but if they become public knowledge, it will make a scandal that would rebound on Grant and on the children.* She was pleased at how composed she sounded.

'Kate, you must write to your brother soon,' Grant said.

'No. I will not write to him. I do not want him knowing anything of my marriage.'

'Kate, why ever not? I would have asked you for his direction and done so myself if I had realised you would neglect to do so. I need to talk to him about the settlements,' Grant said. 'And I assume he is holding money for you that will be released on your marriage. I seem to recall you saying something.'

*Did I? How foolish.* 'There is virtually nothing. I do not want to make a fuss about it. He has control until I marry with his approval, that is all.'

'You think he will object to me? He may not know me by reputation, but he is hardly likely to turn up his nose at an earl.'

'He would be delighted with an earl,' Kate said drily. 'But he will be unpleasant. If you must have the truth, Henry has an expensive wife and ambi-

tions beyond his means. He is quite unscrupulous.'
That was all true enough. 'If he discovers who I
have married, he would ask to borrow money—
which I doubt you would ever see again. To en-
courage him to sponge off you would not be right.'

That was harsh, but it was a mild version of the
truth. Henry would hold the scandal of Anna's
parentage over Grant, try to entangle him in that
mire. He would get a surprise if he tried it, she
thought grimly. Grant would probably throttle him.
But then there was the blackmail. What if Grant
thought he must inform the magistrate? He was an
honest, straightforward man. There was no way he
could ignore it, surely? Then he would be smeared
by association, by his marriage.

'He is my brother-in-law. I would not like to be
unreasonable. Do not sound so apologetic, my dear.
Brothers-in-law are almost expected to hang on
one's coat-tails.' The tolerant amusement in Grant's
voice was no help. 'Besides, there is the matter of
the settlements, which I really should discuss with
him. You should have what is yours.'

'It is very little, a few hundreds.'

'Settle it on Anna if you do not want it. It is always a mistake to neglect financial matters, however minor.'

Kate wondered suddenly just how wealthy Grant was. There was no stinting about the household, the land was obviously in good heart. But that might simply be because he was expending all he had on keeping things just so. Now, on top of the risk of her dubious brother touching him for loans, which would never be repaid, she had saddled him with the expense of a wife and a child. She had removed his opportunity for a much more advantageous marriage and all she could offer were the skills of any competent mistress of a country house.

For how much longer could she put Grant off about contacting Henry? Or could she add to her deceit, tell Grant that she had written to her brother, but that he had cut the connection?

But then Grant would still want to pursue her money for her and, she suspected, he would try to heal the breach. And behind those fears was the lurking terror that sooner or later he would ask her to accompany him to London, take her place beside him in society as his hostess. Inwardly she quailed. A country mouse contemplating life amidst the birds of prey of fashionable London could not have felt as inadequate. She could not even dance the waltz, Kate reflected with a descent into gloom. The faint smile felt as though it was pinned to her face. She would manage if she had to. Somehow. But if Lord Baybrook was there…

'Kate, is something wrong?' Grant had obviously noticed the artificiality of her expression.

'No, of course not.' She made the effort to smile with her eyes when all she felt was queasiness.

'There is no need to be anxious.' There was something warm in his expression, some meaning in his tone. Kate stared back, puzzled, as he added, 'About tonight, I mean.'

*He is talking about bed, about making love. Does he mean not to be anxious because he will come to me…or that he will not? I hope he comes.* There was no hiding the truth from herself that she was attracted to this man, this stranger-husband. She felt the blush rising up her face and with it the shame that Grant would see her eagerness, think her a wanton. Or perhaps he would welcome that, expect her to be very experienced and to possess sophisticated skills in bed.

It was difficult to understand this feeling. After all, her skills were non-existent and she had no idea what would be involved in sophisticated love-making.

'I am not anxious about tonight,' she said, rather too loudly.

'Dinner is served, my lady.' Grimswade somehow managed to sound even more smoothly efficient and bland than normal. When had he appeared in the doorway behind her? Had he heard? She wondered if it was possible to pass out from sheer embarrassment. Henry always said that one should treat the servants as though they were furniture and would discuss anything and everything in front of them—from an embarrassing rash to his gaming losses.

'Thank you, Grimswade.' She found a smile for the butler as she began to rise to her feet, then almost jumped in surprise to find her husband by her side, his hand outstretched.

'My dear.'

*My dear. A conventional phrase, that is all. He means nothing by it.* She put her fingertips on his wrist and resisted the urge to curl them around the strong tendons, to feel the jut of his wristbone. When she had seen him this morning her eyes had been drawn to his bare, tanned hands, a sharp contrast with her smaller, paler hands beside his on the rug. What would those long fingers look like on her body? How would they feel? Now she told herself that she could detect nothing through the fine kid of her evening gloves, not his body heat, not the pulse of his blood.

'I do hope you like the new recipe for veal ragout Cook has been trying,' Kate remarked as they walked through to the dining room. 'It is an old family one I remembered.' Discussing the food was utterly banal. He would think her so dull. But it was safe.

Giles the footman stepped forward to pull out her chair at the foot of the table for her, but Grant was before him. He pushed it in carefully as she sat, then laid one hand on her shoulder in a fleeting caress before taking his own place at the head of the long board. 'I am certain that whatever you suggest will be delightful.' That warmth was back in his eyes and behind it a question that had not been there before. Or perhaps a doubt.

Conscious of the attendant footmen, of Grimswade bringing the decanter to fill Grant's wine glass, Kate closed her lips on the impulsive questions—*What do you want of me? What do you expect of me?*—and focused her attention on the dishes arrayed on the table. At least her husband would have no reason to complain of her supervision of the kitchen, whatever he felt about her presence in his bed.

# Chapter Nine

Kate was nervous. That blush when he had mentioned *tonight* had not been the faint glow of anticipated pleasure, but the embarrassment or nerves that Grant might have expected from a virgin. But she was not untouched—the presence of little Anna was proof enough of that. So what was it? An aversion to him, or painful shyness? One would be easy enough to overcome, the other, less so.

'Have you been dining here in lonely state every night?' he asked, casting round for some innocuous topic to discuss in front of the servants. He could send them away, of course, but that might only aggravate whatever fears Kate was harbouring.

'Usually I invite Mr Gough to join me. I find he is an intelligent conversationalist. Once a week we have an early supper with Charlie in the small dining room with all the leaves taken out of the table. He enjoys the grown-up treat.'

Grant felt a jab of something unpleasantly like jealousy and instantly regretted it. His wife had been lonely, Gough was a gentleman, intelligent and doubtless pleasant company, and he, too, was probably lonely and welcomed the opportunity for conversation.

But something in his expression must have betrayed that instinctive, possessive reaction. Kate bit her lip and glanced uneasily at the footmen as though expecting a rebuke in front of them.

'An excellent idea,' Grant said with casual approval. 'My grandfather would dine with Gough when he did not have company visiting and often when he did. I am glad you had congenial adult companionship.'

'We had a lot to discuss about Charlie's lessons. Mr Gough follows your instructions carefully, of course, but there is so much day-to-day detail. I hope you do not feel I am encroaching?'

It was a question, not an apology, and Grant was careful to keep his own tone light. 'Certainly not. You are his stepmama, after all, as I am sure you would have reminded me if I had objected to your involvement.'

Kate flushed up at that, but her voice was confident as she raised it to give an order. 'Grimswade, that will be all. We will serve ourselves and ring when we require dessert.'

'My lady.' The butler gestured to the footmen and closed the door softly behind the last liveried back.

Kate put down her fork and fixed him with a direct gaze, compelling his attention. 'My lord, I think we should be frank. I have a great deal of experience of being a daughter and a sister and of the limits of my authority and freedom in those roles. Since I have been here at Abbeywell I have gained several months' worth of knowledge of how to run a large country house. But I have no experience of a husband, of the limits he will impose on my actions, of his expectations of me.'

*Ah, so now the recriminations come.* Grant chewed his mouthful of beef, swallowed and decided that dodging the issue would not help. 'In effect you feel I abandoned you.' He had done just that, but he was damned if he was going to justify himself. Which was a good thing, because he was not certain that he could. He had left Abbeywell because he knew, once he was not drugged with exhaustion and grief, that he could not bear to be there. Now he was going to have to make himself endure. He owed it to Charlie, to the estate and to his neglected wife.

Part of him had been running away from confronting what he had done by marrying a woman
without the qualifications necessary for a countess.
He was beginning to suspect he was wrong about
that judgement, but confessing that he had believed
it could only be deeply wounding to Kate.

'You had a great deal to do in London, many re-
sponsibilities in connection with the earldom. I am
not reproaching you, my lord.' Her smile was sudden, vivid, and took him completely by surprise.
'I merely explain my own…limitations.'

'I wish you would use my given name.' Grant
smiled back, charmed, and realised he had never
seen that open, uncomplicated smile from Kate before. She smiled at the children, at the servants, but
never at him.

But why would she? He had hardly seen her except as a desperate woman in the throes of labour,
or an exhausted one in its aftermath. Even that
morning her smile had been polite and dutiful. But
this expression transformed her. Strangely it did
not enhance her beauty, as a smile usually did for
a woman. Instead it emphasised the slight irregu-
larity of her face, it crinkled up her blue eyes and
showed the little gap between very white, otherwise

even, front teeth. And yet…*charmed* was the only word for his reaction. This was a real woman, not a pretty, regimented society doll. A real woman he knew not at all.

'I see no limitations, Kate. There is nothing we cannot deal with by a little discussion, an exchange of views, greater familiarity.' He chose the final word deliberately.

That produced a blush that he had no difficulty interpreting as anything but one of sensual awareness. Kate's lips were parted and she did not meet his gaze, but glanced up, above his head, blushed even more rosily and reached for her water glass.

Grant suppressed the instinctive movement to turn and look at the wall behind his chair. Of course, that was where his own portrait hung. So what was there about that to make her colour up? Unless she had spent every mealtime sitting just there, looking at his image and liking what she saw. He bit his lip to repress a grin that could only be unworthily smug. He was used to hearing himself described as a good-looking man, women seemed to like to flirt with him, but he felt no conceit about that. He looked like his grandfather at the same age, which was good fortune and no merit of his.

He could feel some satisfaction at the appreciation shown by his lovers, however, because he was confident that was due to practice and an interest in his partner's pleasure as well as his own, rather than to heredity.

His first wife had been more prone to burst into tears or tantrums at the sight of him than to blush prettily. The marriage had been an arranged one and they had hardly known each other before it. Grant had come to the conclusion that Madeleine was simply averse to sex and hoped that he was not the cause, but that it was something inbuilt in her character. She had been stiff and unresponsive in bed from the first, informing him, when he had asked her what was the matter, that her mama had explained to her that she must endure her marital duty and that was what she was doing. Enduring. It was hard work being a sensitive and imaginative lover in the face of that. And then he had made the grave tactical error of getting her pregnant too soon...

Grant pushed away the memory and focused on the very different wife facing him down six foot of polished mahogany. It occurred to him that it would be a pleasant novelty to be wed to a woman who took an interest in the physical side of marriage.

He allowed himself to smile and decided that Kate was decidedly flustered.

*Slowly, slowly, don't startle her, you are almost a stranger in her eyes,* he reminded himself. Just because she showed sensual awareness did not mean that she was not shy. He must court this woman even though she was already his countess. 'I hope you will always feel free to discuss any thoughts you have about Charlie. As for the household, it is yours to command, and if the allowances I give you for those expenses and your own expenditure are inadequate, I will certainly amend them.'

'Thank you.' Kate had recovered her composure, it seemed. She took a sip of wine. 'It would be helpful to know when we might have regular discussions about day-to-day issues.'

'Of course. Would around ten each morning suit you? I am usually back from my morning ride about then and the steward and estate manager come to see me after luncheon.' She nodded, apparently happy with the proposal. 'Of course, we will have much more time together to discuss more…intimate matters.'

The charming smile vanished, but the equally charming blush persisted. How far down did it go? Below the decorous dip of her black silk evening gown? Down far enough to tint those sweet curves with rose? Grant shifted in his chair, feeling again the lash of his own arousal. Slowly, slowly might be wise, but the seduction of his countess promised to be a leisurely pleasure.

Kate watched her husband's face and tried to read the thoughts behind that handsome, intelligent surface. She suspected that he was clever enough to hide whatever emotions he did not want her to read, although the warmth in his gaze and the faint curve of his lips when that gaze strayed downwards from her face were less revealing of deep thoughts than of basic masculine instincts, that was certain.

She wanted him, although now the man was before her in the flesh and not simply as a fantasy fuelled by a two-dimensional image, that wanting was tinged again with apprehension. Kate reached for the silver bell that stood before her place. 'Time for dessert, I think, my lord.'

One dark brow lifted.

'In front of the servants I should not be too familiar, Grant,' Kate said repressively and was rewarded by a fleeting, wicked smile that vanished into an expression of aristocratic calm when the footmen re-entered.

\* \* \*

Somehow Kate's increasingly fevered imagination had carried her directly from the dining table to the bedchamber and it came as a shock to see Grimswade setting the decanters on the sideboard when the dessert dishes were cleared, just as he always did when Mr Gough dined with her.

'I will leave you to your port, my lord.' She rose and Grant stood, too. She caught his reflection in the glass of the watercolour that hung by the door as she left and saw he was still on his feet, watching her. The glimpse of dark, shadowed eyes made her shiver deliciously.

Now what? Mr Gough would linger only long enough to drink one glass, more out of custom than pleasure, she suspected. Then he would join her for an hour, bringing journals with items he thought might interest her, or some written exercise of Charlie's that he knew she would approve.

She had come to enjoy the harmless, companionable interludes that were such a pleasant novelty. Her brother had never scrupled to leave the ladies waiting for him if he had a male companion to talk to or when he found a female guest tiresome. Sometimes, he would not join his wife and sister at all, disappearing to a cockfight in the village or to join his cronies for a game of cards without as much as a by-your-leave.

Kate picked up her embroidery, regarded the unsteady line of French knots with dismay and began to unpick them.

'If you scowl at that unfortunate piece of work much longer, it will scorch,' a deep voice remarked from just behind her.

She jumped, drove the needle into the ball of her index finger and said a naughty word under her breath. She switched the glare to Grant, who moved, soft-footed, to stand in front of her.

'You have pricked yourself. My fault for startling you.' He hunkered down, the silk of his evening knee breeches straining tight over muscular thighs, and took the wounded hand in his. 'Let me kiss it better.'

'I— Oh!' He lifted her hand, pressed his lips to the tiny bead of blood and then sucked the whole top joint of her finger into his mouth. Kate stared down at the fashionably barbered dark head bent over her hand, the wide shoulders in their blue superfine, the elegance of the man performing a small, insignificant, utterly indecent act.

Because it was indecent, she had not the slightest doubt of it. His fingers clasped lightly around her wrist, the ends over her pulse as if to monitor the effect he was having on her. She was shackled by the encircling grip as securely as if by iron manacles, because she could no more have moved her hand away than flown.

The sensitive tip of her finger was encased in the wet heat of Grant's mouth. His tongue caressed the pad until the sting of the needle prick was lost in the soft touch. She could sense the sharp edge of his teeth, carefully kept from her flesh as gradually, so very gradually, he drew her finger into his mouth as far as the middle joint. The suction pulsed, moving it in and out, his tongue tip curled and the heat rose through her as she realised what this action mimicked.

She needed to move, to squirm in her chair and push him away, draw him closer. She needed—

Grant sat back and she jerked her hand back against her bodice, the damp finger leaving a mark on the silk for a moment. 'Has that taken the sting away?' His lids were half closed, his eyes dark, his parted lips a little moist.

*As if he has been kissing me,* she thought wildly. *This is what he will look like when he holds me in his arms, when his body comes down over mine, pressing it into the bed. His* naked *body over mine, hot and hard and aroused.*

Somehow she found the composure to murmur, 'Perfectly, thank you', as though he had merely dabbed at the little puncture with his handkerchief. 'So careless of me. I might have got blood on the linen.'

Grant's lids lifted, his lips closed as he smiled and he stood up, looming over her for a moment. Kate found her eye level was precisely right for her to see that whatever he said, however coolly he might smile at her and however steadily he got to his feet, he was aroused. Impressively, alarmingly, aroused. *Just like my fantasies.*

'I think I will retire now.' It was the instinct to escape, to be alone to come to terms with what his touch was doing to her, but as soon as the words were out of her mouth she saw that Grant had interpreted them as an invitation, a direct response to what had just happened. Kate folded her embroidery into a careful square, put it into the sewing box and made herself rise with leisurely grace. Anything but let Grant see how excited and panicked he made her. Why she must hide it, she was not sure, because instinct told her he would welcome her awareness. It was pride, perhaps, or apprehension of her own limited experience disappointing him. Or was it fear that her own confused and heated fantasies would prove false and she would feel as let-down and unsatisfied as she had with Jonathan?

'Goodnight, my... Goodnight, Grant.'

His crooked smile was teasing. 'Goodnight, Kate.'

*He doesn't mean it as a farewell. He'll come to my room,* she told herself as she climbed the stairs and hurried to the nursery for Anna's goodnight kiss and a quick word with Jeannie. Then to Charlie's room, her fingers crossed that he would be asleep and there would be no battle over lights out. But he hardly stirred as she brushed the hair back from his forehead, kissed the smooth skin and pulled his tumbled covers back over his sprawled body.

Wilson, her maid, was already in Kate's bedchamber, alerted by the downstairs staff. 'The new lawn nightgown—' Kate began, then saw that it was already laid out on the bed, its matching robe beside it. Of Kate's usual comfortable plain cotton nightgown there was no sign. 'You already have it,' she observed lamely.

'Yes, my lady. With his lordship being home, I assumed this would be the right one.' The woman said it without the slightest hint of embarrassment.

Apparently she took it as a matter of course that her master would visit his wife's bedchamber and that her mistress would want to look her best.

*And why shouldn't she?* Kate told herself, attempting to look as nonchalant as the maid about the fact she was preparing to receive her husband. *She thinks we are an established married couple who have been separated for months, not two virtual strangers who have not even exchanged a kiss.*

She submitted to the bath and the hair brush, made a choice at random from the array of scent bottles presented to her, rejected the robe and climbed into bed, wishing she had not read so many Gothic tales where the heroine, a virgin sacrifice clad all in white, awaits the arrival of the mysterious dark man, who may be the villain, or, perhaps, the hero.

She tried to calm herself with thoughts of her youthful fantasies about marriage. It had been a sheltered life in the Essex countryside. Motherless, her behaviour had been subject to more scrutiny by her father and brother and the neighbouring matrons than it might otherwise have been. So flirtations were very mild, her social circle limited, her daydreams of a husband vague and romantic. No wonder she had fallen so hard for Jonathan.

Minutes passed. Kate reached for the novel she had been reading and tried to focus on it so that she would not look too eager, or too nervous, when Grant came in. She read the same page four times. The clock struck the half hour. He would have gone to look in on Charlie and perhaps also Anna. He would have bathed, or at least washed. Shaved, perhaps. He was, she suspected, a fastidious man. *Another half hour, he'll come within the next half hour,* she told herself and frowned at the small print that seemed to dance before her eyes.

She pushed one shoulder strap down, then pulled it back. *Ting,* went the clock on the mantelshelf. *Ting, ting...* Kate counted to eleven. Grant was not coming. She tossed aside the book and made herself go through all the perfectly acceptable reasons why he might not. Then she threw back the covers and slid out of bed.

No patience with slippers, no patience with a wrapper and certainly no patience with a husband who'd left her for months, then behaved in a manner enough to fluster a nun, let alone a wife, and who then left the aforesaid wife to a lonely bed and a very silly novel.

Kate opened the connecting door without bothering to knock. Grant was sitting up in bed, bare-chested, the evening beard still shadowing his chin and what appeared to be a most absorbing book in his hands.

He looked up as she stepped into the room, but he did not let go of the book.

'What are you reading?' Kate demanded.

'Constitutional procedure,' he said so calmly that she wished she was wearing slippers so she could throw one. How dared he be all relaxed when she was a positive tangle of emotions? 'I am attempting to get my head around some of the trickier aspects of the working of Parliament.' He closed the volume. 'Why? Are you looking for something interesting to read?'

'No. I am attempting to get my head around the trickier aspects of marriage,' Kate retorted. 'I see I may have to consult an encyclopaedia.' The door, when she turned and stalked back into her bedchamber, slammed with the most satisfying bang.

It opened again before she reached the bed. 'Perhaps I might assist,' her husband offered.

# Chapter Ten

Kate kept walking on shaky legs, climbed into bed and only then turned. Grant was dressed, somewhat sketchily, in a heavy green silk robe, belted loosely at the waist over what appeared to be nothing but bare skin.

She took a strengthening breath down to her diaphragm. 'Assist? You, my lord, are the source of my confusion.'

'Because I did not come to your bed?' He moved to the foot of it, sat with his back against the post, legs stretched out parallel with hers, and studied her face.

Kate made herself lie still and not acknowledge the insidious pressure of his body. One long, bare, elegant foot pressed against her hip bone. She wanted to run a finger along the sharp cords of tendon, the curve of his instep. Instead she said,

'I told myself that Charlie might have had a night-mare, or that you were so tired after your journey that you had fallen asleep or that a crisis might have occurred on the estate. All those were per-fectly reasonable excuses for flirting with a wife you had not seen for months and then failing to… to join her. But constitutional procedure? I am not a vain woman, but really, I had not placed myself below turgid reading matter of that sort.'

'I was employing it to take my mind off your presence in the next room. It was not very success-ful, and if I had been aware of that nightgown, it would have been even less so.' As Grant leaned back, the front of his robe gaped open to reveal the side of his muscular chest, dusted in dark hair.

'Why?' It seemed she was only capable of enough breath for one word at a time.

'I thought you were nervous. Shy. Flustered.' He shrugged and the robe gaped more. Kate held her breath. 'I did not want to pressure you.'

'Of course I was…*am* shy. I do not know you. We have never even kissed, let alone…that. How am I supposed to feel?'

'You are not a virgin,' Grant pointed out. He looked faintly wary, she was glad to see. *So he should be. He is lucky I am not throwing* The Caledonian Bandit *by Miss Smith at his head. It is all it is fit for.*

'Clearly not.' She had her breath back now the robe had ceased its descent. 'But I am not at all experienced. I…I became pregnant very quickly.' She tried to recall what she had told him about her lover. Lying was so alien and so difficult. 'And we could not meet often.'

'I'm not a virgin, either, of course. I don't expect you to hold that against me. But you are not at all experienced?' He seemed to be pleased by that. Men were strange creatures.

'Yes. I mean, no.' It had been lovely to be in Jonathan's arms, to be able to show her feelings for him, of course it had. While it lasted, before disillusion set in. But even at the height of her short-lived infatuation he had never made her feel so agitated, so confused as this did. And it had not been such a wonderful experience that she was desperate to repeat it, so why did she want Grant to shrug off that robe, come to bed and just— 'So, yes, I was apprehensive. I am still. But now I think it would be better to simply get it over with.'

'Get it over with,' Grant repeated, his voice flat. 'Your expectations do not appear to be very high.'

His hands had gone to the ties of his robe. Now they stilled.

'I am sure you make love very nicely,' Kate said politely, wishing the soft feather mattress would simply swallow her up. Now she had insulted him. No man was going to take well the suggestion that his lovemaking was anything but magnificent. *Very nicely? Of all the things to say...*

'I have not had any complaints recently.' Grant straightened up from his relaxed slouch against the bedpost.

*Recently? From his mistress, I suppose. Does that mean his late wife...* Pride made her bite back the question. 'I just thought it would be better to—'

'Get it over with. Yes, I grasp the point that flirting and courting and giving you time to get accustomed to me may not be the best way to go about this and that you really wish it was all over.' He stood up and tugged the knot in the sash free. 'But you do wish me to come to your bed?'

'Yes. Of course. Lights?' It came out as a squeak. The branch of candles was still alight on her dressing table and the little oil lamp by the bed cast a warm, but revealing, glow over the snowy expanse of sheets.

'We have confided that neither of us is a virgin. I

think we can cope with the shock of nudity.' Grant shrugged off the robe. He sounded less than happy.

Kate closed her eyes, then, when there was no sound of movement, opened them again. Grant was standing there, hands on lean hips, waiting, she supposed, for her to faint, scream or dive under the covers. She did none of those things, just stared at his admirably flat stomach, then, when she thought her breathing was under control, let her gaze slide lower.

He was not as aroused as he had been in the drawing room when he had been sucking her finger, but then he was probably finding her so infuriating that it was killing his desire. Kate realised suddenly that she did not want that. She wanted Grant to make love to her, here, now and with enthusiasm. His eyebrows lifted as she threw back the covers, reached for the hem of her nightgown and dragged it over her head in one ungainly movement.

When she made herself meet his gaze she found he had not moved, but the green eyes were dark beneath lowered lids and his mouth was curved into a crooked smile that held both approval and a promise.

'Right from when we first met, I knew you had

courage,' Grant said as he closed the distance between them. He lay down beside her and, to her enormous relief, pulled the covers up over their bare bodies. She was very aware that the last time she had lain with a man she had not given birth to a child and that this man had once been married to a woman who, if Kate had discovered nothing else about her, had been a beauty.

The warmth of his body as he lay beside her was comforting, but her nerves were jangling and she just wished he would get on with it. 'Have you changed your mind?' she asked.

'No.' Grant turned so he was on his side facing her and moved closer, until the evidence of just how much he had *not* thought better of this was branding itself to her hip. 'I was giving you the opportunity to dive out of the other side of the bed if you had changed yours.'

Afterwards Kate had no idea whether it had been nerves, hysteria or simply her old sense of the ridiculous reasserting itself, but she found herself laughing. 'Like a scene in a French farce,' she managed between gasps of mirth. 'In and out of bedrooms, in and out of bed...'

'You have obviously been watching far more *risqué* farces than I have,' Grant said with a grin, and then, before she had stopped laughing, before the nerves could seize her again, he rolled her on to her back and kissed her.

Kate was open-mouthed on a gasp of laughter and Grant took advantage of her parted lips to take possession, his tongue sliding in to stroke hers, his lips warm and firm and demanding. For a first kiss it was anything but tentative, but nor was it impatiently demanding. *Here I am,* Grant seemed to be saying. *I want you, you want me. Shall we?*

Her body knew the answer, it seemed. Her arms curled around his neck, pulling him closer as her tongue stroked against his. *Yes.* He felt so different, so new. Taller and more muscular than Jonathan, his hands slower, yet more assured, his taste absolutely new and very arousing. Her hands slid over his shoulder and the right one encountered long, rough tracks of scar tissue. Grant shrugged away from her touch and she took the hint, curling her fingers around his neck instead. Then she forgot all about scars.

When Grant broke the kiss, gathering her in against his chest, she rubbed her cheek against the dusting of coarse hair, learning his scent. Citrus from the soap he had washed with, a faint hint of leather, a distant tang of brandy, a musk that was very male, very much him. The scent she remembered from that long desperate night when he had sat close beside her and she had clung to his hand, patterning it with bruises, spiced now with arousal.

'That tickles,' he said, his voice a rumble under her cheek. His hands were beginning to stray, down over her hips, up across her ribs, curving around her buttocks. Kate let her own fingers wander, exploring the flat stomach, dipping into his naval, which made him gasp with laughter, running up and down the thicker line of hair, not daring to follow it all the way.

Grant seemed content to let her roam, but his own hands became more purposeful, stroking up over the curve of her breasts, rubbing across her nipples just enough to make them peak and tingle, then down to brush the curls at the apex of her thighs.

Kate began to move, restless, and found her fingers were gripping Grant's hips. Jonathan had been faster, more urgent, rougher. Did Grant not want her with the same desire?

His lips closed over one aching nipple and she moaned, arching up against him. She felt his lips curve into a smile and then shivered with nerves as he shifted and pressed one hand gently between her thighs, opening her.

'Oh, yes,' he said, the words vibrating against the puckered skin of her nipple, and his teeth nipped gently as he slid one finger into her. Then his thumb found the place that Jonathan had rubbed against so impatiently. Only, Grant was gentle, teasing, and the raw, almost intolerable sensation became one of pulsing sweetness mixed with a desperation that had her squirming against his hand.

'Shh, slowly, slowly,' he murmured against her neck.

But she did not want to be slow. She wanted him now, wanted the *more* that she could sense, just out of her reach. Her right hand moved from his hip, stroked down, touched the heated flesh and stroked again until he groaned aloud.

'If you do that—'

'Yes,' Kate urged. 'I want...I don't know. I need...'

Grant's weight was a fresh arousal as their bodies touched down their entire lengths, hot skin against hot skin. He shifted, lifted on his elbows and then, holding her gaze with his, sheathed himself within her.

'Ah...sweet Kate.' He closed his eyes, dropped his head so his forehead rested on hers and held still. She felt the tension vibrating through him as she grasped the broad shoulders, tilted her head so her lips found his. The urgent need to move became a longing for peace as she lay there, so close, so much at one with him. She let her body encompass his, ease around it, holding him within her.

When he began to move it was at first so slow, so gentle, that she hardly realised that her own body was rocking with his, yielding to the slow thrusts, the need building again as she released the hard flesh only to accept him back with a soft gasp of pleasure. The rhythm increased until she was clinging to him, gasping as they rode the gathering, building storm together.

Grant shifted, lifted her against him, and the pressure built until she was curled around him, her ankles locked at the small of his back, striving desperately to catch hold of whatever it was that was tormenting her so deliciously, promising something that was just out of reach. And suddenly she broke apart, heard herself cry out, felt Grant tense and arch over her, and then the world went black, save for the lights in the darkness behind her lids as she let go and flew.

What had just happened? Kate lay in the circle of Grant's arm, her cheek against his chest. His skin was damp, his heartbeat strong, rapid, but slowing as she sensed him drifting into sleep.

What had *happened*? she asked herself again, lying wide-eyed in the flickering candlelight. She hardly knew this man except as the Good Samaritan who had saved her that bleak Christmas. Saved her, saved her child, turned her life upside down. Yes, he was an attractive man, but a man with secrets, a man with barely hidden darkness in his soul.

She had married him, accepted the protection of his name, his status and his wealth. Accepted, too, that she had a duty as his wife to lie with him and perhaps, if she was fortunate, to bear a child of his. *And I had become excited by the thought of him,* she admitted to herself. *Aroused.* Which was good, because it would have been hard to accept lovemaking with a man for whom she could feel no attraction.

But this wonderful physical experience—where had that come from? She had known Jonathan a little, liked him, thought she loved him, considered him a handsome man and had been eager to go to his arms. Yet his passion had left her strangely untouched, unsatisfied, confused. *I talked myself into love with him, didn't I?* Kate told herself. But she did not love this man, either, so what was the difference? *Why did I not burn up in Jonathan's arms as I did with Grant?*

*Because Grant is the better lover, of course.* So it was all a matter of technique, of arousal, and in her imaginings when she met Jonathan she had told herself the romantic lies that it was all about love.

Kate turned away from the comfort of the warm, strong body beside her to lie on the edge of the bed on cold sheets. *I deserve the chill,* the nagging little voice of her conscience chided. *Wanton.* 'Jonathan,' she whispered. What a fool she had been, how eager to experience love, when really what she had been seeking was this, this physical delight. And as a result of her naivety and Henry's cynical scheming she had been ruined and was now hundreds of miles from home, living a lie.

That had been…incredible. Grant let himself drift in utterly relaxed drowsiness, his body boneless with sensual pleasure. He had never expected it, never thought that Kate would catch alight in his hands, that her body would answer his with that joyful, urgent sensuality.

She curled against him now, warm, soft. Kate, his wife, who did not react to his kisses and caresses as though forcing herself to yield to her duty, but as though she wanted to join him in creating magic. To find a compatible lover was not such a novelty, but to find that, quite by chance, he had married a woman who took and gave with such sweet, almost innocent, eroticism, that was a miracle.

Kate moved, turned away, and he woke fully to see she was lying, her back to him, on the edge of the bed. 'Oh, Jonathan...' He caught the faint whisper and even with that thread of sound, the unhappiness.

Something cold and heavy lodged in his stomach. Disappointment? Jealousy? So, Kate was still in love with Anna's father, still mourning him, which must explain her shyness and confusion earlier. Now she was feeling guilty for enjoying making love with her husband.

Because she had enjoyed it, that was not arrogance on his part—even the most accomplished courtesan could not have feigned that reaction. Grant reached out his hand to touch her shoulder, then drew it back before his fingers reached the curve of exposed skin. Reluctant to intrude, he turned on his side away from Kate's tense body and pulled the covers up over both of them. If he touched her now, she would think it was a demand for more sex. If he tried to console her, then she would know he had heard that whisper. He had no idea what to say to make things any better. At least now he understood her strange mood, the evidence of interest, of arousal, and yet the fear that forced her to ask for his presence in her bed had driven her to want to *get it over with.*

Grant got up, went to snuff the candles, doused the bedside lamp, pretended that he believed Kate was fast asleep as he fought down the dark mood that threatened to grip him. It was unreasonable, to feel…hurt. He was not in love with Kate and she had made no pretence of marrying him for anything other than the protection of his name for her child, so in no sense was he betrayed or deceived. She did not dislike him, he was certain, and she was certainly not repelled by him. It was simply that she had been in love with someone else, someone for ever out of her reach. And now she was making the best of the circumstances. In effect he had married a widow and done so before she'd had a proper chance to mourn.

But how to mend this marriage? He had the summer and the autumn, that was all. Then they must go to London, he would take his seat in the House of Lords and Kate must learn to be a peer's wife, a society hostess. They could do it as virtual strangers—after all, many marriages functioned like that—but it was not how he wanted his marriage to be and it was not how he wanted the children to grow up, in a household with parents who were distant and cool with each other.

A hideous accident had taken Madeleine before Charlie's life could be blighted by his parents' unhappiness, but Grant was not prepared to risk it again. He could live without a wife's affection, certainly without her love, but somehow, for the sake of the children, he was going to have to make this work and make Kate happy, or, at the very least, content.

## *Chapter Eleven*

When Grant opened his eyes on to the dawn light he found that, against all expectation, he had slept without his dreams being full of heat and flames and he had woken knowing how he was going to deal with his marriage. He would not let Kate guess he had heard her last night, he would not mention her lover, he would apologise for his long absence in London and then he would simply carry on as though everything was normal. He would make love to his wife, he would talk to his wife, he would ask his wife's opinions—and he would keep her so busy out of bed, so well satisfied in it, that she would not have the energy to mope over the man who had fathered Anna.

Beside him Kate stirred. He curled his arm around her and pulled her round to face him. She mumbled sleepily, eyes still closed, hair tousled, but she did not resist. Grant tightened his grip and bent to kiss her. 'Good morning, Lady Allundale.'

*If she seems the slightest bit reluctant, then we'll have to talk...* But Kate's lips opened under the pressure of his and her arms came up around his neck, her fingers sliding into the hair at his nape in a way that made him shiver with anticipation. It was a start. *Make love to her until she's dizzy,* he told himself, inhaling the scent of warm, sleepy woman. That would be no hardship.

Kate woke, stretched, blushed. She was alone in her bed, but Grant was still a powerful presence in the room. Her body ached pleasurably in the most intimate places, the musk of their lovemaking was heady in the air, the bedclothes were a tangle and, when she turned her head to look at the pillow where his head had rested, there was a single dark brown hair that curled around her finger when she touched it.

So, last night had not been a dream. They had made love twice and Grant had seemed to be very satisfied with the result. She most certainly was— physically satisfied, that was. Mentally she felt happy, guilty, confused and apprehensive. Happy, because to take that much pleasure in one's husband's arms must be a blessing—and the greatest good fortune. But she did not understand how it could be that she could do so. She did not love Grant and he did not love her. Would this last, or had it been a fluke? She wished she could talk to him about it, but how could she?

The conversation would be impossible. *I am overwhelmed by how good it is to make love with you. But why did I not feel like that with the man who took my virginity? Is it always going to be like that? Am I very ignorant and unskilled? Will you become tired of me soon? Am I disgracefully wanton?*

What if he agreed that, yes, she was lacking skill and sophistication, yes, the experience had been nothing out of the ordinary for him? 'I would sink with shame,' she murmured.

'My lady?' Wilson had entered from the dressing room with her usual quiet efficiency. The mistress of the household might have had the most wonderful and confusing night of her life, but the routine continued as usual.

'Nothing.' Kate cast a despairing glance around the bedchamber as the curtains were drawn back and light flooded in, revealing the wrecked bed, the sash of Grant's robe, her own nightgown tossed to the floor. Wilson merely glided around, gathering things up. She folded the sash neatly and set it aside.

'Would you care for breakfast here in your room, my lady? Or will you be taking it in the breakfast parlour?' That was where Kate normally took it, along with Charlie and his tutor.

'His lordship—'

'His lordship rode out about an hour ago, my lady. I understand from his man that it is his usual habit when in residence here.' There was not the faintest suggestion in her voice that his wife might be expected to know this. But of course, Grant had spoken of it last night and she had forgotten. For the past few months she had felt in control of herself, of this household. Now the arrival of one man meant, it seemed, that she could not even recall last night's conversation.

'I will take breakfast as usual in the parlour, after I have seen Lady Anna.' And Grant had suggested that they meet at ten to discuss practical matters. That had seemed an excellent idea at the time, now she could not imagine producing one coherent word when she had to face him again.

\* \* \*

The harmless meeting still did not seem anything but an ordeal to be survived when she tapped on the study door on the stroke of ten.

'Come in!'

She pushed the door open and Grant came to his feet behind the big desk. 'My dear Kate, you have no need to knock.'

*My dear Kate.* 'Thank you.' She made herself meet Grant's eyes and smile. She at least felt rather more composed now she was dressed and had made a neat list of things to talk about. It was amazing how clothes made a barrier to hide behind. Last night she had been naked with this man, clawing at his muscled back, revelling in the hard thrust of his body.

Kate took a firm hold on her imagination and forced herself to be practical. This was broad daylight. She was the mistress of the house, coming to discuss harmless domestic matters. She should not feel awkward—after all, up until yesterday she had not needed to knock on any door in this house. Except for the one Grant kept locked. Bluebeard's chamber. Madeleine's rooms. She took the seat on the other side of the expanse of polished oak. 'I have several things I would like to discuss.'

'So do I. An early ride gives me the opportunity for some uninterrupted thinking, so I made some notes.' Grant picked up the sheet of paper from the blotter in front of him, frowned at it, then abruptly screwed it up and tossed it into the hearth. 'And I thought I had worked it all out, a plan for this marriage.'

'A plan? Why do we need a plan?'

'I did not think we did. I thought I would come back here for the summer, join my wife and family, spend a pleasant few months getting to grips with the estate and then take us all back to London after Christmas when Parliament reconvenes. Then you could enjoy the Season.'

'And that is no longer your intention?' *Please, not London.*

'Certainly it is. And I thought that it would be easy enough to find a way to live together, to co-exist and form a household, despite the way our marriage started.'

Her mouth felt dry. Kate willed herself to say calmly, 'So what has changed?' What had gone wrong that he had brooded about on his morning ride?

'Last night—' He broke off, looked out of the window and then back at her as though making the effort to meet her gaze. 'I was not going to say anything. I thought we could coexist, work together and simply put the past behind us. But in the light of day, I wonder if that is the best way forward for us.' He picked up a quill without looking at it and Kate watched as it bent in his grip. When it snapped Grant glanced down as though he was unaware he had been holding it.

'I see.' She could hear that her voice was colourless, but for the life of her she did not know how to inject any warmth into it. 'You must find me inexperienced, lacking in…sophistication.'

'In bed? Oh, hell.' Grant got to his feet, came round the desk and sat on the edge of it, close to her. 'No, that is *not* what I mean. Last night was very pleasurable for me, Kate. Very. But I heard what you whispered afterwards. You are still in love with him, aren't you? You are doing your duty as my wife, but you still love Anna's father.' He said *duty* as though it was a dirty word.

'I… No, I don't.' She realised how important it was to make Grant understand that. He did not love her, he was not asking or expecting her to love *him*, but he must loathe the thought that he had taken to his bed a woman who was gritting her teeth and doing her duty—even if she discovered she enjoyed it.

If Jonathan had been a groom from the stables, a local farmer, a merchant from King's Lynn—any of those—she could tell the truth, admit he was alive and had refused to marry her. But how could she confess that her lover had been an aristocrat who was in all probability known to Grant? The awful thought struck her that they might be friends. What if Jonathan had confided in him? *I'm being blackmailed by some dirty little worm and his two-faced bitch of a sister.*

She had to keep lying even though she hated it. 'I had thought I must still love him, but I am not in love and perhaps I never was.' She stared up at Grant, trying to find the right words, create a safe fiction that would protect her—and him—from the humiliation of the discovery that he had married not just another man's cast-off lover, that he had given his name, not to some fatherless baby, but a child with a parent who could very well support it. A man who would probably want to see her and her brother tried for blackmail.

Kate tried to find a story that would satisfy him. 'Jonathan was going to America, and then he would send for me. But when no letter came, when I realised he must be dead, lost at sea, then I was frantic with worry. But not with grief. I was sad, but I wasn't devastated. And I would have been, wouldn't I, if I loved him?'

It was partly true. When Henry told her that Lord Baybrook had refused to marry her she had been frightened, but she had been more fearful that Henry would challenge him to a duel rather than shattered by his betrayal. If she had loved him, truly loved him, his refusal to protect her should have broken her heart. And when she had found out Henry's infamy, if she had loved Jonathan she would have gone to him, done everything in her power to put things right. As it was, to her shame, she had done nothing until she realised that Henry was a threat to her unborn child.

'I see.' Grant lifted a hand as though to touch her, then let it fall back to rest on his thigh. The broad hand gripped the buckskin-covered muscle and the movement sparked a dull gleam from the signet on his finger.

She could not raise her gaze from his hand. 'You are shocked.' Of course he was, what did she expect? 'It was scandalous enough that I slept with him, but if I did not even have the excuse of loving him… And now, to find such pleasure with a man I hardly know? You must think I am a wanton.'

'I think I am a lucky man.' Kate jerked up her head and saw Grant's smile—sudden, dazzling. Confusing. Then he bent down, pulled her into his arms and up to perch on the desk beside him. 'You are not wanton, Kate. You are sensual, passionate and desirable. I thought I was marrying a woman with courage and intelligence who would be a good stepmother to Charlie. I rather think I have been more fortunate than I deserve.'

'Desirable?' She was no traditional beauty, she knew that. And childbirth had made changes to her body, even though she had ridden and walked until her figure was trim again and her muscles taut.

'Desirable,' Grant confirmed and bent his head to snatch a kiss from her lips. 'Did you not notice how much pleasure you gave me last night?'

Kate felt ready to sink, but Grant was being frank with her, and very understanding, so she owed it to him to be equally frank. Besides, his arm around her waist, the pressure of his body against hers, gave her courage. 'I thought men didn't mind very much who they were with, once they were actually making love. That any woman would do.'

Beside her Grant made a sudden, suppressed

sound. Laughter or outrage? 'Believe me, we mind.'
It had been laughter. 'And, no, any woman will not
do. Except for the sort of rutting beasts whom I
hope you will never encounter.'

'You do not find being married to me as bad as
you feared, then?' She let herself lean into him,
reading his mood through the feel of the big body
more easily than she could interpret his expression.

Grant stiffened, then she felt him relax. *He has
decided to carry on being truthful.* 'I foresaw dif-
ficulties, and the bedchamber was one of them. I
am much reassured.'

'And the others included the fact that you thought
me plain, awkward and unfit to be an earl's wife?'
Kate prodded.

'As you observed yesterday, neither of us was at
their best last Christmas.'

'So you left me here rather than allow London
society to see who you'd married.' As soon as she
said it, she knew the fact that he had left her here
had been a blow to her pride, even as she had been
so relieved that he had done so. And it was very
poor tactics to make him think she wanted to go
there now.

Grant got to his feet and began to pace around the
study. 'I could not… It was too soon after the birth

for you to travel.' Perhaps he was not prepared for total honesty after all. At least, she pondered, he was careful not to hurt her feelings.

'You could have sent for me when Charlie went to London for the second time.'

'I told myself that Anna was too young, that she was better here in the country air.'

'You told yourself?'

Grant swung round and she saw his expression was rueful, not angry. 'You listen to what is behind the words, don't you? Yes, I *told myself* we were better apart. My reasons for marrying you were good, I knew that. But the risks, the drawbacks, seemed greater the longer I was away from you.'

*And you did not come back, you left it months. Why?* 'And now?' *This is the rest of our lives, the choice between happiness or, at best, a bitter toleration.*

'Now I wish I had come back sooner, begun to know my wife sooner. London and the Season may be a trifle…sticky, but we have months to build this marriage to be too strong for gossip to break it and for you to become a confident countess.'

*It is to be happiness, then.* She pushed away the thought of the Season, the threat implicit in those words. 'I have a list,' Kate said and smiled at her husband. For the first time since she had woken up to the enormity of what she had done, the word *husband* did not fill her with apprehension. And London was a long way away, time to worry about that later.

'And what is on this list? An increased dress allowance? I'm to make numerous morning calls with you?' He was teasing her, but his eyes held that familiar reserve. What did he think she would demand?

'I want you to show me the house and the estate yourself. Tell me about it and what it means to you. Let me see it through your eyes.' That was what she had wanted, for all those months. She needed to understand Abbeywell and its importance to Grant and Charlie, then she would know how to live here, not as a visitor, but as part of it. There were changes she could see that needed making, projects that would improve the life of the tenants, the ease of using the house, the beauty of the estate, but she had no right to make them without consultation and some she would not even suggest if her idea for diverting the stream to make a water garden meant drowning Grant's favourite boyhood hideout or the suggestion for building a communal laundry for the village was simply too expensive. Opening the door to Madeleine's rooms was far down the list of what she could venture upon, even though it was becoming something dangerously like an obsession.

'You want me to show you around? But you have been here for months, running the household. Charlie must have dragged you all over the grounds, Mrs Havers will have covered the domestic side of things.'

'Yes, but it is your *home*, you grew up here. Now I am your wife I need to understand it as you do, if that is possible.' Grant still seemed surprised. 'It will help me understand you, too.'

'If that is what you would like, then of course.' He sounded merely polite, but Kate thought he was pleased. 'You realise that you will be undermining the main complaint of husbands everywhere—*my wife does not understand me*?'

'Is that what you men say to each other in your clubs to justify lurking there, drinking and gaming, or is it what you whisper in the ears of ladies who you hope will take pity on you and share their favours?'

Her relief at the change of mood between them had carried her into dangerous waters. Grant raised one dark brow and was suddenly no longer the amused, slightly flirtatious husband of a moment ago. 'Are you asking me if I am faithful to you?'

Kate slid from her perch on the desk. It was no longer the time and place to sit swinging her feet, behaving like a milkmaid with her swain. She must remember that she was a countess. 'No, I am not asking you that question and I do not think I ever would. But if you are asking if I wonder about other women, then, yes, of course I do. I know that men are not designed to be celibate, even the best of husbands.'

'I keep forgetting that you do not know me,' Grant said and she saw from the set of his mouth that she had managed to insult him again. 'I take marriage seriously. I may not have made vows to you in church, but I will act as though I have. I will be faithful to you and I have been since we wed, if you are wondering about a mistress in London, or even less reputable arrangements.'

'Thank you...' Kate managed. Her sister-in-law, Jane, had confided that no man could be trusted to be faithful, that it was in their very nature to seek out new excitements, new women. She had shrugged in the face of Kate's shocked disbelief and incoherent protests about honour and love matches. Men, Jane maintained, were all tomcats by nature and male honour did not preclude infidelity. Either her sister-in-law was wrong, or Grant was telling her what she wanted to hear. She trusted his honour, she realised. Grant would keep his vows.

'And I am sure I do not need to say that I do not subscribe to any fashionable tolerance in regards to my wife.' He waved a dismissive hand when she opened her mouth to protest. 'I am sure you will be as faithful as a wife can be, Kate. I am just saying, for the record, that I will call out any man who lays a finger on you—and do my damnedest to kill him. And if your Jonathan had abandoned you and not drowned, then I would go after him and kill him, too.'

They stared at each other for a long moment, then Kate said, slowly, 'You may trust me with your honour and mine and I trust you in the same way.' She would never betray him with another man—but the pit was gaping at her feet. She had lied to him, she continued to lie to him, and if he realised that her lover was alive and was being blackmailed by her brother, she did not know what he would do.

'Enough of this serious stuff.' Grant's sudden grin caught her off balance as it had done every time he had surprised her with it. 'What is the first place you want to explore with me?'

'The water garden.'

'We do not have a water garden,' Grant pointed out.

'I know. I think we should, don't you?' *He need never find out.* She forced herself to smile and found it was real. Tomorrow might never come, Christmas was a long way off and, for now, they were happy.

# Chapter Twelve

Grant came with her to visit Anna, who delighted him by smiling and gurgling and gripping his fingers. He picked her up, despite the nursemaid's warnings about babies who had recently been fed, and tossed her up to make her laugh.

'Never mind, my lord,' Jeannie said consolingly, ten seconds later. 'I'm sure it will sponge off.'

By the time Kate had found her bonnet and cloak, Grant had surrendered his milky coat to a silently disapproving valet and changed to a battered old shooting jacket and well-worn boots. 'I have a suspicion that water gardens mean bogs,' he said as he joined her on the steps down to the rear garden. 'At least the sun is shining.'

Kate led the way across the formal parterre to the lower level where a lawn, uneven and rank despite the gardeners' best efforts with scythe and roller, sloped away from the woods.

'The view from the parterre in this direction is dull and this lawn leads nowhere except to that boggy patch just inside the woodland. See, where all the alders are, and those rushes, beyond the bank?'

'There's a spring there. I remember that it used to be a good place to find frogs. I think Grandfather had the bank thrown up to keep the water from the lawn.' Grant strode towards the woodland, then stopped as his foot sank into mud. 'And not very effectively, by the looks of it!'

'We can skirt round.' Kate was already leading the way and scrambled up the bank. 'I thought if the bank was breached and the spring water channelled, then it would come out here. We could excavate a chain of ponds across this lawned area and puddle the bottoms.'

Grant had walked further along the top of the bank, but he turned to look back at her. 'And what do you know about puddling bottoms, Lady Allundale?'

'I read about it in a book I ordered on making artificial water features. You need a great deal of stiff clay, then it is spread across the bottom of the hollow and trampled down by lots of men in stout boots.'

'Lots of men?' Grant was frowning now.

'I thought it would be valuable employment for the local people. But if you think it would be too costly, of course I understand.' How foolish to allow her imagination to run away with her when she had no idea how far Grant's resources would stretch. He had this estate and a London house to maintain, a son to educate and now a wife and daughter.

'It sounds like an excellent idea. I was simply disappointed that when you said *we*, you meant a gang of hefty labourers. I had assumed you and I would be puddling in the mud.'

'Us?'

'Mmm.' Grant seemed oblivious to her gasp of scandalised laughter as he looked around the boggy patch and then further into the woods to where a shaft of sunlight lit up one of Kate's favourite places, a glade of soft grass spangled with wild flowers. 'I like the idea of getting very wet and very muddy with you. I appreciate your eye for landscape as well, my dear. What do you make of that sunlit patch through there?'

'It is lovely and usually quite dry underfoot because it is on a slight slope. I would not like to damage it if we do make the water garden.'

'It merits further inspection.' Grant held out his right hand. 'Let me help you around the edge of the mire.' Intrigued, Kate followed. 'How very wise of you to bring a cloak,' he observed as he turned to face her and she caught her breath at the wicked intent in his expression.

'Why?' Although she could already guess and his fingers were at the ties at her neck.

'Because we do not want grass stains on the back of that charming walking dress, do we?'

'Grant! In the open? What if someone sees us?'

'Who?' He looked up from spreading the cloak on the grass. 'No one can see this spot from the house—I used to hide here often enough as a boy.'

'I don't know! Gardeners, gamekeepers. Poachers,' she added wildly as her husband tossed aside his coat and began to untie his neckcloth.

'The gardeners are scything the front lawns. The gamekeepers are chasing the poachers over there.' Grant knelt down and gestured vaguely to the east. 'I am tired of being serious and sensible. I am tired of duty. I want to be utterly frivolous with my wife.' He held out his hand. 'Do you want to be frivolous with your husband?' he asked as his fingers went to the fastenings of his falls.

An hour later Kate flopped back on to her crumpled cloak beside the long, naked body of her husband as he sprawled face down, half on and half off the cloak.

'That,' he observed without moving, 'was excellently frivolous.'

'I would never have thought it.' Kate snuggled against Grant's flank, glad of the heat of his skin. The breeze was cool through the trees, despite the sun almost reaching its height. 'If I had been asked to describe you, *frivolous* would be one of the last words I would have thought of.'

'I used to be wild, a rakehell in training, my grandfather always said.' Grant rolled over on to his back. 'When I was at university with Gabe and Alex and Cris they called us the Four Disgraces. That's why he did not oppose my attending medical school. He said a few years in cold, dour Edinburgh delving into cadavers would sober me up better than anything short of a spell in the army and with less chance of him losing his heir.'

'Did it sober you?' Kate buried the chilly tip of her nose in the angle of his neck and shoulder and smiled as he muttered in protest. He stopped complaining when she slid her hand, palm down, across the flat planes of his chest and began to play with the curls of hair.

'Coming home and finding my grandfather recovering from a heart seizure did that. I was needed here and I couldn't expect him to carry the burden of the estate and all its business while I pursued an interest that could only ever be that—an interest.'

She sat up, but stayed close to his warmth as she admired the lean, masculine beauty of the body lying beside her. The only flaws were the raking scars from his right shoulder, disappearing down to his shoulder blade. That was what she had felt the first time they had lain together.

Kate leaned over and touched them. 'You said you were in the army for a while. When was that?' She could feel him bracing himself against the desire to shrug her hand away.

'I volunteered in '15, when Bonaparte escaped from Elba. I was at Waterloo and escaped with my life and a healthy horror of warfare.'

'So you were wounded and these are battle scars?'

'No.'

She stared at them. There was something familiar about them, the way the flesh had been damaged, the way the weapon had raked through the flesh. Then she remembered Jason Smith, who had been Henry's groom years ago. He would get drunk and pick fights and he was, from all the rumours, a nasty dirty fighter when he'd taken drink. Then one evening he had come staggering into the kitchen, pouring blood, and Kate had helped the housekeeper dress the wounds. Long, raking parallel cuts like these, the result of a slashing blow from a broken bottle. Surely Grant was not the kind of man who got involved in barroom brawls? But that flat negative had been a clear warning, and if he had wanted to explain the scars, then he would.

'And then you married?' she asked as though her questions had not interrupted the story of his life.

'Yes.' There was no change in Grant's tone, but he sat up and reached for his clothes. The affirmative had been as flat as the negative and just as clear a warning. *No trespassing.* 'You are getting chilled, best to get dressed before the gardeners decide to scythe the back lawns, as well.'

He helped Kate with laces and pins, exhibiting the facility with feminine garments that she had noticed back in the bothy. If she had felt a little more confident, she might have twitted him gently on the subject, but she had strayed far enough into dangerous waters with that question about his first marriage.

'We need a summer house, you know.' Grant sat on a tree stump to pull on his boots. He pointed at a flat area in the centre of the clearing. 'If we built one there, it would have a view down to your new water gardens.' He stood and stamped his feet firmly into the battered old boots. 'Then we can be frivolous whatever the weather and with less chance of scandalising our innocent staff and the not-so-innocent poachers.'

'Classical or rustic?' Kate laced her half-boots, determined to be as sophisticated about the prospect of future al fresco lovemaking as Grant was. The prospect was delicious in itself, but most of all she treasured the fact that he was becoming so relaxed with her. Surely, soon, the scars from his unhappy first marriage would fade?

'Classical,' Grant said. 'A little temple in the woods. It will have a fireplace and an inner chamber we can lock and a room for picnics on warm rainy days.'

They strolled back up to the parterre, hand in hand, bickering gently about how a chimney could be incorporated into a classical temple, and were met by Charlie, his tutor at his heels.

'There you are, Papa! Have you fallen off your horse? Your hair is on end and your hat has gone. And, Maman, did you know your cloak is inside out?'

'Lord Brooke, we have discussed the fact that a gentleman does not pass personal comments on the appearance of others, have we not?' Mr Gough was so straight-faced that Kate was certain he had a very good idea of just what his employers had been doing.

Charlie grimaced at the formal address, the signal that he was in the wrong. 'I am sorry, Maman, Papa. Only, I was looking for you. The post has come and there are letters with Uncle Alex's seal on, and Uncle Cris's and a very splodgy one that must be from Uncle Gabriel, I think, because he told me he had lost his signet ring whilst dicing with a German count and—'

Mr Gough cast up his gaze as though in search of heavenly assistance. 'Lord Brooke, we will return to the schoolroom and you will translate *I must not speculate on other people's business* into Latin and then write it out twenty times in a fair hand.'

'Ouch,' Grant remarked when his son had departed with the air of a condemned man heading for the gallows. 'I am not certain I could translate that with any elegance these days.' He ran a hand through his tousled hair, twitched off Kate's cloak, shook it out, draped it over his arm and opened the door for her. 'Those letters, I hope, are the replies to my invitations to our first house party.'

Kate was conscious that he was watching her for a reaction. Did he fear she would be unable to manage a small, informal gathering, or was it his guests' reactions to her that gave him more concern? No man would want his closest friends to think he had made a poor marriage, that his wife was not good enough for him.

*I* am *good enough,* she told herself. *Good enough for him and for his friends. And I can manage a country house party more easily than he thinks.* The thought of confounding Grant with her ability gave her an inner glow of unworthy satisfaction, even if it was only a small thing. Henry liked to entertain his friends and his wife, Jane, uncomfortable with country gentlemen and their hearty manners and unsophisticated pleasures, had been more than happy to unload the burden of organisation on to Kate.

If truth be told, it was the thought of female guests that gave her the most apprehension. Men, if they were comfortable, well fed and provided with plenty of sport, tended to be uncritical of their hostess. Ladies, on the other hand, were not. Polite, charming—and if they sensed a weakness, as relentless as a flock of pigeons pecking away at a pile of wheat grains until there was nothing left but the husks.

'Let's hurry and open them,' she said and was through the doorway into the shadowed hall with, surely, enough enthusiasm to convince Grant that she was not nervous in the slightest.

'Alex and his wife can come,' he said, studying the first letter. He opened the others. 'So can Cris and Gabriel. But they both say they will not be accompanied by their sisters. Gabe, in language I will not use to my respectable wife, assures me he will inflict neither his latest *chère amie* upon us, nor a respectable fiancée—which it is unimaginable that he will ever have, by the way—and certainly not his unmarried sister.' Grant folded the sheet with its sprawling black handwriting and grimaced. 'Now I come to think about my last encounter with her, that is probably a good thing. She can talk the hind leg off a donkey and needs diluting with a very large pool of other guests. Cris merely thanks me most properly for the suggestion, but tells me that he will be unaccompanied, as his sister is newly betrothed and will be staying with her future in-laws.'

Grant handed her that letter and Kate scanned the elegantly written page. 'He sounds somewhat cool,' she ventured. 'Is it the prospect of meeting me?'

'He always sounds cool, although this does seem more detached than usual.' Grant took the letter back and read it again. 'It isn't us, it is him. Something's wrong, I think. He's been in Russia or Denmark or somewhere in that direction, doing a vaguely diplomatic job for the Foreign Office.'

'Not as an ambassador?'

'No, far more undefined than that.' Grant looked thoughtful and Kate did not probe. If his friend was engaged in espionage, he certainly would not want to speak of it. The poor man probably needed some peace and quiet and homely comforts after the stress of a foreign court.

'I suggested May 20 and they all say they can make that. Is it convenient for you?'

Two weeks? 'Certainly,' Kate said with a sense of fizzing excitement. Her first house party as mistress of Abbeywell and the chance to understand Grant much better through his friends. She could hardly wait. 'That will be no problem at all.'

* * *

The house was quiet, finally. Grant leaned back against the door of his bedroom and yawned. Charlie, still overexcited from the day before at the prospect of all his favourite honorary uncles arriving at the same time, had been difficult to get to bed. Anna, with the knack of small children for knowing when adults were tired and distracted, decided to wail endlessly and Kate had been absent-minded throughout dinner. And, to put the cap on a wearisome evening, she had indicated in an embarrassed murmur that it would not be a good time for him to visit her bedchamber.

So now he was feeling selfish for feeling disappointed when she was obviously self-conscious and uncomfortable. The decanters had been set out and he went to pour himself out a finger of brandy, shifting his shoulders under the heavy silk of his robe in an effort to ease the ache in the right one, which always complained when the weather turned cold and damp.

He'd been short with Kate yesterday when she had asked a perfectly reasonable question about the scars. On an impulse he tossed back the brandy and strode to the door, stopping only to remove the key from its hiding place in the indented base of a Japanese bronze figure and to pick up a three-branch candlestick.

It was over a year since he had been in the empty suite. The door swung open with a faint creak and the cold, stale air hardly moved the candle flames. He could still smell burning, he was convinced, even though all the fabrics and carpets had been torn out and destroyed, the walls and floor scrubbed. The seat of the fire was obvious from the heavy charring of the floorboards in front of the hearth and near the door where the edge of the rug had been was a dark patch. His blood.

He made himself walk further into the room, telling himself that he could not hear the crackle of the fire, the screams, the child's wailing cries. He could not smell the smoke, the burning brandy... But they were there, in his head, the memories mixed with the sounds and stench of the battlefield, the screams of the dying, and afterwards, those hideous pyres...

Then he was through into the bedchamber. It was still furnished, for the door had been closed that night and the smoke and flame had not penetrated here. It smelt of dust and old polish and faintly, unmistakably, there was the scent of jasmine in the air.

There were sounds here, too. A woman crying.

Screaming. Sobs and reproaches. Pain and grief. To pull himself back into the present left him sick, but he made himself walk around the room checking coldly, methodically, for damage, signs of damp, of mice or mould. These chambers were spaces, that was all. They had no memory, no life of their own. The phantom sounds and smells were all in his head and he could overcome them, drive them out with the laughter of a son who was healthy and happy, the scent of a woman who found joy in his lovemaking, the smiles of a baby who reached out when she saw him. He had experienced no nightmares since he had returned to Abbeywell—he was healing, even if his lacerated shoulder never would.

He walked back, locked the door behind him, returned to his room. Yes, he could sleep now.

## Chapter Thirteen

Kate woke, blinking at the darkness. Something had roused her. A shout? All was quiet, but instinct made her get up and tiptoe to the dressing room door, which stood ajar. Anna was fast asleep and there was no sound from Jeannie, who slept in a small room just along the corridor.

It must have been an owl, or a vixen's strange cry. Then she heard it again, distinctly now, unmistakably a human voice.

'Charlie!' It was Grant and she ran to the connecting door, threw it open expecting to find some emergency—a sick child, sleepwalking, an accident—her mind ran through the possibilities. But the room was dark and still, except for the sound of muttering and movement from the bed.

'Grant?' There was no reply. A cold finger of unease moved down her spine. Kate backed away into her own chamber, found by touch the candle and tinderbox by the bed and, hands shaking, struck a light. 'Grant?' This time she could see him naked on the bed, the sheets a tangle around his legs, trapping him. He seemed to be trying to drag himself towards the edge of the bed.

'Charlie. I'm coming. Charlie...' He was deep in the throes of a nightmare.

Kate bent over him, put her arms around his shoulders and tried to make him lie down, but he was too strong for her. 'We have Charlie. He is safe, quite safe,' she murmured, then repeated it loudly, but it did nothing to calm him.

Then something in the tension of Grant's body changed. 'Dream,' he muttered. 'No.'

He knew he was in a nightmare, Kate realised, and he was fighting against it, forcing it back with the strength of his mind as much as his body. She held on tightly, pulling the rigid body against hers, stroking down his back. When she touched the scarred shoulder she felt him flinch as though the wounds were raw.

With a heave Grant threw off her restraining hands, fell back against the pillows. 'Couldn't help her,' he muttered. 'Charlie...'

'He is here. You saved him. Charlie is safe.'

'I know,' he answered her rationally, irritably, even though he was asleep. 'Damned dreams...' And then he was still, relaxed, deeply asleep.

Shaken, Kate backed away from the bed, the candle flame wavering. She put up a hand to shield it and realised it was her own panting breath that made it move. Grant had been dreaming about the fire that killed his wife, she was certain. Dr Meldreth had said something about Grant being injured during the fire, but the only scars she could see on his body were the slashes on his shoulder and they were not burns. How could a fire cause those? But a weapon could, a broken bottle could.

None of it made sense. Kate stood watching her sleeping husband, then, once she was certain he was deeply unconscious, she pulled the covers up over him. Should she stay? No, she decided, staring down at his profile, stark against the white of the pillows. He had dragged himself out of that nightmare by sheer willpower, as far as she could tell. He would hate to know she had been watching his struggles against it.

But what had triggered it? she wondered as she turned away. She had seen no sign of bad dreams when they had slept together. The candlelight caught a glint of something metallic on the little table by the door and, curious, she went to see what it was. A key. A door key very much in the style of those for all of the bedchambers on this floor. It was in her hand before she realised that she had moved to pick it up. It was not the key to this room, that was protruding from the lock right in front of her, Charlie's room was never locked, in case of accidents. Hers, too, was unlocked.

*Madeleine's suite.* It had to be. Kate hesitated for perhaps ten seconds. Grant did not want her, or anyone, in those rooms. But whatever had happened there had scarred him, mentally and perhaps physically. It was giving him nightmares and the experience had been so bad he could not tolerate any mention of it. How could she help him if she did not understand?

The door opened with a faint creak like the protest of her conscience, but Kate kept going. This was the lesser of two evils and Grant need never know she had been in the rooms, she told herself.

The forbidden door opened easily and she stepped on to bare boards. The air was cold and dry and, stripped of its furniture, the room seemed enormous and overscale, like something from a fairy tale. *Bluebeard's chamber.* The light of the single candle that she held created deep pools of shadow in the corners, the edges swaying as her hand trembled. Something dark spilled like a puddle in front of the hearth and for a moment Kate thought it was a body fallen there, draped in a black velvet cloak.

'Nonsense,' she muttered and shook off the superstitious dread. 'Too many Gothic novels, you will be seeing ghosts next.' Even so, it took resolution to walk towards the pool of blackness. She stopped, her toes at the edge, and saw that the boards at her feet were charred by the heat of an intense fire. Instinctively she stepped back, repelled by the thought of her bare skin touching the blackness. There was another patch of darkness by the door and she made herself walk to that. There was no charring here, the boards were intact, although scrubbed until the grain showed. She had the cold certainty that this was blood, but there was no way of telling in the dim light.

The bedchamber door was closed. It yielded to her cautious push and Kate stepped into Madeleine Rivers's most intimate world. The room was feminine, exquisite in every detail, decorated in shades of blue with touches of silver, tarnished now, but still catching the light from the candle flame.

The dressing table held its array of bottles and jars, a silver-backed hairbrush and hand mirror.

There was just the lightest film of dust, so whatever Grimswade said, one of the servants was coming in to keep the rooms clean. Then Kate saw a single line, fresh-traced through the dust. She held the candle flame close. It looked like the mark of a fingertip that had come close to one perfume flask. *Essence de Jasmine.*

There was a large mirror on a stand and Kate looked up to see herself reflected in it—pale-faced, pretty enough, dressed for warmth and comfort in a sensible nightgown, bare feet showing beneath the hem. The woman whose room this was would have scorned to look like this, she sensed. She glanced at the dressing room door, but did not try to open it. The thought of prying into the other woman's clothes was abhorrent.

Slowly, forcing herself not to run, Kate closed the door, crossed the sitting room and let herself out into the familiar world again. She turned the key in the lock and tiptoed back to Grant's bedchamber, laid the key down where she had found it and retreated to her own room.

What had that taught her? *Nothing,* she concluded as she climbed into bed and pulled the covers up tight to her chin, although the room was not cold. There were marks of a fire, possibly of blood. But she had known that already. She had intruded into Grant's private nightmare, against his wishes, and she had discovered nothing that might help.

*Let that be a lesson to you,* she would have said to Charlie if she had caught him prying. Now she had a guilty conscience, a definite case of the shivers and another secret to keep from Grant.

*May 20—Abbeywell Grange*

Grant strolled through the rooms of his home and shook his head with bemused pleasure. Kate had seemed understandably nervous when he had first come home, not just of him, but at the thought of making any changes to the house. With the confirmation of the house party all that reserve seemed to have been swept away, although he worried that she was overdoing things. It was almost as though she had flung herself into the preparations as a way of burying her nerves.

After he had visited Madeleine's rooms the nightmare had resulted in the inevitable headache and bad dreams every night afterwards. He fought both nightmares and the pain as he always had, but the relief when Kate shyly asked him back to her bed was acute. Somehow making love to his wife kept the demons at bay and he had not dreamed again.

But Kate was working too hard and he worried about that. When he waylaid her in the corridor and swept her into either his or her bedchamber, lists and note tablets would scatter along with her stockings and petticoats as he undressed her. Whichever room he walked into appeared to have a member of staff—some of them unfamiliar to him—working away. The billiard table was brushed to a perfect nap, while new blocks of chalk stood aligned under the racks of cues. His study acquired three more comfortable leather armchairs.

Grimswade was found in solemn consultation with his mistress on the correct number of packs of cards to order and brand-new umbrellas were set in stands by all the outer doors, along with every walking stick the house could muster. When Grant caught his wife emerging from the backstairs and kissed her, she tasted of sugar and cinnamon, but when he began to kiss with more enthusiasm, and the intention of licking it all off, she batted him away and scurried off muttering, 'New recipes!'

Charlie entertained them before his bedtime every evening with an entire repertoire of poems and recitations, Anna acquired at least half a dozen new dresses and the small drawing room was declared out of bounds to men as it was transformed into a ladies' boudoir.

'Grant! Oh, there you are.' Kate hurried in, seized his hand and began to pull him towards the door. 'I need you to come upstairs immediately.'

'An admirable idea,' he agreed, allowing himself to be steered towards the stairs. 'But have we time? I expect they will begin arriving in about an hour or so, and your hair looks dashed complicated to fix if it comes down.' As it would, if what he had in mind—

'*Grant.* I want you to look at the guest bedchambers, not to…well, not to do anything else.'

He loved the way he could make her blush, while at the same time she threw herself into whatever amorous idea he had in the most enthusiastic way. And she was beginning to have ideas of her own. Grant paused on the landing, happily recalling the uses to which a set of library steps could be put, and was ruthlessly tugged to the first set of rooms.

'Is this all right for Lord Avenmore? He is the one I am most worried about. Lord and Lady Weybourn are newlyweds, so I thought what we would like and arranged their suite accordingly.' That produced an intriguing pink glow over her cheeks. Grant thought again how satisfying it was that he could make Kate blush. It made him think about making love to her...

'Grant, are you attending?'

'Yes, my dear.' It was his best husbandly voice and it usually worked whenever he had lost track of the conversation in erotic daydreams.

Kate gave him a decidedly old-fashioned look. 'And by the sound of it, Lord Edenbridge values comfort and informality, so his rooms were easy. But Lord Avenmore...'

Grant surveyed the room. It had always been an elegant chamber, but now it was decidedly masculine, with the landscapes replaced with large architectural engravings and all the Dresden china swept away to be replaced by Chinese blue-and-white export porcelain. It would suit Cris de Feaux's austere tastes very well and he said so.

'I didn't know what to do about books, so I have selected a mixture for all of the rooms. But I think we should consider redecorating some more suites very soon, because the rooms I have allocated to Lord Edenbridge are really almost shabby, and if you want to entertain larger parties in the future, it will be difficult. There are your grandfather's rooms, of course—but I hardly like to suggest making changes there if you would find that upsetting.'

'No, you are quite right. They would turn into three respectable guest rooms. I'll have the personal items moved to my rooms and the study. The study and the library are the places that remind me most of him anyway. I have no sentimental attachments to the bedroom suite.'

He was rewarded by a warm smile and glanced at the clock on the overmantel. Perhaps there was just time.

'And then there is the suite next to yours,' Kate said with the air of a woman steeling herself. 'The one with the locked door.'

'No!' He swung round away from her, his vision blurred by the smoke, his ears full of the obscene crackling laughter of the fire, the screams… the screams and the air full of the smell of brandy and burning and the pain in his shoulder and head so bad he could not focus, could not make that hellish decision…

'I realise there are sentimental reasons why it would be difficult, but it is a large suite, and if we were thoughtful with the decoration and furnishing, there need be nothing to remind you,' Kate continued. The sensible, slightly nervous voice flowed on, the remarks perfectly reasonable. Grant hauled himself back from the edge of his waking nightmare and made himself stand still, listen to her.

'How do you know it is a large suite? Have you been in there? I told the servants that the door was never to be opened except for a monthly cleaning.'

'I know.' He realised that Kate was standing her ground with an effort of will, that he was probably frightening her. He made himself step back, widening the space between them, and saw her make the effort to relax her hands from their tight grip on her skirts. 'But…I assumed, from the space I have been given for my suite. And it is obvious the areas that those rooms occupy, one only has to look at the adjoining rooms.'

'No,' Grant said. 'No, it is not obvious.' The angle of the external walls was deceptive at that point, the arrangement of the inner rooms, confusing.

Kate was not blushing now. She was pale and stammering, the picture of guilt. She made no attempt to deny that she had entered the suite. 'But… sooner or later Charlie is going to wonder why that door is locked. What will you tell him? Do you want to make it into some s-secret chamber of horrors to give him nightmares?' Kate was regaining her confidence now, he saw, driven by the force of her argument. She took two rapid steps forward, caught his hands in hers. 'Grant—'

'That room *is* a chamber of horrors,' he said between lips that seemed frozen. 'And it gives *me* nightmares. You've been in there, I don't know how, but you have been, against my expressed wishes. Now, do you want to probe any more? Do you want to dig out secrets that don't concern you, pry into my feelings and thoughts? Because the answer will be *no*, I tell you now.' He flung his hands apart, dislodging hers. 'You had no right, *have*—'

Grant broke off at the sound of a very heavy footstep outside the door. As he turned, Grimswade appeared in the opening. Somehow he bit back the demand that the butler go to the devil. 'Yes?'

'A carriage is approaching, my lord. I believe it is Lord Weybourn's conveyance.'

'Thank you. We will be down directly.' He followed Grimswade along the corridor without turning to see if Kate was following him, without a word to her. He was dimly aware, through the crashing headache that had descended as he lost his temper, that he should go back, apologise to her. Try to forgive her, if he could, for that intrusion. He kept going, down the curves of the front stairs, across the marble floor, the percussion of his boot heels on the stone like daggers stabbing behind his eyes.

Footmen flung back the double doors as he approached and sunlight streamed in, blinding him. Instinct took him out on to the top step, the swirling lights that distorted his vision revealing the shape of the approaching carriage like an image that had been torn across and reassembled out of true.

He was conscious of a presence at his side, of Kate's delicate scent. She made no move to touch him. Then the shape that was the carriage stopped. Footmen hurried down the steps, Grant fixed a smile of welcome on his lips. His vision was failing as the circle of broken, dancing lights enclosing nothing but blackness moved inexorably outwards. In a moment he would be blind.

'Grant! Are we the first?' It was Alex.

'Yes, you are. Welcome.' A figure in green wavered beside Alex and he broadened the smile, painfully. 'Tess, you are more than welcome to Abbeywell. Come and meet my wife.'

Then they were up the steps and beside them. He managed not to retch at the waft of rose scent as Tess stood on tiptoe to kiss his cheek. Alex gripped his hand and, turning, tucked it through his own. 'Migraine?' he murmured. Then he raised his voice.

'And this must be Lady Allundale, you clever devil, Grant. Ma'am, I am Alex Tempest and this is my wife, Tess. I am delighted to meet you at last.'

Alex swung round, taking Grant with him to stroll into the hall. 'Ladies, you will excuse us, but I must be off to consult Grant's valet this minute—I have a hideously uncomfortable nail working through the sole of these new boots.'

Grant found himself climbing the stairs and managed to get out, 'What the blazes—'

'You are blind with a migraine, Lady Allundale is as white as a sheet and Grimswade looks as though he has sat on a poker. What's wrong? No, don't try to talk. Same room as usual?'

Alex steered Grant into his bedchamber, pushed him on to the bed, pulled off his boots. 'Lie down, I'll send your valet in.'

Grant tried to sit up and was ruthlessly shoved back. 'I can't… You are guests, Cris and Gabe will be arriving…'

'We're friends, not guests. Leave it to me.' There was a rattle of curtain rings, the light against his eyelids was reduced. Then silence, broken only by the soft-footed entrance of Griffin, who pressed a glass into Grant's hand.

'Willow-bark powder, my lord.'

He gulped it down, wincing at the bitter taste, lay back and tried to make his mind blank, relax his tense muscles. As soon as he could see, he would have to go downstairs and, somehow, come to terms with Kate.

## Chapter Fourteen

'Here they are.' Lady Weybourn turned to the door. 'Or, rather, here is mine. Where is Grant, Alex? I didn't think he looked well.'

'Migraine.' Alex Tempest strolled in to the drawing room and smiled reassuringly at Kate. 'Haven't seen him blind with one for a while. I've sent his valet to him,' he added as Kate jumped to her feet with a murmur of distress. 'He'll be fine as long as he's quiet. There's nothing to be done.'

With him on his feet the only courteous thing to do was sit down. Griffin would send for her if she was needed and probably the last thing Grant wanted was his unsatisfactory wife fussing over him. She sat and Alex dropped his elegant length into a chair. 'He is subject to migraines? I did not know.' It was his anger at discovering her trespass into the forbidden rooms that had triggered it. And Lord Weybourn said he was *blind* with it.

'Only occasionally. It is very stressful situations when he can't act to resolve things, that's what usually sets them off. If he can act and *do* something, then Grant copes with anything.' Alex Tempest smiled his lazy, reassuring smile again. 'And he's a stubborn so-and-so. He'll be on his feet the minute he can see clearly, even if his head still hurts. I don't expect that blow he got in New Town helped any.'

'No, probably not.' She wrenched her thoughts away from guilt and worry and focused on her guests. 'Now, would you like to take some refreshment, or shall I show you to your rooms first?'

'Some tea would be very welcome.' Lady Weybourn unpinned her hat and set it aside, then peeled off her gloves as Kate rang for Grimswade.

'Tea and some food, Grimswade. Do you know where Lord Brooke has got to?'

'I do not, I regret to say, my lady. However, I venture to suggest that the production of cake will cause him to appear.'

'Uncle Alex!' Charlie erupted into the room and leapt at Lord Weybourn, who caught him, stood up and held him upside down by his heels.

'Good afternoon, Lord Brooke.'

His wife rolled her eyes at Kate. 'Do put him down, darling. He'll be sick.'

Eventually order was restored, Charlie was silenced by the threat of the withdrawal of cake and Kate once more embarked on making polite conversation with these two very informal strangers.

'You have known Grant for a long time, Lord Weybourn?'

'Alex, please. Yes, since university, along with Cris de Feaux and Gabriel Stone. We were known as the Four Disgraces, but I assure you we are sober and responsible now.'

Lady Weybourn snorted inelegantly. 'Nonsense, darling. You are merely better at hiding the insobriety and irresponsibility these days.' She turned to Kate. 'I think we are very brave, taking on two of them. We must see what we can do about finding nice civilising wives for the others, don't you think, Lady Allundale?'

'Oh, Kate, please. I don't know the others, so I really can't say.' The thought of Grant being a Disgrace would be funny if she wasn't feeling so apprehensive and guilty.

'These days we think of ourselves more as the Four Elementals, because of our names,' Alex continued, ignoring a whisper of, *And because that's the name of the inn in Ghent they meet up in*, from Tess. 'Tempest—wind, de Feaux—fire, Stone—earth, and Rivers—'

'Water,' Kate finished, relaxing a little. It was almost impossible not to, around these two. They would be good for Grant, she knew it.

'Two more carriages are approaching, my lady.'

'Thank you, Grimswade. We had better have more tea and cake brought in.'

'I'll come out with you,' Alex offered as she stood up with a murmur of apology. 'You can't be expected to greet those two by yourself.'

'They are quite safe really.' Tess walked beside her to the front door. 'At least, *mostly* safe. Gabriel is unsettling and Cris is terrifying, but just pretend you don't notice.' She waved enthusiastically as the two coaches, both driving at breakneck speed, came to a crashing halt.

*Pretend I don't notice? How?* Kate waited with butterflies somersaulting below her diaphragm as a footman opened one door and the other was thrown wide. The man who climbed languidly down with a nod to the footman was, Kate realised, probably the most handsome man she had ever seen. He was also glacially blond, blue-eyed and dangerously composed. Why dangerous?

'That's Crispin de Feaux?' she whispered to Tess.

'Indeed it is,' the other woman whispered back. 'I always think of archangels and flaming swords.'

He strode up the steps and bowed over the hand that Kate, expecting to shake hands, had extended. 'Lady Allundale, I am delighted to meet you at last.'

'Kate, allow me to introduce the Marquess of Avenmore,' Alex drawled. 'Cris, Lady Allundale. Grant's flat on his back with a migraine.'

'The prospect of losing to me at cards again, I assume.' The dark, loose-limbed man one step below the marquess needed a shave, a haircut, and had obviously chosen his expensive clothing for comfort. He smiled at Kate, a wolfish baring of his teeth that had her stiffening her spine before she offered her hand.

'Edenbridge, at your service.' He took her hand and neither kissed nor shook it. 'Clever, clever, Grant,' he remarked, closing his long fingers possessively around hers.

*Oh, yes, this is definitely the unsettling one.* 'Do come in.' Kate tried to look sophisticated, as though dark-eyed men with feral smiles murmured ambiguous compliments to her every day. He released her hand and she even managed not to snatch it back and hide it behind her back. 'There are refreshments in the drawing room, unless either of you would like to be shown to your rooms first?'

They all voted for refreshments, trooping after her into the drawing room, as much at home as she was. *More so,* she thought, nerves jangling as she worried about Grant, fretted about her marriage, restrained Charlie from causing havoc and somehow made conversation. She was certain it was thoroughly banal and that four people who obviously knew each other well would much prefer to be talking amongst themselves rather than answering her polite enquiries about their journeys.

And upstairs her husband, whom she had tried to deceive, was lying blinded by pain and she could do nothing to help him.

'Do have another ginger biscuit, Lord Avenmore. Such fortunate weather for your journey, was it not?'

Grant lay with hard-learned patience and watched the plaster details of the ceiling over his bed gradually come into focus. His head still felt as though it was gripped in a vice and pain stabbed behind his eyes, but the worst was over. The attacks were always short and savage and it took a while before bright light and loud noises were tolerable.

Normally he would sleep for several hours until the sickness and nausea were gone, but somewhere downstairs Kate was greeting his three best friends and he understood her well enough now to guess that she was doing so with poise and grace despite the ordeal. Because it would be an ordeal, meeting people who knew him better than anyone and far better than she did.

And then there was her unfamiliarity with high society. Cris, simply by standing around, had been known to make dukes run a nervous finger around their neckcloths. Gabe was enough to make any relatively unsophisticated lady flustered and Alex and Tess were so head over heels in love that they could only serve to point up the deficiencies in his own marriage.

And Alex had seen at once that something was wrong. Grant shifted cautiously and, ignoring the way it made the room move about, sat up. He had to get down to Kate. The acid anger still churned in his stomach as he forced himself to his feet and he stopped his unsteady progress across the room to his boots to analyse it.

His wife had disobeyed him, deceived him, so why did he feel guilty about being angry with her? He stared into the mirror at his narrow-pupilled eyes and rigid mouth. The sight made him feel considerably worse. He needed to think, but it was hard enough staying on his feet. Yet instinct told him to move. He reached for his boots, winced as he bent his head and made the effort to pull them on. Grant got to his feet and made his way downstairs, steeling himself against the tide of talk and laughter, punctuated by Charlie's whoops, that rose to meet him.

'Grant.' There was anxiety on Kate's face, as well as relief in her voice. She half rose from the chair, then sat down again, and he realised that, thankfully, she was not going to make a fuss over him.

Neither Cris nor Gabe stood. They knew too well that getting up, slapping him on the back or shaking his hand just now would make his head feel as though it had fallen off. Cris waved a greeting with a stylish turn of his wrist, Gabe merely smiled his pirate's smile. Charlie opened his mouth and was promptly scooped up by Alex, who wagged a finger at him until he subsided.

'My apologies for not receiving you. One of those confounded migraines.' They had left his usual chair for him, so he sat down and tried to focus.

'Charlie, take your father his tea, please.' Kate handed the boy a cup and turned back to her interrupted conversation with Gabe, which, to Grant's amazement, appeared to be about *vingt-et-un* and the calculation of odds. Perhaps he was hearing things.

Ten minutes later Mr Gough came down to remove a reluctant Charlie and give the adults some peace. Then his guests decided that they should retire and wash off the dust of the road. They left, waving him back into his chair when he would have risen. 'We're family, remember,' Alex said airily. 'We'll find our way, Kate, never fear.'

It left him, head still pounding, sitting opposite his wife. She looked decidedly pale now the animation of talking had left her. 'Kate.' He realised he had no idea how he felt about her.

'Please don't. You could not reproach me half as much as I am reproaching myself. We were building trust between us, weren't we? And I destroyed it.' Bravely, she kept her gaze on his face and he remembered that it was her courage that had first impressed him.

'No, we were not.' It came out more harshly than he had intended, a snarl at himself as much as at her. Kate bit her lip and Grant closed his mouth before he said anything else unconsidered.

'I am not going to apologise any more.' She

levelled a steady look at him across the teacups. Grant looked down and saw her hands were shaking. When Kate saw the direction of his gaze she curled them loosely in her lap as though willing them to stillness. 'I have said I am sorry, and I am, but my motives were good. Mostly. I cannot acquit myself of some curiosity.'

She admitted inquisitiveness and he knew she wanted to remodel that part of the house, but neither of those could be described as a *good* motive. Grant almost said as much, and then he saw the anxiety in her eyes, stopped thinking about his own feelings and saw hers. *Because if the positions were reversed, I'd have done the same thing.* Of course he would.

If Kate had been hiding some secret that gave her nightmares, made her short-tempered and laid her low with migraines, he would have done anything that he could to discover what it was and try to set it right, whether she said she wanted him to or not. She was too important to him now—he would not have shrugged and ignored her pain, left her to carry the burden alone. Which meant that he was important to her. He knew himself well enough to recognise that when he was angry it took nerve to stand up to him. Kate had risked his anger and so he must forgive what she had done.

Forgive. And that meant telling her the truth, because otherwise she was going to fret herself to flinders over him. *Hell.* The thought made him nauseous all over again, his shoulder seemed to flare with remembered pain. What would she think of him? That he was as good as a murderer? It was, after all, what he thought of himself often enough as he lay awake long into the night, because that was better than sleeping and the dreams that came with sleep.

With another woman he would never have the confidence in her discretion and her understanding, but he could trust Kate, he realised.

'Yes, I can see that your motives were good.'

Kate's expression changed subtly. Relief, possibly. Anxiety about what he would reveal? Or regret that she had pushed things this far? He had always known her to be self-contained, now he could not read her thoughts, interpret her emotions, and he knew he should be able to. This was his *wife*, he should be able to understand her because that was what happened in real marriages and he wanted this one to be real.

Grant forced his reluctant tongue to form the

words. 'I would not let you in to my secrets. Where's the trust in that? And you were not idly curious, I know that. You wanted to help, despite my best efforts to keep you out.'

'Most husbands would maintain that a wife must obey them,' Kate ventured. He thought of someone edging out on to thin ice, testing each step, listening for the ominous cracking. He had failed her by not trusting her before. Now she was wary of how far this tolerance went.

'Even if they are wrong. Yes, I know. I do not want to be a husband like that. Will you come here, Kate?'

She stood up, looking demure, except for the hint of a smile, and he realised with a flash of insight that she was relieved and something more positive than that. Happy? The relief at being able to understand her made his own lips curve in response.

'You have a headache,' she said.

'So don't bounce.' Grant opened his arms and Kate curled up on his lap, her head on his shoulder, and he gathered her in tight, tucked her head under his chin and thought how right she felt there, how perfect her weight on him was.

'Have you had these headaches all the time we have been married?'

'No. When we first got here I was so busy that I was too tired to dream. I had them in London, now and again, but they are always worse here.' He felt the familiar guilt at his own weakness, even as the rational part of his brain, the part that had studied medicine, told him that it was not something he could control by willpower.

He could almost hear Kate working it out. 'You have slept with me every night since you returned from London and you have not had nightmares, not ones that disturbed your sleep and woke me.'

'I suspect that sex helps,' Grant said, hoping he had not shocked her. It had occurred to him, these past few days when he woke refreshed after a solid night's sleep.

'Of course!' Kate sat up, bumped his chin with her head, murmured an apology. 'The night you woke me up because you were dreaming and I went into your bedchamber and found the key was the first time since we had been sleeping together that we…haven't…' She seemed to find it difficult to select the right word. 'Made love.'

'Well, there's the answer,' he said, feeling, for the first time since that confrontation upstairs, like smiling. 'Lovemaking as often as possible.'

'It will cure the symptoms,' Kate said seriously,

apparently not ready to joke about it. 'But not the cause. Have you talked to anyone about what happened when Madeleine died?'

'My grandfather, when it first happened. The other three.' He gestured at the ceiling, but she knew what he meant. The other three of the close band of four friends.

'Did you tell them what happened or how you feel?' Kate asked.

'How I feel? No, of course not. I told them the facts.'

Kate pushed at his chest until she was sitting upright, her expression wry. 'Men! Tonight, when we go to bed, tell me what happened and tell me how you felt, how you still feel.'

'I realise I owe you an explanation, that I can't make a mystery of this any longer, but what the devil do my feelings have to do with it?'

'I want to understand,' she said as she slid off his knee and stood up. 'How is your migraine now?'

'Better.' He rolled his head and flexed his shoulders. 'My neck's stiff, but that's usual afterwards.'

'You should take a hot bath.' He almost smiled again at the confident tone. Planning and making decisions seemed to cheer Kate up as much as it did him. 'And we'll take our time changing for dinner.

Let's look in on Anna and Charlie on our way up,' she suggested. 'With our guests and our plans for later, I think this should be an evening for adults, don't you?'

'Oh, yes,' Grant agreed. 'Most definitely.'

# Chapter Fifteen

Kate accepted a shelled walnut from Cris de Feaux, who was cracking them with one hand while moving the cruets around the table to demonstrate some obscure point about the Schleswig-Holstein question that her husband and Gabriel were arguing about.

'Thank you,' she murmured, too engaged with the argument to feel shy with him any more. He was beginning to intrigue her, with his sharp intelligence and sardonic observations. But he was unhappy, she sensed. It was hard to tell with such a controlled, contained man, but she thought he was acting, putting on a false front of normality for his friends. She wondered whether he resented the fact that two of them had married and there was certainly something in his eyes when he looked at

Alex and Tess, but she thought it was pain rather than resentment or jealousy.

'The convolutions in a walnut are as nothing compared to Gabriel's mental processes,' Cris observed, breaking into her musings. 'Of course the Danes have a good claim to the territory,' he added as Alex joined in the argument. 'But the German states…'

Kate met Tess's eyes and smiled. She had been pleased with herself for remembering to rise and nod to Tess when everyone had finished dessert and she had been taken aback when the other woman said airily, 'Must we? It is only us after all.'

'Why, no, I would be happy to stay if the gentlemen are not inhibited by our presence.' They certainly would not be removing a chamber pot from the sideboard to relieve themselves, as she knew Henry and his male guests did as soon as the ladies were out of the way, because her wary inspection had revealed that was not done in this household. On the other hand she had always assumed that the men liked the freedom to discuss sport, politics and women.

'I would wager that you and I know quite enough about politics to keep our end up in a discussion,' Tess had announced. 'And if they want to talk about bare-knuckle boxing or duels, then I am all agog to hear about them, too.'

'But that means we won't be able to discuss opera dancers or our latest flirts,' Alex Tempest said plaintively and was punished with a well-aimed walnut thrown by his wife.

But, despite the teasing, the arguments were anything but frivolous. From her hours of lonely reading Kate realised that they were all travellers who knew the Continent well—and that included Grant, although she knew he had not been abroad since their marriage and she had no idea why he would be travelling across the Channel in any case.

'After the way we treated Denmark during the war, I am surprised they are a friendly nation now,' she remarked, making herself join in the discussion and not spend the evening silently puzzling over her husband.

'The fact that we bombarded Copenhagen twice?' Grant asked. 'Things in that part of the world are so complicated, even after the Treaty of Vienna, that they are probably grateful for a friendly trading partner who doesn't want to realign their boundaries.'

'You've never had any problem buying horses in

Holstein, have you?' Gabriel Stone reached for the decanter and refilled all the glasses within reach.

'None. You'll have to come down to the stables and look at my latest crosses with Yorkshire coach horses. They are going to be the carriage horse of choice if I have anything to do with it.'

So that was what the handsome bay horses down at the stables were. They were not riding horses, she knew that, but not being a good horsewoman herself, she had never been curious enough to ask about them. Now it seemed that Grant was enthusiastic about horse breeding and she'd had no idea. Another side of her husband that was unknown.

The men got up, lost in an intense argument about something new that had escaped Kate's notice whilst she was brooding. 'Come and look at the atlas,' Grant was suggesting as he headed towards the door. 'It should be clear on a large-scale map.'

She and Tess were alone, one at each end of the table. 'That's done it,' Lady Weybourn remarked. 'They are off on the subject of Waterloo and we probably won't see them until breakfast time now. I shudder with relief every time I remember they were all four in that hell and none of them was wounded.'

'Shall we go into the drawing room?' Kate suggested and was surprised, and pleased, when the other woman took her arm in a companionable manner.

'Is Grant better now? He looks it.' Tess kicked off her shoes and curled up in an armchair in a scandalously casual manner.

Kate remembered something that Grant had said about Alex's wife being born on the wrong side of the blanket and never having a come-out. Despite that, she seemed relaxed enough about her place in society, which was encouraging. If she could do it, so could Kate. And then she remembered that she would have to negotiate London society while avoiding one particular aristocrat and it all seemed impossibly difficult again.

'Grant is much better, I think.'

'Had you had a row?' Tess asked with a cheerful lack of restraint. 'I thought you both looked positively stony with each other when we arrived, but of course that might have been his headache and your nerves at the thought of us all descending on you.'

'A row?' Kate temporised. She was not going to be indiscreet about Grant, but she did wish she had someone to confide in, at least about her husband.

'He's not like Alex. We have rows at least once a week and no one's any the worse for it and we usually end up laughing our heads off, or in bed. Or both,' she added with a wicked smile, apparently not noticing Kate's flushed cheeks. 'But Grant is so self-contained. Alex says he virtually never loses his temper—not to show, in any case. But you are obviously doing him good.'

'I am?' Kate murmured, lost in the face of so much frankness.

'When I first met him I had sprained my ankle and he was very kind to me, but his eyes held so much sadness, even when he was smiling. That's gone now.'

There was the fleeting memory of that look in his eyes when they were in the bothy and, afterwards, when they reached Abbeywell. She had thought that the haunting sadness had gone because he was home again, and with Charlie, but Tess implied that it had been there for longer than just that difficult journey from Scotland. 'I know the look you mean. And you are right, it isn't there now.'

'That's love for you,' Tess said, her smile tender and secret.

'But it isn't,' Kate protested. 'We're not in love. Surely Grant told you all in London about how we met, why he married me? This is not a romance, this is a marriage of practicality.'

'Well, yes.' Tess sat up straighter, the smile gone. 'But he did not have to *marry* you to get you out of the fix you were in. There were all sorts of things he could have done to help you. He must have been attracted to you right from the beginning. And the way you look at him…'

'He needed a stepmother for Charlie,' Kate said stiffly. 'I needed a father for Anna and there was no time to discuss all the options, she was about to be born. And I don't love him.' *Do I?* Tess arched one dark brow. 'And Grant does not love me,' she added with rather more certainty.

'I am sure you know better than I,' Tess said, but the smile was back.

'Knows better than you about what, my darling?' The men were back in the room before Kate could answer that sly remark. 'Surely no one knows better than you about anything,' Alex Tempest added.

'Wretch.' Tess tilted her head back to look up at her husband. 'Have you men finished fighting the battle again to your own satisfaction? Because if Kate will excuse me, I am for my bed. It has been a long day.' She paused as she passed Kate. 'But I am right, you know, about at least one of you.'

Tess's departure broke the party up. Alex, it seemed, was not prepared to let her go up to bed without him, Gabriel suggested that Lord Avenmore come up with him so he could lend him a book he had just finished and, with the departure of her guests, Kate wanted nothing more than to get Grant alone upstairs.

'My chamber or yours?' he asked as they climbed the stairs.

'Yours.' He would be more relaxed there, she sensed. *I don't love him, I am not in love. I like him, I desire him, I am so very grateful to him, but...love? I still hardly know him and, anyway, I am not very good at recognising love.*

'I like your friends,' Kate said and went to help him out of his coat when he dismissed the waiting valet. 'Let me untie your neckcloth.' She enjoyed the closeness of standing toe to toe, unwinding the body-warmed muslin from around his neck, exposing a glimpse of skin beneath.

'Good.' Grant bent to nuzzle her temple as she stood folding the cloth. 'They like you, but then I knew they would, all being men of taste and discrimination.'

They undressed slowly, helping each other, pausing between garments for a lingering caress, a kiss. But without any spoken agreement Grant reached for his heavy silk robe when they were naked, while

Kate retrieved her own robe from her room. She sat down facing him across the width of the hearth, studying the austere profile, the straight nose and firm mouth. He was a handsome man, her husband, and, yes, she looked at him and enjoyed doing so, just as Tess had observed. That did not mean she was in love with him.

'I married very suitably and far too young,' Grant said without preamble. 'We were *both* too young and I had very little experience of well-bred young ladies beyond the ballroom. I was disappointed that Madeleine seemed so cool, but she had seemed willing enough to marry me, and neither of us had been brought up to expect some passionate love match. We rubbed along well enough until Charlie was born and, naturally, I would not have dreamed of returning to the bedchamber for quite a while after that.'

'It sounds like a very lonely marriage,' Kate ventured.

Grant's shoulders moved in the ghost of a shrug. 'It is what we both expected, what I had grown up with. Then I visited her room one night and was told that she had done her duty by bearing me an heir and surely, if I wanted to *indulge my male lusts*, I could set up a mistress. I pointed out that sex within marriage was not a question of lust, and besides, I wanted more children and surely she did, too.'

He turned his head against the back of the chair until he was staring into the cold grate. 'I asked myself if I had been clumsy or insensitive in bed, I thought about Charlie's birth. I wondered, even, if there was another man she loved, had loved all the time we had been married. But she denied there was anything. Sex, she thought, was squalid and *animal*. Childbirth was *horrid*, especially as she really had little interest in children. Of course there was no one else—she had been reared to do her duty and she thought she was doing it. But if I felt she was not, then, naturally, she would resign herself.'

'Not very encouraging,' Kate murmured, secretly appalled. She could understand Madeleine's fears about childbirth, but why hadn't she confided in Grant, talked about it, rather than erected that wall of icy rejection between them? And her husband might have acquired a little more experience since his first marriage, but surely his lovemaking could not have changed *that* much? Perhaps, she mused, some women simply did not enjoy the physical side of marriage.

'No, and in retrospect I can understand her. She had been raised with no expectations of marriage beyond status—that was how she measured a successful match. A good wife gave her husband an heir, and, she reluctantly accepted, a spare. Her mother had instilled in her the belief that men were essentially bestial in their desires and that a lady endured their attentions out of duty. From the beginning she was expecting it to be a painful, distasteful, messy business. But the rest of her duty came easily to her. She knew how to behave impeccably in public, she enjoyed enhancing my standing, and with it her own. She loved to spend my money to make herself a decorative and fitting accessory at my side. But I failed to see all that. I thought another child would kindle warmer feelings, both for it and for me. Madeleine became pregnant within months and the birth was complicated. She lost the baby.'

'I am so sorry.' And he had lost a child, too, although she doubted anyone had comforted him about that.

'After that she became…difficult. She began to drink, to behave wildly. In public she was as impeccable as always, but in private it was a nightmare. The staff tried to keep drink from her, but she would find it. I never left her alone with Charlie and I certainly did not go to her bedchamber again. Grandfather would lecture her on her duty and she consigned duty to the devil.'

'You must have been tempted to have her committed to some form of care.'

'She was my wife so I did my best to look after her. I blame myself for getting her with child too soon, for not being able to save the baby.' He closed his eyes as though trying to block a vivid memory. 'I worked with Meldreth, did what I could, but he had to try to turn the baby and they were both so exhausted, mother and child. It was a miracle Madeleine lived. She was so angry with me for getting her pregnant again, it was as though she was fighting me. Every time she cried out it felt as though I had just, that moment, inflicted the pain on her. I still do not know whether it would have been better to have left the room, got out of her sight. Was I there because of my conscience, flagellating myself, or was I doing the right thing? I still do not know.'

His expression was so bleak it was hard to speak. Kate reached for the right words. 'Of course it was the right thing to do. You had some medical training, Dr Meldreth needed your help, your strength.

But how could you be expected to have succeeded when an experienced practitioner could not?' She remembered the strain on his face, the shadows in his eyes as he worked to save Anna through that long night in the bothy. 'It must have been so hard for you to help me as you did.'

'No. That was a blessing, something I could do. There was no one else, I could hardly make things worse and I might make things better. And once she was born and I knew it would be all right, then it felt so good, as though I had been given a second chance. Up to that point, I admit, it was difficult to push the fears away.'

'But you kept on trying, you kept my spirits up and never let me see you were afraid of the outcome.' He smiled at that and she sensed it was a comfort. 'In the end, what happened?' she prompted when Grant fell silent.

'Come to her rooms.' Grant stood, took a key she recognised from his pocket and led the way the short distance along the passage. Kate saw his hands were steady as the key turned and the door swung open. They both carried branches of candles and she set hers on the hearth, while Grant placed his near the door.

'My wife died in this room,' he said, his face

stark, his voice harsh. 'She died in front of my eyes and I did nothing to save her.'

'And that is only half the story,' Kate said when she could speak again. 'I know there is more to it than that, there has to be. Tell me.'

'I came home one night from dinner at a neighbour's house. Grandfather was beginning to fret because it was late and Madeleine had Charlie with her and when the nursemaid went to take him to bed she wouldn't let the girl in. I knew then there was something very wrong, because she hardly ever kept him with her or spent any time playing with him. The door was locked. I could hear him crying, so I broke it open.'

Grant walked into the room, towards the cold, empty hearth, where Kate waited, silent. 'It was hot, the fire was roaring in the chimney. Charlie was crying on the sofa that was over there, but it was angled away from me so I couldn't see him.' He gestured towards the side of the room away from the chimney. 'He sounded fretful and hungry, but not frightened.

'Madeleine was standing there, just where you are. The tray with the spirits was turned over at her feet, the liquid soaking the carpet. She had a cut-glass decanter in her hand.' He closed his eyes again and spoke without opening them. 'I think she had been drinking directly from it. She was certainly drunk. I walked across.' He moved as he spoke, blind, lost in the memory. 'I tried to take the decanter from her and she swung it at me. It hit the side of my head and smashed.' His left hand, fingers spread, speared into his hair. 'And then she must have panicked, I think. I tried not to hurt her, to take it from her gently, but I was half stunned. She swung it again and it hit my shoulder, cut down through my coat to the skin, and I fell.'

Kate glanced at the dark patch on the boards that endless scrubbing had not removed. She had been right. It was blood. Grant was still speaking, eyes still closed.

'I think I was knocked out for a moment. When I came to there was blood everywhere and there was screaming and Charlie crying. For a moment I was back on the battlefield with the noise and the smoke and the dreadful smells...' He stopped and opened his eyes. 'You do not need to hear it all. The brandy had splashed all down Madeleine's muslin gown, the carpet was already soaked. She must have staggered back towards the fire and her skirts caught. The carpet was ablaze. I crawled across, got Charlie and dragged him back. The door burst open and help was there, but it was too late for her.'

What to say? *How terrible. How tragic. Poor woman.* All so obvious and so meaningless. She would say what she thought, what concerned her, even if it was not the comforting platitudes that convention expected. 'You know you did the right thing, don't you? To go to Charlie and not to try to save Madeleine?'

'Yes.' Grant almost smiled at her. 'Yes, I know. I only had so much strength, I was bleeding like a stuck pig and she was probably beyond saving, even if I had gone directly to her. I had to get the child to safety.'

'Then, if you know that, accept it—'

'What is the problem? The problem, my dear, is that while my rational brain accepts it while I'm awake, my dreaming mind does not, it seems. A policy of *out of sight, out of mind* has worked to an extent so far, but you are right, I cannot continue like that, ignoring the existence of this room, ignoring that night.'

He stood up and held out his hand to her. 'Come, sweetheart. Let us go to bed, lock this door on the horrors of this room for another night.'

## Chapter Sixteen

Grant kissed her, gently, sweetly, when they reached his bedchamber again. They shed their night robes and Kate climbed into bed beside him and lay on her stomach, her chin propped on her hands as she frowned at the harmless stack of pillows. 'So, what do you want to do? Leave the door locked for ever?'

'No. You are right, I cannot risk Charlie becoming curious.' He began to play with the ends of her hair as it spilled across the sheets. 'He is growing up and I need to deal with this for all our sakes.'

'Let us be practical, then,' Kate said, lifting her chin to look at him. He was stretched out, hands behind his head, the muscles of his upper arms and shoulders in strong relief. A wave of desire washed over her and she suppressed it. They could make love when this was decided. 'Pull the house down?' she suggested to shock him into suggesting a counter-solution.

'Demolish it? Rather an extreme solution—besides, I am fond of all the rest of the old place, so is Charlie.'

'Rip out those rooms, tear up the floorboards, get rid of the fireplace and everything in the bedchamber, put new dividing walls in to change the space completely.'

'That would work,' Grant said thoughtfully. 'And what do I tell Charlie?'

'Woodworm?'

'That's a lie.'

*And Grant hates lies.* 'Tell him that the floor is dangerous. And it is. Dangerous to your peace of mind, dangerous to his if he ever sees it and asks what the marks of fire are, what that dark stain is.'

'Clever.'

'Of course.' Kate said it smugly to make him laugh and, to her great relief, he did.

'Come here.' He hauled her up unceremoniously to lie on top of him. 'Thank you. I was beginning to think I was losing my mind. A man ought to be able to cope with such things.'

'Not everything, not horrors, not unless he is an unfeeling brute.' She laid her cheek against his chest and blew gently into the dark hair, smiling as his nipples contracted tightly. 'I think you feel more guilty because you did not love her.' It was dangerous to talk of love. As soon as she used the word, she had a horrid feeling that Grant might think she was fishing for him to say that he loved *her*. Which of course he didn't. Nor did she expect it. It was not as though...

'Is that some feminine logic that escapes me?'

'You cannot mourn her, only her unhappiness and the unhappiness she caused you. You dare not think too much about her in case you find you are relieved at her death.'

Beneath her the long, hard body had become very still. Kate could feel the thud of his heart, the slight rise and fall of his breathing. Then Grant said, 'You hit hard, do you not, honest Kate? You drag out thoughts that I had not even acknowledged.'

'I like you,' she said and raised her head to look deep into the troubled green eyes, half shielded by dark lashes. 'I hope I am your friend as well as your wife and your lover. Who can be honest if not your friends?'

'My closest male friends do not suggest such things.'

'Because they are male. Does Alex confide how

much he loves Tess? Does Cris admit that he is in love?'

'Is he?' Surprise seemed to jerk Grant out of his inward-looking thoughts.

'I think so. He is certainly not happy, although he hides it well. I cannot be certain, of course, but there is something in his expression when he looks at Alex and Tess, and I saw it once, reflected in a mirror, when he was looking at us. Happy marriages. I cannot believe that he would be unhappy over not being married, because he could remedy that soon enough, he is so very eligible after all. Which makes me think he loves someone and it is not returned. Will he tell you about it?'

'Poor devil. I never thought to say that about Cris, and as for confiding, at knife point, possibly, otherwise, not,' he admitted with a faint smile that vanished as he frowned, back searching into his memory. 'I was not relieved she died. No, never that. If I could have gone back in time, never married Madeleine, then perhaps I would have done— but then I would not have Charlie, would I?'

Kate felt him relax as he thought of his son, then he smiled properly and she sensed the loosening of his taut body. 'We'll turn that space into rooms for the children. A bedroom each, a schoolroom, a nursery. That will chase the ghosts away better than any exorcism.'

'Grant, that's a brilliant idea.' Kate wriggled up to kiss him and realised that he had relaxed enough to be thinking of his new wife, not his old—or perhaps it was just his body that was doing so. She slid her tongue between his lips and snuggled her hips closer against his and smiled as her husband rolled her over with a possessive growl. He would not have nightmares tonight.

But, as she went down into the whirlpool of sensation with him, the thought flickered through her mind that they were making love without restraint and without care for the consequences. Strange that she had never given it a thought before tonight. The children's suite might need more rooms one day…

'You are happy.' Tess linked her arm through Kate's as they strolled across the parterre.

'Yes,' she admitted. 'We…confronted our problem. Look, you see that rough lawn down there? We are going to turn that into a water garden.'

'I'm so glad—about both the problem and the water garden.' Tess was not easily diverted from her theme. 'And I am happy for both of you. I only met Grant fleetingly before I married Alex, but I liked him very much. I am so glad he has found someone to love, someone who loves him.'

'I...' *Oh, why deny it? You are head over heels in love with the man.* 'Grant does not love me. I told you the truth, that it was a marriage of convenience. We hardly know each other yet.'

'Alex and I did not know each other very long before I knew that I loved him. Mind you, it took an awful lot to make him realise that he loved me, even when I set about seducing him,' Tess admitted with a candour that made Kate smile despite everything. 'Men are not very bright about emotions of that sort.'

'Nor am I. I don't want to have my heart broken. I thought I was in love before, with Anna's father, but I was not. Now I feel like this about Grant and it can be wonderful in... I mean, it is wonderful being with him.' She must be the colour of a peony.

'Wonderful in bed?' Tess teased. 'For me, too. Aren't we lucky? Such *talented* men.'

'Yes. But Grant doesn't expect love in marriage. He certainly didn't find it with his first wife and that was a disaster that's haunting him still. He really did not want to marry again, not for himself. He did it because he wanted to rescue me, and because Charlie needed a stepmother and because he had promised his grandfather.' She watched a rabbit hop across the grass, stop to eat something, then, suddenly alarmed, make for the woods. That was how she felt—calm and content, then frightened by fears she could not quite name, doubts she could not express.

'I should be happy with what I have—a good man, two lovely children, security, physical bliss. And yet…'

'And yet you want it all and it will hurt all the more if he does not love you, because you can see so clearly how it could be.'

'And Grant says that *I* hit hard,' Kate said with a rueful smile.

'I was brought up by nuns to be painfully honest and it is difficult to remember tact sometimes. Are you sure he does not love you?'

'Quite sure. I believe he thinks he did the right thing in marrying me, which is something. But if I vanished off the face of the earth tomorrow?' She shrugged. 'He would be truly sorry, but his heart would not be broken.'

'What will you do?' Tess took off her bonnet and began to swing it from its ribbons, turning her face up to the sky.

'You will get freckles,' Kate warned. 'Do? Why,

nothing. I can't imagine ever having the courage to tell him. He would be so kind about it.' She shivered.

'Yes. Horrible,' Tess agreed. 'He would pussyfoot around being nice to you and you would never know what he really felt.'

'I think we should go through the things in Madeleine's bedchamber,' Kate suggested as she and Grant found themselves alone in the dining room waiting for their guests to join them for luncheon. 'Do you think there might be items you could give to Charlie as a memento of his mother? He would treasure that.'

'You wouldn't be jealous?' Grant seemed puzzled. 'He's never known her, he can't really remember her and he loves you. Why do you risk that by making her more real for him?'

'What he feels for me cannot be diluted by what he feels for anyone else. He loves you, he loves me, he loves his grandfather's memory and he can love his mother—that makes more love, not less.' *Tess was right,* she thought, *men really are confused about love.*

'I suppose that is true.' Grant caught Kate around the waist and pulled her into his embrace, to the imminent danger of the nearest place setting. 'He won't love you less—you are here and you are easy to love, Kate.' He said it with a smile as he dipped his head to kiss her and Kate lurched back clumsily, sending a knife clattering to the floor.

There was the sound of someone clearing their throat and Cris de Feaux remarked, 'My dear Grant, we are more than happy to take luncheon on the terrace—you only had to drop a hint, you know. But I'm sure a fully laid table is a most uncomfortable place to...er...bill and coo.'

Grant released her, scooped up the knife and waved the others into the room. 'If a man cannot kiss his own wife in his own dining room without being accused of disgusting practices, things have come to a sorry pass,' he remarked as he held a chair for Kate, then walked around to take his own place. 'Billing and cooing indeed. Where on earth did you pick up such a bourgeois expression?'

Gabriel Stone sat down next to Kate and gave a snort of laughter. 'I would pay good money to see the Marquess of Avenmore billing and cooing.'

Kate kicked him sharply on the ankle.

'Ouch,' he murmured. 'My dear Lady Allundale, if you wish to flirt, might I suggest that firstly you *caress* with your delightful foot and secondly that we do it away from your husband's jealous eye? I have no desire to face him at dawn. The man is too good with a firearm.'

'Oh, stop it,' Kate whispered back. 'I do not want to flirt with you, Lord Edenbridge, and you know it. Kindly do not tease the marquess.'

'Why ever not?' He turned his wicked smile on her. 'Teasing Cris keeps him human. He'd be too perfect to be true if we didn't.'

'He has feelings,' she said vehemently. 'Even if you do not.'

'Ah, Lady Allundale, just because you are in love, you do not need to wish the affliction on everyone.'

'It is not an affliction,' Kate snapped.

'No?' The dark, knowing gaze moved from her to Grant, who was engaged in an energetic argument with Alex Tempest at the other end of the table. 'If you say so, sweet Kate, I must believe you.'

*Infuriating man.* Kate passed Gabriel the bread and butter with more force than elegance. *He knows I love Grant. Which means if both Tess and he can see it, then Grant must be able to see how I feel, as well. On the other hand,* she mused, pushing a slice of cold chicken around her plate, *perhaps Grant* doesn't *see, any more than he and Lord Edenbridge can perceive that Lord Avenmore is suffering.*

She was making herself dizzy, going in circles. Kate made a superhuman effort, pushed all thoughts of her marriage to the back of her mind and enquired about Lord Edenbridge's family home in repressive tones that managed to curtail even *his* tendency to tease.

'We need a builder,' Grant said a week later as they stood and waved goodbye to the three carriages.

'Not an architect?' Kate shifted Anna into a more comfortable position and kept an eye on Charlie, racing down the drive for a last wave to his favourite 'uncles'.

'No, the sketches we did will be enough for a good joiner to work from.' Grant turned back to the house. 'I thought to ask Wilson to sort all the personal items from the bedroom. The gowns, perfume bottles, the curtains, all of that kind of thing will go anonymously to charities in Newcastle for them to sell.' He hesitated. 'There's a miniature of Madeleine. Should I give it to Charlie now, do you think, or wait until he is older?'

'Now, I think.' Kate moved close to his side. 'You remember that tomorrow I have a number of ladies visiting for tea? I met them at Mrs Lowndes's charity sewing circle. Some of them are bringing children with them, which will keep Charlie occupied. That will give Wilson the opportunity to tackle the room.'

She stopped in the doorway and called to Charlie, who came racing back with Rambler, the elderly pointer, at his heels. The secrets and ghosts would soon be gone from this house and from Grant's heart, driven out by sawdust and hammering, plasterers and cheerful, noisy builders. Summer was coming, the valley was blossoming and her children were, too. Her husband seemed happy and she was learning to live with loving him in secret.

Christmas, and London, were a very long way away, Kate thought as she turned back to the hallway and her waiting husband. A long way. Grant would see how happy they all were here and it could only get better. When autumn came he would not want to leave this place for the dirt and noise and artificiality of London.

She held out her hand and he took it and, as he bent to kiss her, there was nothing but warmth in the green eyes that smiled into hers.

*November 23—Abbeywell*

'Lady Mortenson is holding a party and we are invited.' Kate waved the letter in Grant's direction.

'What date is it?' Grant looked up from the copy of the *Times* that was folded beside his plate.

'The eighteenth of December.' Kate spread damson preserve on her toast and passed her wardrobe in mental review. She would definitely need a new gown and probably some evening slippers, as well.

'That's a pity, we'll miss it.' Grant was still intent on the Parliamentary news.

'Why?'

'We will be in London by then, of course.' He looked up as if surprised she even had to ask.

'*London?* But you never said anything about London.'

'I most certainly did.' Grant tossed the newssheet aside. 'When I came back in May I said we would have the summer here, then go back to London.'

'After Christmas.' Somehow she stopped her voice rising to a shriek. 'You said *after* Christmas.'

'Yes, but the building work is proving far more disruptive than we thought with all the work they are doing on the chimney flues.' He was using what Kate thought of as his *husband being reasonable* voice. It usually amused her, especially as she won half of the battles that necessitated the use of it. Now she dropped the toast, jam-side down, on to the plate and stared at him as he continued, just as reasonably. 'We can't use half the downstairs rooms because we can't light fires there and the house is getting colder and colder. And you said yourself only the other day that it is making a lot of work for the staff, trying to keep all the dust under control. If we weren't here, they could shut up all the rooms, put dust covers on the furniture, retreat into the warm part and let the builders get on with it. I thought we could go down next week.'

'Next week?' Kate echoed faintly. Over Christmas week London would be quiet and starved of fashionable company because most of the *ton* would be at their country estates. But at the beginning of December she was sure the capital would seem as busy as always. It might not be the Season, but society would still be there in force.

'I'm sure I said something.' Grant shrugged. 'Perhaps I just remarked about it to Grimswade and Bolton. And Wilkinson.' He picked up the paper again. 'I'm sure I mentioned it to Wilkinson.'

'My lord.' Kate kept her voice level because it would not do to shout in front of the footmen. 'You may have told your butler, your secretary and your bailiff, but you did not tell your *wife*.'

'There is no need to worry, my dear.' Grant seemed blissfully unaware that he was within an inch of having the jam pot thrown at him. 'The staff are well practised in getting packed up for London. We'll take the chaise for ourselves and the travelling coach for the children and Jeannie and Gough, and then another coach for the luggage. This fine dry weather seems set to hold.'

'Thank you, Giles, that will be all.' Kate waited until the footmen had gone out and the door had closed. 'My lord, I do not want to go to London.'

'Why ever not?' Finally she had his full attention. Probably the repeated use of his title gave him an inkling that all was not well.

'Because—' *My lover will be there. Anna's father. The man who ruined me and who has every cause to wish to see me in prison. My brother might be there and will try his damnedest to ensnare you in his schemes. Because you'll find out that I told you a pack of lies. Because I am terrified that everything we have built is going to fall apart.* And she could say none of that.

The six months that Grant had been at Abbeywell had been months of contentment. They had grown closer and had fallen into a domestic routine that appeared to please both of them. Their nights were filled with passionate lovemaking and Grant showed no sign of tiring of her, even though he had not declared any feeling for her beyond affection. The children were flourishing.

*We have become a family,* Kate thought, *but it is all founded on lies. My lies.* They were companionable, but sometimes that companionship felt merely polite and distant and Kate knew there was an invisible barrier between them that stopped them achieving the closeness that might lead to a mutual love. She suspected it was her own guilty conscience that had raised that sheet of glass. She dared not break it and the more time went past, the harder it became to even contemplate telling him the truth. It was as though the right moment had slipped through her fingers and was now vanishing, too far gone to catch.

The marriage was like a house built of cards. If Grant discovered the truth, then it would all come tumbling down—their family life, the children's security, Grant's reputation if, as she suspected he would, he insisted on confronting the criminality of what Henry had done. At some level Grant must sense that she was holding something back from him, but he was too much the gentleman to force the issue.

*Or perhaps he does not care enough,* she thought in her darker moments. He must have had enough drama and emotion with Madeleine not to want to demand a confrontation with her. Surely now he wanted only a quiet life with a wife who satisfied him in bed and loved his children. *But it is so lonely sometimes.*

'Why are you so reluctant to go to London?' Grant asked.

'Charlie will miss Christmas at home.'

'The town house is familiar to him now—besides, this house at Christmastide can only hold bad memories for him. Let him have this year somewhere entirely different and then the following year the recollections will be dimmer, the house will be much changed and we can enjoy the festive season here.'

That was perfectly, unarguably, reasonable. Kate tried another tack. 'I'm shy of London. I won't know how to go on there.'

'Of course you will.' Grant was beginning to look impatient now. 'You are quite at ease with company in the neighbourhood, you are well informed on the issues of the day, you make excellent conversation and you dance very well and you'll have fashionable gowns—there is nothing at all to be alarmed about.'

'I can't help it,' she said. 'I am.'

He was puzzled now, she could tell, and in a moment he was going to move from puzzlement to suspicion. 'Where is the courageous woman I found in that bothy?'

There was nothing for it. Unless she developed a disfiguring rash or broke a leg, she was going to have to face London society. 'Facing critical leaders of fashion is far more alarming than giving birth, believe me,' Kate said with a laugh that she hoped rang true.

Grant visibly relaxed. 'I will be there by your side.'

*That is what I am afraid of.* 'Of course.'

## Chapter Seventeen

Something was wrong with Kate. Grant paced along the terrace, welcoming the cold, rolling his shoulders to relax them after two hours of solid work in the study with his bailiff and secretary, sorting estate matters out so that he could safely go away for a few months. Was whatever had made her so wary of London related to the reserve that was always present just below the surface, however cheerful she seemed, however lost in the passion of their lovemaking?

He wanted to trust her totally and yet, somehow, he could not. Was it the ghost of his first marriage haunting him, holding him back from that complete act of faith? He only wished she would tell him what it was that put the shadow in her eyes, those moments of constraint when he sensed she was holding back from telling him…something. It was hard not to think, *Confess something.* He told himself it was not jealousy that he felt, that she was not still pining for Anna's father. After all, she had told him she had not loved the man, and besides, what did it matter if she had? Theirs was a practical, companionable marriage, not a love match. Kate was passionate and responsive in bed, and that was what a man needed, not some foolish romantic fantasy with moonlight and roses. And heartbreak.

'My lord?'

He turned to find Jeannie standing outside the long window to the drawing room, Anna in her arms. 'Yes?' He strolled across to tickle the baby under her chin and she laughed at him and held out her arms.

'Could I leave Lady Anna with you a moment, my lord? I brought her down for an airing, but there's much more of a nip in the air than I realised and I want another shawl for her.'

'Of course. I'll wait with her in the drawing room.' He took Anna, who immediately fastened both chubby hands on his neckcloth and proceeded to demolish it as he carried her into the warmth.

'You, madam, are a menace to any gentleman with pretentions to elegance,' he chided and held her away while he went to examine the damage in the mirror. Not so bad, at least she hadn't chewed it this time. Anna laughed up at him and he smiled back, then sobered as a thought struck him. What if Kate's reluctance to go to London was a fear that a lack of resemblance between her husband and the child might be noticed? After all, Anna had reached the age when a proud mama might be expected to produce the child for a few minutes for morning callers to admire.

Their local acquaintance had known Anna as she grew up and, presumably, were used to her and accepted her as Grant's child without question. Now he shifted Anna until he could hold her up facing the mirror beside his own face and compared their features—straight brown hair in a shade nearer his dark tones than Kate's lighter tresses. A face that would, he was sure, echo her mother's as she grew out of babyhood and the promise of height that would fit well with both her assumed parents.

And green eyes. He shifted her round again so he could study them more carefully. Several doting matrons had remarked on those eyes—'Green, just like her papa's!' That was useful.

Anna was watching him now, eyes wide, and he realised that her eyes were not like his after all. They were a paler, clearer green with gold flecks and a dark rim around the iris. The effect was beautiful and unusual and when she grew up he imagined they would give her a unique charm. He checked his own eyes in the mirror—a darker green that verged towards hazel when he was tired or angry, so he'd been told. No gold flecks, no dark ring. But that was not a problem, Anna was like enough in various characteristics to both of them not to raise the slightest suspicions. It might be a different matter if she was a redhead or a pale blonde. He was conscious of disappointment that he had not found the reason for Kate's anxiety.

'Here we are, my lord, her warmest shawl. I'll take her now, shall I?'

Jeannie bore Anna away to the terrace, leaving Grant frowning at his own reflection in the mirror. Kate was perfectly competent socially, she was intelligent enough to learn and adapt quickly and she was usually confident enough to be aware of that. Could it be that she feared encountering her brother? He knew he should have insisted on making contact with the shadowy Mr Harding of somewhere in Suffolk, but he had managed to forget all about Kate's brother and she had done nothing to remind him. He should confront her about all of these things, but he sensed that if he did he would destroy the happiness they now had, perhaps simply for a phantom of his own imagination. He would watch and think and see how she took to London, see what clues he could discover.

He strode out of the drawing room and along to the little room Kate had claimed as her writing room, tapped and went in. 'Kate.'

She jumped, blotted her page and tutted irritably at him. Sometimes he made her cross simply because it was so rare to see her lose her self-control and he wanted to see the real woman that she kept so carefully hidden behind the facade of the good wife and mother. She revealed that face in bed, when she lost all inhibition with him, and she had shown it when she had helped him fight his demons over Madeleine, but there were times when he thought she was moving further and further away from him.

'I'm sorry.' He moved to stand behind her and ran the back of one finger down the exposed nape of her neck, enjoying the sensual little shiver she gave. 'Were you writing poetry? I am sorry if I have made you blot the final stanza.'

Kate gave a little snort of laughter, the irritation vanishing as fast as it always seemed to. 'No, I am not writing poetry. This is a shopping list for the linen warehouse. There hardly seems to be a decent sheet left in the house.' She twisted round to look up at him and he kept his hand where it was so that his fingers trailed round her neck as she moved. 'Do you think I should be writing odes to my husband's eyelashes?'

'Are they so worthy of praise?' He felt absurdly anxious that she should say so.

'They are indecently long and thick.'

'Are they indeed? Indecent, eh? All the better to tickle you with.' The confrontation he had come for was less interesting than the possibilities presented by a flustered wife, a comfortable chaise longue and the thought of how his eyelashes might be employed.

'Grant!' It was accompanied by a most encouraging blush. He turned the key in the lock, twitched the nearest curtain across the window and advanced on the desk.

'Grant—only half the window is covered.'

'If anyone is standing in the middle of the flower bed, on a box, contorting their neck in an effort to see in through the uncovered area of the window, all I can say is that we have more flexible staff than I imagined.' He stripped off his coat and waistcoat as he advanced. 'Am I going to have to chase you round the desk?'

'Do you want to?' Kate slipped off the chair and retreated to the far side. 'I warn you, I have a quill and I know how to use it.'

Grant hopped on one foot, then the other as he tugged off his boots. Kate was not making much of an effort to escape, which was interesting. He had never tried to make love to her downstairs and he had expected her to be shy of doing so in broad daylight. When he emerged from the folds of his shirt and prowled towards her clad only in his breeches she edged away around the desk, then, when he was within arm's reach, extended the quill like a rapier and flicked his right nipple with the point of the feather.

*'Touché,'* Grant conceded, moved his right hand and, when her eyes flickered to follow the movement, lunged, caught Kate around the waist and bore her off to the chaise. She tried to bounce up. He flipped her skirts up over her head and, as she struggled to extricate herself, pressed a kiss into the exposed triangle of curls at the junction of her thighs.

Kate went very still, but did not resist as he eased her knees apart, settled his shoulders between them, bent his head and brushed his lashes up the inside of her thigh, over the white, soft skin. There was a sudden heave and the skirts settled over his head plunging him into semi-darkness as he shifted the subtle caress to her other thigh.

That convulsive movement was all the resistance she gave as he worked his way up, fraction by fraction, towards his goal. She was aroused, there was no mistaking that. Grant parted the delicate folds, touched once with his tongue, and Kate came apart in his hands. He used his lips and mouth in a long, demanding kiss that had her writhing on the couch before he shook off the folds of her gown, pulled down his breeches and sheathed himself in her pulsing, hot body in one hard movement.

'*Grant.*' Her face was buried in the angle of his neck, her arms locked around his shoulders as he thrust. 'Grant, I—'

'Come again,' he demanded, controlling, somehow, his own need. 'Come for me again. *Now.*'

And she did, pulling him with her into the maelstrom.

*I almost told him I loved him,* Kate thought as she cradled her husband in her arms in blissful discomfort. The sofa cushion, a hard, cylindrical bolster, dug into the base of her spine, her corset was doing its best to stop her breathing and Grant, though without any spare flesh on him, was a significant dead weight on top of her. *Thank goodness I didn't.*

'Kate.' Grant's voice was muffled and he heaved himself up until he was sitting on the end of the chaise. 'You were trying to say something just then.'

'Probably *more*, or *again*,' she temporised. 'Goodness, after that, how do you expect me to recall my own name?'

He grinned. 'Flatterer. Kate…' That change of tone from teasing to serious within the space of two words was ominous. She braced herself. 'Is the problem about going to London because you fear coming across your brother? I know you haven't written to him. Perhaps we should make contact now, before we go.'

'No.' She pushed down her skirts and scrambled to sit upright at the end of the chaise. 'Please, Grant. It will be too awkward. I cannot forgive him for how he behaved and he will not forgive me. Let sleeping dogs lie.' He still looked unconvinced as he refastened his breeches. 'It isn't as though my parents are alive, or that I have other siblings.' Which was true. She had cousins, but they were even more country mice than she was.

'If it upsets you so much, I will not insist.' Grant pushed his fingers through his hair, the habitual giveaway that he was frustrated. He would circle round, come back to this, she knew.

'And Henry would be a most unsuitable uncle for Charlie, a really bad influence.' That went home, she saw. 'May I have the carriage tomorrow? I need to go into Newcastle to have my hair done.'

'Surely the coiffeur will come here, or it can wait until you get to London?'

'Oh, did I not tell you?' She had not, quite deliberately. 'I saw an advertisement in the *Newcastle Courier* that Monsieur Ducasse, late of Monsieur Maurice's establishment in Bond Street, has set up in Newcastle. And Monsieur Maurice advertises in all the best journals—*La Belle Assemblée* and so on. I would feel so much more comfortable with a fashionable style. I wrote to reserve a private parlour at the King's Head and he will attend me there.' Grant opened his mouth and she said hastily, 'Wilson will accompany me, of course.'

'Then of course you may have the carriage.' Grant got to his feet and lifted her hand to kiss the tips of her fingers. 'Not that you need any changes to make you look quite delightful, my dear.'

'Flatterer.' She laughed up at him and pulled his hand back to rest fleetingly against her own lips. *I love you and now I will lie and deceive and do whatever it takes to get through this ordeal without you ever discovering who the woman you married really is.*

'Kate?' Grant stopped dead in the hallway, then advanced slowly, like a cat who has seen something that may be prey, or may be something alien and dangerous. 'What have you done?' he demanded as he completed the circle.

Grimswade, who had appeared the moment the carriage drew up, effaced himself, closely followed by Wilson clutching Kate's bonnet, pelisse and reticule.

'Monsieur Ducasse gave me a new style.' She smiled brightly at him and fluffed the soft curls that framed her face. 'I think it's very dashing.'

'He's cut it.' Grant's green eyes were narrowed as he studied the effect.

'Just the front. I knew it would curl if he did that. The back is still long, so it can be put up. You see?' Kate turned right round, skirts belling out.

'It changes the shape of your face.'

She still couldn't work out whether he liked it or not, or whether he realised that she had plucked her eyebrows into a finer arch. 'I think it shows off my cheekbones. I didn't know I had any before.'

'And the colour…' Grant was prowling again.

'Just a shade darker. Monsieur Ducasse said it would make my eyes look bigger.' He came to a halt in front of her and she widened her eyes at him. 'And bluer.' And he had stained her eyebrows to match. Wilson had the little brush and bottle safely tucked away.

'You look more sophisticated,' Grant said at last, when she thought she would go dizzy from holding her breath.

'Is that code for *older*?' She hoped it was. She wanted to look as different as possible from that wide-eyed, unsophisticated girl who had been the bait to catch a lord in a blackmailer's snare.

'Just a trifle.' Grant seemed to have relaxed, lids heavy over his green eyes. 'It certainly makes you look more…experienced.' There was a wealth of hidden meaning in the one, drawled, word.

*He likes it.* That was a relief.

'Maman!' Charlie appeared, at the run as usual,

skidded to a halt and stared. Then he circled her, just as his father had done, but with his mouth open.

Grant laughed. 'Your *maman* has had a haircut. Fancy, isn't it?'

'It's prime!' Charlie approved. 'Is it for London?'

'It is.' Grant's gaze met hers over the boy's head. 'I'm glad you are getting into the spirit of the London expedition, Kate. It is past your bedtime, Charlie, off you go.'

'I'm doing my best.' She bent to kiss the boy before he ran off to the stairs, then slid her hand through the crook of her husband's elbow and leaned in a little, enjoying the smell of leather and the hint of coffee and the familiar, beloved scent that was simply *Grant*. She had been away all day and she had missed him, even for those few hours.

He turned his head from watching Charlie's retreating form, looked down at her and became very still. His eyes, which were usually green, darkened to hazel, as they did when he was tired, or angry or aroused. And this was definitely arousal, reacting to something he saw in her expression. 'Kate.'

Her chest was so tight that her lungs felt hollow. He was going to kiss her, here and now in the hallway, and she was going to say it, tell him she loved him, and she could not, must not. Not when she was lying to him, deceiving him. 'Of course, it will mean a great strain on my dress allowance and my pin money.' She fluttered her eyelashes outrageously. 'Will you increase it, or will you be mean and beat me if I overspend?'

'I might do both,' Grant said, low-voiced. 'I might increase it so you may buy outrageous garments and then spank you just for the hell of it.' His expression promised considerably more pleasure than pain and she knew he was not a man who would raise a hand to a woman in anger. Was spanking another of those erotic games he was beginning to show her?

'That sounds interesting,' Kate murmured. 'But you'd have to chase me first.'

'That can be arranged.' Grant looked up. 'Yes, Grimswade, what is it?'

'Should I tell the kitchen to put dinner back, my lady, seeing as you have only just got in?'

'Goodness, is that the time?' For a moment she had thought the butler had overheard Grant and was suggesting delaying dinner while she was pursued around the bedchamber by a playful husband. Really, she must get a grip on her imagination! 'I'll go straight up now. Don't inconvenience Cook, thank you, Grimswade.'

'Thank you, my lady.'

'Coward,' Grant whispered in her ear as she passed him.

*If only you knew, my love. Pray heaven that you never do.*

# Chapter Eighteen

*December 15—Grosvenor Street, London*

'More treasures?'

Kate nodded to Wilson and waited until the maid closed the bedchamber door behind her before she answered. Grant was standing at the foot of the bed and eyeing the heap of packets and bandboxes that the footmen had just brought up. She rather thought he was on the verge of smiling, but she could not be certain—after all, she had spent almost a week doing nothing else but shop.

'Yes. And you have bought a stack of neckcloths and at least two waistcoats, and a new evening suit and three pairs of boots.'

'I have.' Yes, his mouth was just twitching at the corner.

'One has to dress,' Kate drawled, risking it. 'At

least that was what I heard one lady say to another while I was in the fitting room at Mrs Bell's.'

'That is absolutely true. Think what a spectacle Bond Street would be if one did not.'

'Especially if Prinny was on the strut.'

Grant shuddered. 'I did not need that image being put into my mind, thank you!' He picked up a large flat box from the floor. 'And what does this contain?'

'Um…I was hoping it was something you wouldn't see in broad daylight,' Kate confessed.

Grant weighed the box on the upturned palm of one hand and looked at the shop stamp on the lid. 'Ah, the cost of this, I imagine, is in inverse proportion to the amount of fabric it contains.'

'It was a *trifle* expensive. I was hoping it might be the sort of thing that would get me chased around the bedchamber.'

'But not spanked?' Grant had a speculative gleam in his eye. 'Try it on for me, and we'll see.'

'At four o'clock in the afternoon?' Her pulse was racing along with her imagination.

'I really cannot persuade you out of the idea that there are *respectable* times and places for lovemaking, can I?' Grant piled the parcels on the bed on to the floor, then sat down and pulled off his boots.

'I can be persuaded.' Kate picked up the box and whisked into the dressing room. 'Close your eyes.'

He was quite correct about the cost. If looked at dispassionately, the negligee consisted of nothing but floating panels of pale blue silk gauze, a large number of silver ribbons and dark blue silk flowers appliquéd in various strategic positions. Crushed up it would fit in a soup bowl and, as a garment, it was utterly impractical for anything except tormenting one's husband. She had thought it delicious the moment she saw it.

When she looked around the edge of the door Grant was leaning against a bedpost, arms crossed, eyes closed. He was wearing nothing but a severe expression. Once, Kate would have been alarmed, now she could read him well enough to know she was being teased, especially as there was nothing to disguise the fact that he was finding this arousing.

She tiptoed up, swirled round so her gossamer skirts whispered across his legs and ran to the other side of the bed. Grant's reflexes were fast and he was on her heels, reaching for her as she scrambled across the bed, silk panels flying. Kate made it to the other side just as Grant somersaulted across the bed and landed on his feet in front of her.

'That is the most outrageously provoking garment

I have even seen.' He was breathing far harder than the amount of activity justified.

'And you have seen many?'

Kate could have sworn he had actually growled, although as she found herself seized, upended and face down over Grant's knees, she could not be certain.

'Now, then, let's check the workmanship.' One large hand at the small of her back was more than enough to hold her down, even if she had wanted to struggle, which she did not. A wriggle or two, though...

There was a flurry of fabric, a whisper of silk, and then there was nothing over her buttocks but air. 'Quite impractical,' Grant observed. 'I cannot imagine how this would keep you warm on a chilly evening.' There was a tantalising pause, then one palm moved slowly over her right buttock. 'This would, though.'

It was only a light smack, more noise than anything. Kate squeaked, then gasped as he did the same to the other buttock.

'Warmer? Certainly pinker.'

What was warm was the thrust of his erection against her stomach. Kate decided she liked this game. 'Beast! Savage!' She wriggled against him and was rewarded by a flurry of light open-handed slaps. She realised the wicked sensation of being powerless while Grant did what he liked was making her excited, breathless and very, very needy. 'Grant?'

'Hmm?' She felt the pressure of his lips on one sensitive buttock. 'Shall I stop? Perhaps you are right and this isn't the thing to be doing in the afternoon. We could get dressed and discuss the Parliamentary report in the *Times*.'

'You haven't checked the design of the front of the negligee. What if they stinted on ribbons?'

'What an appalling thought. I would have to wrap you in a cloak and take you straight back to the shop to demand a refund.' He turned her so she was sitting on his thighs and tipped up her chin. 'A very becoming shade of rose. Are you flushed because you enjoyed being spanked, or at the thought of being carried through the streets in nothing but this flimsy thing and a cloak?'

'Both,' she admitted as he began to untie the ribbons, counting as he went.

'…nine, ten…' His voice was not quite steady as he gave up on the little bows and lifted her, then brought her down so she was straddling him as he sat. 'I need to see it in motion,' he said, his voice husky as he lowered her with aching slowness until he was sheathed inside her. 'Like that.' She held him, burrowed close against him so the friction of the fine gauze fretted her nipples, and his, and felt the control he had been tantalising her with snap. *'Kate.'* He broke in six powerful strokes, took her with him into the whirlwind and then stayed, deep inside her, his arms around her, his forehead on her shoulder.

Just as she was sliding into sleep Grant murmured, 'I didn't hurt you, did I?'

'Of course not. I knew you would never hurt me.' She sat back, ran one finger down the straight line of his nose and smiled when, eyes still closed, he put out his tongue to catch the tip. 'And you aren't cross about all my shopping?'

'Of course not.' Grant opened his eyes and fell back on to the bed, bringing her with him. 'I've kept you locked up in Northumberland away from all the shops for months.'

'I've been extravagant, though.' He shook his head, but she persisted with her confession. 'I'm… nervous. It took my mind off things. It's quite dangerous really, spending all that money. It must be like gambling or drink.'

To her surprise he didn't laugh at the notion. 'You

are probably right. But don't worry, if you can see the danger, then I doubt you are in it. But don't be nervous, Kate. I'll look after you. I won't let the society sharks near you.'

'I know.' *But you can't protect me from the monsters I've unleashed myself, my love.*

Grant climbed to the next step on the grand staircase leading to the ballroom of the Marquess of Larminster's ballroom, the setting for the marchioness's 'surprise' birthday reception for her husband. The event was a surprise for no one, least of all the long-suffering and newly sixty-year-old marquess, but he enjoyed indulging his wife and she enjoyed parties, the larger the better.

It was not the event that Grant would have chosen for Kate's introduction to London society, for the place was full to bursting and the noise level indescribable. It was also packed with the important people Kate needed to make a good impression upon if she were to obtain the entrée to the right circles and the friendship and approval of the ladies who made society go round. And they were married to the men Grant mixed with socially at his clubs and would be forming alliances with, and against, in the House of Lords.

As he stood with as much patience as he could muster in the receiving line, he looked down at his wife again, still coming to terms with how sophisticated and elegant she looked. It occurred to him that the height of his hopes had been that she would 'do', pass muster, not be a disaster. How little faith he'd had. Somewhere, always in the back of his mind, was the image of the bedraggled, exhausted, desperate woman in that bothy, the knowledge that she was not trained up for this world, that she carried scandal with her.

Despite coming to know her—her courage, her humour, her intelligence, her breathtaking natural eroticism—he had still taken it for granted that she could not cope with this world with its dagger-sharp criticism, its rivalries and sophisticated pleasures.

'Grant,' Kate murmured. 'We're moving again.'

Up another step, almost at the top now. She was still nervous, he could see the almost imperceptible tremor of the beading around the bodice of her gown, but she looked magnificent. Not a traditional beauty, she would never be that, but somehow something better. *Elegant, charming, warm,* he thought. *And sophisticated with her new hairstyle. And the minx has been colouring her lashes with lampblack and, if I'm not very much mistaken, she's using lip stain.*

Like a soldier she'd put on her armour to go into battle for him. *She makes me so happy.*

The realisation hit him as though someone behind him had punched him between the shoulder blades. Happy. He was actually, positively happy. Not just now and again, like when he was playing with Charlie, or feeling the wind in his hair when he galloped unchecked across the moor, or won a hand of cards against Gabriel, but bone-deep happy. That had come with this marriage. Somehow he had moved, without him realising it, from simply coping with life and snatching what pleasure he could, to a feeling of inner contentment. But he had not been conscious of feeling happy. *When did that happen? Just now? Yesterday? Weeks ago?*

A sharp elbow nudged him in the ribs. *'Grant, it's us.'*

'Sorry, air-dreaming.' Hell, in a minute he'd be shouting with laughter, capering like a fool for a fascinated audience. Grant found a social smile from somewhere, plastered it on and advanced on the marchioness. 'Lady Larminster, may I introduce my wife, Catherine?'

'Lady Allundale.' The marchioness raised artfully curved eyebrows as she studied Kate. 'Delightful,' she pronounced.

'Lady Larminster.' Kate's curtsy was perfectly modulated.

'Larminster, here's Allundale's wife at long last.' The marquess inclined his head and beamed at Kate, who curtsied again. 'You've taken long enough bringing her to town, Allundale.'

Grant had no trouble interpreting that as, *So what is wrong with her?* 'All due to my sins, ma'am. I'm greedy, jealous and possessive and don't want to share her.' As he spoke, he realised that was all quite true. He wanted to scoop Kate up in his arms and sweep her off back home. He wanted to do something about this strange fizzing joy inside him.

'Well, now, there's a declaration of the kind one doesn't hear enough of in these cynical days. Do you hear that, Larminster?'

Beside him he could almost feel the warmth of Kate's blushes, but when he walked her away from the receiving line and could look at her face he saw the light dusting of rice powder had subdued the colour, or else she was pale through nerves.

'She's a bossy old besom,' he said as he steered her into the reception room. 'But she means well.'

'I'm sure she does.' Kate's chin was up. 'That was very gallant of you, to say those things.'

'I meant them.' *You make me so happy. You have transformed my life.* How the blazes did one say these things to one's wife in the middle of this scrum? Surely there was a withdrawing room somewhere? Gabriel would have slipped a coin to a footman and would know the location of hidden nooks before he had even sized up the ladies at any social event. Alex, in the old days, wouldn't have been much slower. But Grant had never enjoyed dicing with scandal under the very noses of chaperons and sharp-eyed husbands and had always conducted his affaires with considerably more discretion.

'What is amusing you?' Kate obviously didn't find anything at all amusing about the hot, noisy throng and was eyeing them with a social smile on her lips and eyes as wary as any gladiator thrust into the arena, wondering where the lions hid and just how hungry they were.

'I'm regretting not bribing a footman, that's all,' he said vaguely. 'Come, let's circulate and I'll introduce you to some people you'll like.'

And, by a miracle, he managed to locate many of the acquaintances he had hoped to introduce to

Kate. The pleasanter young matrons with small children of their own, the cheerful chaperons whose gossip was friendly, not vicious, and several gentlemen he could trust to treat her to polite and harmless flirtation or intelligent conversation.

After half an hour he felt she had relaxed enough to leave her with a group of his friends while he went to find her a glass of ratafia. When he got back she had Mr Whittaker choking with laughter over her description of their vicar confronted by the flock of sheep that wandered into the church during his sermon, pursued by a very amorous ram. By her side the Reverend Herbert, one of the Bishop of London's more irreverent curates, was extemporising a sermon of his own on the subject of lost lambs while making eyes at two young ladies who appeared very willing to stray in his direction.

Grant had never realised that Kate was a natural raconteur before, but she was holding her small audience gripped while, with perfect poise, she spun the tale in such a way that the poor vicar was described kindly and yet the scene was irresistibly funny.

'Do let me introduce you to my sister, Lady Allundale. She pines for witty conversation.' Whittaker took her arm, removed the ratafia glass from Grant's hand and steered Kate off into the crowd. She seemed more than happy to go with him.

'You look as nervous as a hopeful mama whose chick has just been launched into the stormy seas of the Season,' a familiar voice remarked.

'Alex.' Grant relaxed a trifle. If Alex was there, then Tess was as well, so that was two more allies. 'I don't know about looking like a hopeful matron, but I'm certainly nervous—Kate is painfully shy about all this.'

'She looks stunning. Very chic. I like the hair.' His friend was watching Kate with the eye of a connoisseur.

Grant narrowed his eyes at him, then told himself not to be ridiculous. This possessiveness played havoc with the common sense. 'She does, but she doesn't look like my Kate any more when she's dressed up like this.'

'Ah. *Your* Kate. I wondered how long it was going to take you to notice.' Alex's mouth twitched into its lazy smile as Grant frowned at him.

'Of course I notice. She's my wife.' He did his best to sound offhand. This new awareness of his feelings was too sensitive to discuss, even with Alex.

'No *of course* about it. Tess says we men have to be hit over the head with it before we realise it isn't lust or liking. When did you get hit with the brick?'

'An hour ago,' Grant admitted. 'At the top of the staircase, two couples from the head of the receiving line.'

Alex's hoot of laughter had heads turning, including Kate's. She raised her hand in a little wave, then turned back to her new acquaintances. 'No wonder you are looking vaguely concussed. Love does that. I assume Kate is aware of your feelings?'

'*What?* Don't be an idiot. Of course I'm not—' Grant managed to get his snarl down to a whisper. 'She makes me happy, that's all. I realised just now that I hadn't felt like this...for ever. And it is due to her. But that's contentment and liking and lus—er, compatibility in bed. It is not love. Ours is a marriage of convenience, you know that. And stop mopping your eyes, it isn't that funny.'

'No?'

'No, it is not.'

Alex rolled his eyes and returned his handkerchief to its pocket in the tails of his coat. 'There have been times when I've been deluded enough to think you quite intelligent, Rivers. I will leave you to stew and go and see who Tess is making eyes at and rescue them.'

'Don't say anything.'

'About what? The fact that you are *happy*? Or the fact that you're an idiot?' Alex strolled off, leaving Grant to practice deep breathing in the middle of the crowded floor in the intervals between greeting acquaintances, bowing to ladies and attempting to get his emotions and his brain into some kind of alignment.

He was an adult male with considerable experience of life and women. He had faced his man in a duel, he had fought at Waterloo and somehow got out of that intact, he had dealt with hysterical mistresses throwing the porcelain from under the bed before now. He wasn't a romantic youth desperate to transform simple liking, affection and desire into some hearts-and-flowers nonsense that could only end in disillusion and anticlimax. He was happy. His marriage made him happy. That was a wonderful realisation and now he could just get on with his life.

# *Chapter Nineteen*

Kate was beginning to relax. In fact, she thought with a small start of surprise, she was actually beginning to enjoy herself. No one had pointed a finger at her, crying *Fallen woman!* or *Blackmailer's accomplice!* as they did in her worst dreams. She could see no one who looked even faintly familiar, except for Alex and Tess, and her new acquaintances were all pleasant and even positively friendly.

Grant had seemed a little strange for a moment while they had been waiting on the stairs, but perhaps he had been nervous for her, which was understandable. She had no idea how her shaky legs had got her up those stairs, but now she was happily answering questions about which days she was at home to visitors and promising to take Anna to call on Mrs Whiting, who had a baby girl almost the same age.

She sensed Grant with a prickling awareness that had her glancing back over her shoulder with a smile, even before he arrived at her side. Was he proud of her? She hoped so, because she thought she was doing very well indeed.

'My dear.' He rested his right hand at the small of her back, a possessive gesture that made her shiver pleasurably. 'I am afraid I must tear you away. If you will excuse us?' He nodded and smiled and was perfectly polite as he detached her from the group and began to walk her back towards the entrance.

'Grant, is something wrong? You haven't had a message about one of the children, have you?'

'No, nothing is wrong. I need to talk with you, that's all.'

*So I must be doing something wrong... No, that can't be it. I know I have not put a finger out of line.* Was he unwell? She looked up at his face as he took her arm as they descended the stairs, then sent a footman for their things. He looked tense, keyed up. It must be one of his wretched migraines, although it had been weeks since he had suffered one. Perhaps anxiety about her had triggered it.

Kate stayed silent and did not fuss, even when they were seated in their carriage. She was finally rewarded for her patience when Grant threw his hat on to the seat opposite, ran both hands through his hair and said, 'I am sorry to have dragged you away. You seemed to be enjoying yourself.'

'I was, very much. I have made some new acquaintances and that will make the next engagement even better. But it is no matter, there will be many other opportunities to talk with them.'

'There is something I need to speak to you about. Something important.'

Not a headache, then. Nor did he seem displeased. 'What is wrong?'

Grant had not put on his gloves and she peeled off her own so she could slide her hand into his. It was warm and steady and closed around her fingers in a reassuring grip.

'Absolutely nothing is wrong, quite the opposite, in fact, but I think I will wait until we are home before I tell you.'

'Very well.' Comforted, she settled back and did her best to contain her curiosity.

In her bedchamber Kate handed over her evening cloak and gloves to Wilson and then dismissed the maid and waited with what patience she could muster.

Grant was normally reserved, she knew that from

experience, but this seemed to be a secret out of the ordinary. Perhaps Prinny had offered him a diplomatic post and he was doubtful whether she was prepared to sail to Brazil. Or he had decided to take Holy Orders. Or buy a very large and expensive yacht. Or...

'Kate. I have never told you this... In fact, I have only just realised it, but this marriage makes me very happy. You make me very happy. I cannot recall ever feeling like this. Not all the time.'

She hadn't heard the door open and, lost in fantasies about sea voyages and cathedral closes, she could only stare at him. For a second she thought she heard him say *I love you*, then her brain made sense of what he had actually said and her pulse seemed to stutter. 'You... Grant, did you just say that I make you happy?'

'Yes.' He raised a quizzical eyebrow, seemingly expecting more of a reaction. 'I realise it is rather a sudden declaration, but is it so surprising?'

'When?' Her voice was strangely croaky. 'When did you realise it? I had no idea you had been feeling *un*happy.'

'I haven't.' He shrugged. 'Well, about Madeleine, of course. But I had become used to thinking happiness was a matter of fleeting pleasures, of the absence of pain. This evening, at the top of the stairs just before we reached the receiving line, I realised that it is a positive thing, something that can fill me—and all because of you. Not the most convenient location for a revelation of that kind, you must admit.'

No wonder he had seemed so strange. Kate realised she was simply staring at Grant, unable to articulate a sensible response. Like, *I love you. And perhaps you are in love with me and don't realise it.*

'I'm sorry to be so dramatic about it.' He came further into the room and the door closed behind him with a click that made her jump. 'But I never speak to you about how I feel for you, how much I treasure what you have done at Abbeywell to make it into a home, how good you are with Charlie. I feel as though you have lifted a weight off my soul that I never realised was there. If that makes me sound ridiculous, I can't help it. I thought I ought to be open about how I felt.'

That was heaping coals of fire on her smarting conscience. Grant was offering her an honest declaration of his feelings when she did not deserve it, when she had lied to him in fact and by omission. But there was one thing she could be honest with him about, something she could give him, a response to his declaration. Not the full truth, of course, not that she loved him. She had been waiting too long for him to say it first, now she suspected he never would and her own love would be a burden to him.

Kate stood up and went to stand in front of him, linked her hands behind his neck and looked up into the steady green eyes. 'You make me happy, too. More than happy. With all my heart I am glad that you married me.'

He closed his eyes and rested his forehead against hers and sighed, a long, slow, difficult breath. 'Kate. Kate, I am sorry I never said these things before. I am not very good at emotions, I don't know how to be.'

'I understand.' She thought she did. He had grown up without his parents' marriage as a model. He had been raised by an elderly widower and married to a woman who had rejected and hurt him. Somewhere, deep inside, in a place he probably didn't even know existed, he had raised barriers to ever making himself as vulnerable as love would render him.

'You don't have to say things, to pretend to feelings you do not have. It is enough to know I make you happy. I just need you to know you make me happy, too,' Kate said, picking her way through, wary of saying anything that would make him suspect she loved him, force him to say the words that would be a lie. 'You were my Christmas miracle when you found me in that bothy and saved us. I am so glad I am your wife.' She stood on tiptoe and kissed him, and after the faintest hesitation he kissed her back, slowly, tenderly.

*I must confess, tell him about Jonathan and Henry now. I can't deceive him any longer. It will hurt him that I have left it so long, but to leave it even longer can only make things worse.*

He lifted one hand and began to pull the pins from her hair, drawing his fingers through it until it fell free on her shoulders. 'I am going to carry you off to bed and show you just how happy you make me, but before I do, I must tell you how proud I was of you tonight. I know you were nervous and unsure, but you did your best in spite of that and your best was magnificent.'

There was so much warmth and pride in his voice. If she did not know better, she might have added *love*. She didn't deserve any of those feelings, and if she told him the truth about Anna, the truth about her brother, then that pride would vanish, he would despise her.

'Thank you,' she murmured. 'It was far less daunting than I feared.' It had been—once she had assured herself that there was no sign of Viscount Baybrook, or of Sir Henry Harding, blackmailing baronet, either. Surely if Jonathan was in London he would have been invited to such a magnificent event as the Larminsters' reception? It was less likely that Henry would be there, but he might be in town if he had been both emboldened and enriched by extorting money from Jonathan, and it would be just like him to extract an invitation somehow.

Grant was working his way into the elaborate fastenings and folds of her gown and she arched her back to help him. *I will tell him tomorrow,* she resolved. *I cannot shatter this moment. I cannot, it is too precious.*

Grant used no erotic tricks, no titillating little games, only the magic of his mouth and his hands and his long, hard body, and Kate realised that she had learned to give with as much passion as she received. When he eased into her, slowly, achingly slowly, she realised that it was the exchange about their feelings that had given them this extra awareness of each other, of what they could be together.

There was no hurry, no rush to climax. Grant would stop moving and simply lie there, his heart beating over hers, his gaze locked with hers, his body filling and completing her. Then he would dip his head to take her lips and move again until Kate was lost in a spell of sensual, swirling pleasure. They were close, so close.

*I love you,* she thought and it was as though it was enough to tip them over into bliss, into a place where they were no longer two people, but one whole being, just as she had dreamed.

They made love again in the morning when they woke, a passionate tussle of urgency and need that left them panting and laughing. Grant ducked a flying pillow and pounced on Kate, tickling mercilessly, then subsided, pulling her against his side.

'I needed to laugh with you, Kate.'

*Yes, I needed to laugh, too. I'll talk to him after breakfast,* she thought as they subsided, breathless. 'Grant—'

'Hell, is that the time?' He rolled off the bed and made for the door to his room. 'I'm due at a meeting at the Lords at ten. Ungodly hour, I know, but I promised Pilkington. I think I will be supporting his group over several important pieces of legislation and we must discuss tactics.' He turned back, looked at her, shook his head. 'Incredible, I don't deserve to be so happy.' Then he was gone.

Kate was left staring at the door. It gave her no comfort, nor any inspiration. Finally she tugged the bell pull for Wilson. She couldn't sit in bed all day, her mind a blank. Perhaps a complete confession was not the answer. What if telling Grant about the blackmail made him an accessory unless he reported it to the magistrates immediately? He was loyal and she could imagine he would struggle with his conscience before incriminating her in such a shameful scandal, but he was also honourable. He could not connive at extortion, so he would have to take action.

Perhaps she could establish Lord Baybrook's situation first. If he was safely married, that was one thing—he would probably go to great lengths to avoid her. But if he were not, he would probably still be smarting from Henry's demands, leaving aside the question of whether he would think her a loose woman on whom he could take revenge of a non-legal kind.

Once she knew the facts, then she could truthfully tell Grant that she had fallen foolishly for Jonathan Arnold, Lord Baybrook, but that, when Henry had approached him to tell him he must do the decent thing and marry her, Baybrook had revealed that he was already betrothed.

But then could she admit to Grant that Henry had known all along about Baybrook's impending betrothal, had set up a trap from the start? That he had demanded money, not as a settlement on the child, but as hush money so that its existence was never revealed to Baybrook's future father-in-law, the famously puritanical, and staggeringly wealthy, Lord Harlington?

Henry had sent her away to Scotland, not to hide her pregnancy, but to hide her from Baybrook and, when the child was born, to keep her out of his reach, to hold as a future threat against payments. When she had protested, told Henry that he should wait, not press demands beyond a decent competence to raise the child once Baybrook was safely married and in funds, he had threatened to take the baby as soon as it was born to make certain he had control and that Kate could not do anything *foolish*, as he put it. *Or honest,* she had thrown at him and he had laughed in her face.

She realised that she did not know what Jonathan's reaction had been to Henry's demands for money. He was a rake, but not a fundamentally wicked man, she was certain. Surely he would have made a reasonable settlement on his love child, as soon as he could afford it. But Henry had no intention of settling for *reasonable*, not with Lord Harlington's fortune shimmering before his eyes. Jonathan might be paying up, being bled, or he might have told Henry to go to the devil.

And if he was paying, then she could not, in all conscience, let the blackmail continue.

Wilson came in, followed by Jeannie, Anna in her arms. 'She's fretting over her little tooth, my lady. Such a grizzle, she is, aren't you, my pet?' Jeannie handed her to Kate, who tried to soothe her and think clearly at the same time. One thing was certain, she thought as she gently massaged the sore gums, it was a recipe for disaster to sit passively waiting for disaster to strike, or to confess all to Grant when she did not know the facts.

After breakfast she checked the *Peerage* and a London directory in Grant's study, then rang for Jeannie. 'I would like you to go to this address in Hill Street and see if it is occupied.' She handed over the direction of what had been Baybrook's town house before his marriage. 'I need to know the name of the owner, whether he is in residence and whether he is married. And I need you to find this out without revealing why you are asking.'

Jeannie knew, she was certain, that Anna was not Grant's child, although it had never been spoken of between them. She met Kate's gaze and bit her lip. 'You'll be looking for a…relative, my lady?'

'Yes, that's it. A discreet enquiry.' She knew she could be putting a strain on Jeannie's loyalty. 'It is something about which I need to have all the facts clear before I speak to his lordship.'

The unease faded from the nursemaid's face. 'Aye, I can see that. Can I leave Lady Anna with you directly after breakfast, then, my lady? I could be walking past on an errand, sprain my ankle and have to hobble down to the area door to beg help from their cook. All kitchen staff gossip if they get half a chance.'

Jeannie came back mid-morning, rather pink in the face and inclined to giggle. 'I've made a conquest, I think, my lady. A Scottish footman at the Hill Street house. I managed to trip on a paving stone outside, right into his arms, and when he heard my accent he carried me down to the kitchen and then back up again after I sat awhile. And he insisted on calling me a hackney.' She sobered instantly when she saw Kate's face. 'I'm sorry, my lady, I'm blathering on. It is Lord Baybrook's house and he's in residence with his wife and they've just come back to London after their honeymoon tour.'

'Thank you, Jeannie. That will be all. I appreciate your assistance.'

So now what? The bad news was that Jonathan was in London, but the very good news was that Henry had not managed to do something so dreadful that the marriage had been called off. Although it still might mean that he was extorting money from the viscount, and if that was the case, then she had to stop it. It seemed, more and more, that she was going to have to approach Jonathan directly, assure him of her good intentions and discover just what her brother had done. The thought of Grant getting in the middle of this unholy mess didn't bear thinking about. He would be furious, he would call Jonathan out—and then someone might end up a widow.

It was a plan of sorts, but it did not make her feel any better. Hiding the truth from Grant had been bad enough, but now she knew the extent of his affection and trust, it felt like the worst of betrayals. But there was Anna, an innocent child to consider. And the equally innocent Lady Baybrook, and her own sister-in-law, unwittingly married to a blackmailer.

Now all she had to do was engineer a meeting with Jonathan and trust to his good nature and discretion. It seemed an awfully big risk.

## Chapter Twenty

Grant did not come home for luncheon, which was not unusual. What was out of the ordinary was the note that arrived from him on Brooks's Club notepaper.

> Today, of all days, when I want to be with you, they ask me to meet the Home Secretary! Goodness knows when I'll get away, but I'll tell you all about it at dinner, I promise.
> Yours,
> G.

Kate rang for Jeannie and for Grimswade. 'I feel like taking the air with Anna. Lord Brooke is going for a walk with his tutor, I believe. Have the carriage sent round, Grimswade, if you please.'

When the butler had gone she turned to the nursemaid. 'I hardly know what I hope to achieve by this, but if I see Lord Baybrook, I will try to snatch the opportunity to speak with him. But I do not want him to see Anna, so you must stay in the carriage.' Jeannie seemed about to say something, but Kate forestalled her. 'I can't go out without a maid or a footman, his lordship would be furious. And there is no one else I can trust. But I probably won't encounter Lord Baybrook.'

'It's a nice afternoon,' Jeannie observed. 'A gentleman might take a stroll to his club.'

'Yes.' *And at least it will get me out of the house. I feel like a turnspit dog on a treadmill.*

Kate gave the coachman a circuitous route that took in a number of shops that she might plausibly want to visit and which brought them via Hill Street to Grosvenor Street. There was no sign of Jonathan's tall and elegant figure sauntering along, nor when they turned down Berkeley Street towards Piccadilly. 'It was ridiculous to think I would see him,' she observed to Jeannie. 'The number of places a gentleman can be in even the small compass of Mayfair must be countless.'

And then, as the carriage slowed to a crawl in the Piccadilly traffic, she glanced up Dover Street and saw him. 'He's there!'

Jeannie tugged on the check string, the carriage pulled over to the kerb and they stared at each other. 'I cannot accost him in the street.' Kate watched as he reached the road junction, a polished wooden box under his arm. 'He's been to Manton's, the gunsmiths, I think. Jeannie, look, he's crossing over to Green Park.'

'Hurry, my lady.' Jeannie opened the door and kicked down the step. 'You can speak to him in the park, there aren't many people around. I'll follow along behind, as if I'm not with you.'

Jonathan was held up by a brewer's dray while Kate, catching the attention of a crossing sweeper, was over the road before him. He went through the gate and into the park, not apparently in any hurry, for he strolled past the reservoir and cut across the grass towards the Queen's Walk. Kate walked briskly, came alongside him when there was no one close and realised she had no idea what to say.

He must have seen her out of the corner of his eye, for he stopped and raised his hat slightly. And then stared. 'Madam, do I know you?' The dawning recognition on his face would have been comical if things were not so serious. *'Catherine?'*

'Yes. Jonathan—Lord Baybrook, I need to speak with you.'

He had his composure back. His voice was icy, but perfectly controlled. 'I am sure you do.' His eyes ran up and down the fashionable outfit she wore. 'I see you have acquired some expensive tastes on my money.'

'No, I have not. Is Henry demanding payments from you? It is not with my agreement, believe me.'

'Believe you? My dear Miss Harding, why should I believe a word you say? The last true thing you told me was that you were innocent of a man and *that* I did not need telling, for you were a most uninteresting tumble,' he drawled. 'Your rat of a brother informed me you were with child. My child. Is that true or have I been paying out every month for nothing?' The mask of unconcern was slipping to reveal the fury beneath.

*Anna. I can't let him find Anna.* 'Yes, I was pregnant. I thought Henry was going to insist that you marry me.' She felt the heat rise in her face as Baybrook gave a bark of laughter. 'I did not think you would. But I thought you would make me a small allowance so I could bring the child up decently. That was all I wanted, all I expected. I had no idea that Henry was…'

'A blackmailer? Oh, really, my dear. Doing it rather too brown if you expect me to believe you knew nothing of this.' His anger was beginning to ride him now, overcome his habitual elegant indifference. 'Well, make your demands, and then I will tell you how I intend to deal with you.'

'I have no demands. I needed to know what Henry was doing—I haven't seen him for a year. I'll stop him, I swear. I'll do everything I can to stop him.'

'Do you take me for a fool, my dear?' He turned to face her fully, his voice a snarl of frustrated fury now. 'Do you think because I sampled your very rustic charms that I can be cock-led into another compromising situation? Have you any idea what life is like lived at the toleration of a Bible-thumping old bigot who doles out his money like drops of his own blood, always alert for any moral lapse that can be the excuse for a sermon or for withholding funds?'

'No, but—'

He caught her wrist, jerked her towards him. 'There are many reasons why I do not drag you down to the nearest magistrate's office this minute, but there are equally many, many reasons why you should be very afraid of me, my dear. Very afraid indeed.'

Over his shoulder she could see Jeannie, her face

a picture of anxiety and indecision. *Stay there, do not try to help. Stay there,* she tried to signal.

Then he was jerked away from her. The wooden box fell to the ground and burst open, two duelling pistols fell out on to the grass, exquisite death glinting in the winter sunshine.

'Take your hands off my wife before I break all your fingers,' Grant said pleasantly, his own hands fisted in the lapels of Lord Baybrook's elegant coat. 'You'll need them to fire one of those pretty toys you've just dropped.'

For a long moment they stared into each other's eyes, almost nose to nose, two male stags in their prime locking antlers over a female. Then, when Kate thought she would burst with the tension, Jonathan stepped back, hands raised in the fencer's signal of yielding.

'Your *wife*? Allundale, is it not? I am Baybrook. My apologies, I had no idea. In fact, I had misread the situation totally. The lady asked me something and I thought—forgive me, madam—that she was…well, not to beat about the bush, I completely misunderstood her status. I could see no one with her. I was deep in thought and most unfortunately leapt to the conclusion that she was…er…importuning me.'

'Lady Allundale?' Grant's rigid formality failed utterly to veil the fury in his eyes.

*He'll kill him,* Kate thought. *If he has the slightest idea what is happening...* Jeannie, thank heavens, was keeping her distance, had turned away from the three of them so the child in her arms was not visible.

'It was, as the gentleman says, a misunderstanding. I was cutting across to the path, stumbled and caught at his arm and must have blurted out some words of apology. When he spoke to me I was confused, I did not realise what he thought and then when I did I was agitated, which made things worse... Jeannie had fallen behind, so I appeared to be unescorted.' She managed a tight social smile for Jonathan. 'Sir, it was entirely my fault. I am quite unused to London.'

He was a quick thinker, she had to hand it to him. And a brilliant actor. He was all contrition, all elegant apologies, and Grant was left with no option but to accept them. He bowed, the merest inclination of his head, and offered Kate his arm. Jonathan bowed in his turn, picked up the pistols and strode off towards the Queen's Walk.

'Did he hurt you?' Grant demanded the moment they were alone. She shook her head and saw him relax a little. 'And what the devil was Jeannie playing at? Well?' he demanded as the maid hurried up to them. 'When you escort your mistress your duty is to stay with her, not stroll about like a moonling.'

'Anna has been very fretful,' Kate said hastily. 'I expect that is what held you up, Jeannie.'

'Yes, my lady, and then when I saw the gentleman, I didn't know what to do. Not when I had Lady Anna, because I thought he would frighten her.'

'Very well. Where is the carriage?'

'Waiting near the palace, my lord, at the end of the Queen's Walk.' Jeannie gave Kate the tiniest of nods.

'I'll go back with you in that case. I was walking back from the Palace of Westminster across the parks. Fortunately.'

'Yes, wasn't it.' Kate clung to his arm and hoped he would attribute her shakiness to the after-effects of the encounter with Jonathan and not shock at his own appearance combined with a hideously guilty conscience. 'That gentleman was not a friend of yours, then?'

'The Viscount of Baybrook? No. I've hardly ever seen him that close to. The man was a gazetted rake, and a wild one at that, before his marriage. I never ran in those circles, even when I was sowing my own wild oats—the gambling was too deep for me, for one thing, and I dislike being sodden with drink half the time. Now his father-in-law holds the purse strings so tight that Baybrook hardly dares sneeze without permission, by all accounts.' They walked on in silence until they were almost at the gravelled walk bordering the high walls of the fine houses that overlooked Green Park. Grant's fingers stroked reassuringly over hers and gradually her breathing calmed.

'It is strange, though, there was something so familiar about him.' Grant shrugged. 'Perhaps I've come across one of his relatives. Society is so interbred, I may know a cousin of his and not even realise it. Now, where is the carriage?'

It was waiting at the end of Milkmaid's Passage, where a footpath led from the park to the front of St James's Palace. 'Why did you not take the groom with you?' Grant demanded as they settled themselves inside.

'Um…idiocy?' Kate ventured and was rewarded with a smile.

'I shouldn't be cross with you. I forget what an innocent you are in London. This is not the moorlands where you may stretch your legs accosted by nothing worse than a flock of sheep.'

'No, my lord,' Kate said meekly and saw, from the smile in Grant's eyes, that she was forgiven. 'Sheep can be very dangerous, you know.' *I don't deserve him. How am I going to get out of this mire without someone getting hurt?* 'How did your meeting go, my lord? It was satisfactory, I hope?'

'Most. I suspect I have landed myself with a great deal of work, but I am interested in social issues.'

She would get the details out of him when they were alone and, perhaps, convince him that she read the newspapers, too, that she had views on social policy and could discuss the problems he was going to be tackling. *If he is still prepared to talk to me.*

Kate stared blankly out at the passing clubs and shops as the carriage climbed the slope of St James's Street. *What am I going to do about Jonathan and Henry now?*

Grant stood in front of his dressing mirror, tying his neckcloth and attempting to pin down the niggling sense of unease at the back of his mind. He had swept Kate upstairs and made love to her so thoroughly that she seemed to be entirely satisfied that he was not blaming her for the Green Park incident. It also served to satisfy his own primitive male feelings of ownership. He grimaced at himself as he acknowledged the response. Still, it could have turned nasty if he had not come across them. The behaviour was typical of Baybrook, by all accounts. The man might no longer be able to carry on his dissolute lifestyle, but he obviously could not resist accosting an attractive woman when one crossed his path.

What was unsettling was that the strange incident had reawakened all his niggling doubts about Kate. He had been trying to suppress them, tell himself that they were simply leftovers from his experiences with Madeleine, and that now he was so happy in his marriage they would vanish. But they had not. Perhaps the lack was in him and he had lost the ability to trust completely.

'Move the candles up, would you, Griffin?' The valet shifted a branch of candles to the left-hand side of Grant to balance those on the right, and he leaned close to the glass to slide in his tiepin. *Just so.* He met his own gaze in the mirror and grimaced. He was turning into a damn dandy, peacocking about for his Kate.

The thought lifted his spirits. Amused green eyes

smiled back and he went still. *That* was what had been nagging away—Baybrook's eyes. For a few tense seconds they had stared at each other, almost nose to nose. And Baybrook's eyes were green, an unusual clear colour with golden flecks and a black rim to the pupil. The colour he had seen when he had compared Anna's eyes to his own. It was too much of a coincidence, that bizarre encounter between the earl and Kate and the colour of the man's eyes. *He is Anna's father.*

'My lord?' Griffin murmured, the equivalent from him of a nudge in the ribs.

'What?'

'Are you quite well, my lord? A migraine, perhaps?'

'No, I'm fine, just distracted by business.' He had to think about this, try to work out just what the other man knew. It was interesting that, although Jeannie had been with her, Kate had obviously not shown Anna to her lover. *Her ex-lover,* he told himself, exerting all his willpower to steady his breathing, his instinctive reactions. *Don't get into a jealous rage over this. There is no way he and Kate have been together since we married. Although what she was plotting now with apparently chance meetings in the park...*

The thought of Kate getting up to something underhand was like a stab. Was this what he had sensed was wrong all along?

He turned away and stood while Griffin eased him into his evening coat. A sliver of doubt seemed to have slid into his heart. She had lied, he realised, told him Anna's father was dead. So what else had she not told him? The cold fist closing around his gut was all too familiar from years of dealing with Madeleine's lies and evasions. *But not Kate. I need to trust her!*

Hell, he would be whimpering next that it wasn't fair, that she had told him she was happy with him. He was a man and he'd show some backbone over this, but he was not going to confront Kate with it, not yet. He examined that decision for cowardly motives and decided it was only right, and fair, to investigate first. If he was wrong about her, then a direct accusation would shatter that miraculous happiness between them for ever.

The place to start was her family. He should have insisted on contacting her brother before now. 'Griffin, fetch Mr Bolton to me at once. He is in, I assume?'

'Yes, my lord. He remarked he had some notes to transcribe. I believe he is in his room.'

When his secretary entered, tugging his sleeves down with one hand and running the other ink-stained hand through his hair, he looked harassed. 'My lord, I'm still working on your notes for this morning. I should have them finished—'

Grant waved a dismissive hand. 'My handwriting is execrable, I know. Some time tomorrow evening will be fine, for goodness' sake. Have your dinner in peace. Thank you, Griffin, that will be all for now.' As the door closed behind the valet, he added, 'In the morning I need to speak to a discreet enquiry agent.'

Bolton's eyebrows shot up. 'My lord? What sort of enquires, might I ask? I will enquire at your solicitor's office, but such men may come with, er, different specialisms.'

'I wish to trace someone, a connection of Lady Allundale's with whom she has lost touch.' He made himself smile. 'A bit of a black sheep, if you get my meaning. I would like to reunite them, but I will need to be satisfied of his character before I do so.'

'Of course, my lord. One cannot be too careful. I assume this will be a surprise for her ladyship?'

'Precisely,' Grant agreed. If she had deceived him about her lover, then had she told him the truth about her brother—the man she was so very reluctant to get in touch with, despite her new position? If Kate was in trouble, he would do whatever it took to get her out of it, but the deceit wrenched at him. And now he was deceiving her and telling himself it was for her own good. Somehow he was going to have to go downstairs, face his wife over the dinner table and put on a mask, pretend nothing at all was wrong.

*Caring is the very devil,* Grant thought as he walked downstairs, schooling his face to reveal nothing whatsoever. Certainly not fear.

## Chapter Twenty-One

'Allow me to summarise and make certain I have this correct, sir.' Mr Martin, the highly respectable and discreet enquiry agent Grant's solicitors had recommended, glanced down at his notes.

Grant, or Mr Whyte as he had introduced himself, sat in the comfortable client's chair in Mr Martin's elegantly simple office off Ludgate Hill and made himself sit still and apparently relaxed as Martin recapped.

'There is a gentleman, probably by the name of Henry Harding, resident, possibly in Suffolk, who entertained Lord Baybrook in the spring of last year. The gentleman is married, has a sister named, probably, Catherine, and is of a somewhat profligate nature. You wish to identify him.'

'That is correct.' Grant was fairly certain that Catherine had given him her correct name, because she surely would not risk the marriage being invalidated by her using a false one. 'How long will it take you?'

'If he is in Suffolk, and he is a gentleman, then not long. But if the information you have been given is incorrect, then I will need to attack this from the direction of Lord Baybrook's movements and that may require some, shall we say, excavation.'

Grant remembered Kate's hesitation in answering his questions. At the time he had attributed that to exhaustion. Now he wondered. 'I would not be surprised if the county is incorrect.'

'Let us say a week, Mr Whyte.'

'So fast?'

The enquiry agent smirked modestly. 'I have many sources, sir. And Lord Baybrook is, or was, a colourful character. I will send to your solicitor as soon as I have news.'

Grant took his leave and hailed a hackney carriage to take him to Brooks's Club. He was avoiding going home, he knew that. He knew he could not make love to Kate and hide from her that something was wrong and so he pretended to have far more work with his Parliamentary colleagues than he was actually undertaking and retired to his study every night after dinner until he thought she would be asleep.

If this went on for more than a week, he was going to be desperate with the need to hold her, he knew that. Kate had shown him happiness, taught him how to trust his heart to someone else. Now he struggled not to flinch back from that trust, like a man who has already been grievously burned and who expects the same pain again when he reaches out. Something was wrong and he would make it right for her, trust that her reasons for pretending that Baybrook had not been her lover were good.

Grant had expected Kate to comment on his absence from her bed, perhaps to fuss that he was overworking, but she did neither. It was as though she was holding herself back from him, but he could not decide whether it was because she was frightened, or ashamed or simply could not trust him with her secret. In the small hours of the night he had lain awake, alone in his big bed, and fought back the suspicion that she did not care for him after all, that seeing Baybrook had rekindled her feelings for the other man.

Now he looked down the length of the breakfast table and felt all his affection for her welling up, forcing back the suspicion and the anger. She was not Madeleine. He should try to trust her and he would not question her, let her see his doubts and how his faith had been shaken.

'My lord.'

He looked up from the sirloin that he was mangling and could not help but smile at the dignified way she addressed him whenever the staff were present. She did not call him *my lord* when she was screaming his name in the throes of passion, her limbs tangled with his, her nails raking his back.

'My lady?'

'I think I would like to take a small trip, have a day or two away from London. I am not feeling quite myself and the weather is so fine, I thought the sea air would do me good.'

'Brighton?' Grant suggested. 'It should not be difficult to get good lodgings at this time of year, but it will be devilishly cold.'

'I really wanted to go now. To Southend-on-Sea, I thought. So much closer.'

'Southend? It is certainly respectable, but isn't it a trifle…dull?'

'I only want the fresh air and it will do the children good, don't you think? We could go on the steamer easily in the day.'

'I doubt I can get away immediately.'

'If Charlie comes, then Mr Gough can provide a male escort and I'll have Jeannie and Wilson. I could even take one of the footmen.' Kate looked anxious, not like someone planning a short holiday.

'Very well, if that would please you.' He looked directly at her. 'I'll miss you. I know I haven't been very good company these past few days, but even so, the house will seem empty without you.'

Kate was colouring up. Where had this sudden urge to go into Essex come from? Did she just want to get away from him, or was there some more sinister reason? He felt suspicion flare.

'Thank you.' She managed a very creditable impression of pleasure tinged with concern. 'If you are sure? Well, then, I'll speak to everyone and organise it. If I write to the Ship Inn for rooms, I should hear tomorrow and we can set out the day after. We had accepted very few invitations for the next few days. London is becoming very quiet now.'

The Ship Inn? Did she know the town or had she been doing some research? he wondered. 'Certainly, and do use Bolton to book the steamer tickets and so forth. He can send your regrets for the various engagements and I'll see which I want to go to by myself.'

'The first post, my lord.' Grimswade proffered a salver.

'If you'll excuse me, I'll take these off to the study and deal with them.' He stood as he spoke, the letters in one hand, one with the distinctive handwriting of his solicitor's head clerk on the top.

He broke the seal as soon as the door was closed behind him and drew out the letter from Martin enclosed in the wrapper.

Lord Baybrook spent a week as the guest of Sir Henry Harding, baronet, at his estate, Belchamps Hall, in the parish of Hawkwell, Essex, in the period specified. I am unable, as yet, to provide you with details of Sir Henry's character and means, but I am able to confirm that he is a married man with a sister named Catherine Jane Penelope.

I have sent my assistant by this evening's mail coach to Rayleigh, the nearest town, with instructions to discover as much as possible of Sir Henry's situation within the day.

Grant reached for Cary's road book from the shelves beside the desk and opened it on the map of southern England. Hawkwell was apparently too small to be shown, but if it was close to Rayleigh, it was also close to Southend. Not more than five or so miles, he estimated by eye. If Kate was going to Southend, then he was going to Rayleigh.

The steamer was an adventure, at least for Charlie, who was so thrilled that he was rendered speechless, although not still. Mr Gough got Kate, Jeannie, Wilson and the baby settled in the warm shelter of the first-class saloon with Giles the footman to watch over them and was then towed from one end of the vessel to the other by his charge. Kate knew this because, with great regularity, Charlie would erupt into the saloon, compose himself with an effort and inform her of some riveting fact concerning the engines or the weight of coal consumed or the potential speed of the ship, then rush out again to interrogate some unfortunate seaman.

'It is very comfortable compared to a coach,' Kate remarked to Wilson, who was sitting bolt upright clutching her mistress's dressing case on her knees and eyeing their fellow travellers with suspicion.

'Indeed, my lady, although what it would be like on the open sea may be another matter.'

'Yes, I am not sure about venturing to Margate,' Kate admitted. 'I have no idea whether I would be seasick or not.'

But the saloon was comfortable, the company, if rather varied, was respectable enough and the speed was astonishing. Kate looked out of the nearest porthole at the passing river scene and told herself that everything was going to be all right. Henry would be at home and he would see reason about stopping his extortion. He might even be persuaded to pay the money back, although Kate was far less confident about that. But the main thing was to make him stop his criminal activity and write assuring Jonathan that he would hear no more from him.

Then, when there was no longer a crime involved, she could confess everything to Grant and just hope and pray that he would understand. In broad daylight when she was feeling strong, she was confident, but in the small hours, as she lay awake fretting about everything from him working too hard to the loss of his faith in her, she could not help but recall his words.

*I am just saying, for the record, that I will call out any man who lays a finger on you—and do my damnedest to kill him. And if your Jonathan had abandoned you and not drowned, then I would go after him and kill him, too.* What if he called Jonathan out for failing to marry her? But, heartbroken as she had been at the time, if he *had* married her they would surely be in an unhappy marriage now, she would never have met Grant—and it was Grant she loved. And Grant who, one day, might love her.

It was only when the hired chaise was bowling across the flat farmlands around Hawkwell that Kate began to think uneasily about Henry's reaction. What, exactly, would her brother do with a sister who turned up, exceedingly inconveniently, and threatened to crack the golden egg he was relying on? She had nothing to threaten him with to make him do the right thing and she would not put it past him to lock her in the attic while he thought out his tactics. It was not as though he had ever expressed any affection for her after all.

She had left Charlie and Anna with Jeannie and Mr Gough at the Ship Inn, but she had not told either of them where she was going, which, in retrospect, was not sensible. She had said nothing last night as they settled into the accommodation— now she knew she should at least have taken Jeannie into her confidence. The low-lying pastureland looked sodden and depressing as she stared out of the window, biting her lower lip as she thought.

'Giles, when I go into the house I am visiting, I

will take Wilson with me, of course. I would like you to remain in the carriage. Let the window down a crack and then you will hear the church clock. It strikes the quarters. If I am not out within an hour, or if I do not send you a note with my name underlined, then I want you to go to Mr Gough with all speed and ask him to come here and demand to see me. He is to take no excuses, do you understand?'

Giles looked appalled. 'My lady, my lord would have my hide if he thought I had let you walk into somewhere dangerous!'

'It is not dangerous, exactly. I certainly would not take Wilson with me if it were, but the owner may want me to stay against my will.'

'I've got a hatpin,' the maid said darkly. 'And I'll use it. No one will hurt my lady if I have anything to do with it. You do as you're told, Giles.'

'Yes, Miss Wilson.' The personal maid to the lady of the house easily outranked a mere footman. It seemed that Giles was more in awe of her than he was of his mistress. 'I'll listen, like you say, my lady, never fear.'

Kate felt easier with some precautions in place, even though she was probably being completely melodramatic and the worst that might happen was that Henry would laugh in her face and throw her out. *And if that happens,* she resolved as the chaise drew into the courtyard in front of Belchamps Hall, *then I am telling Grant everything.*

Leaving Giles anxiously listening for the clock, Kate marched up to the front door and beat a tattoo with the knocker. The heavy oak door creaked open and she found herself face-to-face with Claridge, the butler.

He said stolidly. 'Yes, ma'am?'

'Claridge, do you not recognise me? Miss Catherine.' She took a step forward as he gaped at her. 'Where is Sir Henry?'

The butler gave way before her, but he still looked utterly taken aback. 'In…in his study, Miss Catherine. But—'

'You were not expecting me, quite. And it is Lady Allundale now, Claridge. There is no need to announce me, I know my way.' Strangely she felt confidence flooding back as she smiled at the butler. She was here to fight dragons, defeat them for the sake of her love and her happiness. She lifted her chin, set back her shoulders, lifted her imaginary sword.

'Yes, miss. I mean, my lady.'

He stepped aside, jaw working as though he was searching for words, and went along the familiar panelled hallway, past the foot of the stairs and the great carved banister rail she used to slide down on her tummy when she was a child. They passed the door into the sunny front parlour, where she would sit and sew with her sister-in-law, and up to the door to Henry's study, not a place in which the women of the household were welcome.

'Make Miss Wilson comfortable if you please, Claridge.'

She entered on her knock and almost stopped dead in surprise. The old gloomy study Henry had inherited from their father had been swept away. Now it was freshly painted and boasted a handsome mahogany desk and chairs in the latest style, new bookcases and an array of books in fine leather bindings. The window had been converted into French doors leading out on to the rear terrace, and as she came in, she saw Henry standing there, the door ajar, apparently letting some chill fresh air into the stuffy room.

'Madam?' He blinked at her and she realised that for a moment he did not recognise her with her smart clothes and the gemstones winking in her earlobes. *'Catherine?'*

'Good afternoon, Henry.' She sat down in the chair opposite the desk, laid her reticule and tightly rolled umbrella on the glossy new leather surface and smiled warmly at him. 'What a handsome study, it must have cost you a pretty penny.'

'What are you doing here?' He stalked from the window and stood clutching the back of his chair. 'Where in Hades have you been?'

'Oh, living my life.' Kate pulled off her gloves, slowly, finger by finger, as she looked around. 'While you have been accumulating the pretty pennies, it seems. What else have you been spending the money on, Henry? Oh, and I would love a cup of tea. And perhaps one of those delicious scones Mrs Hobhouse always used to make.'

He was so taken aback that he yanked the bell pull without arguing. Claridge must have been standing right outside the door. 'Sir?'

'Tea. Scones.' Henry flapped a hand at him and sat down. 'What are you doing here? And where did you get those clothes and those jewels?' He flung himself back in the chair and laughed. 'Oh, I see. You've found yourself a cosy little niche as some man's ladybird, have you? You're cleverer than I thought if you've fallen on your feet that way. Or should I say, on your back?'

'Don't be coarse, Henry.' Kate took the little silver case from her reticule and tossed a card across

the desk to him. 'My husband would not appreciate it.'

He picked up the card and stared at it, the paste-
board creasing in his grip. 'Lady Allundale? *Lady
Allundale?* How the devil? He knows about the
brat?'

'What brat would that be, Henry? My husband's
daughter?'

He stared at her. 'You couldn't have convinced
him it was his, you were too far gone when you
ran off.'

Claridge came in, placed a tray on the desk in
front of Kate. 'Thank you, Claridge, that will be all.
Tea, Henry?' she asked sweetly as the door closed.

'Damn the tea.' He watched, drumming his fingers on the arm of his chair, while she poured herself a cup, taking her time. She pretended to hesitate
over a choice of scones until he demanded, 'What
do you want?'

'I've come about the blackmail, Henry. It has to
stop.'

'What blackmail?' He tried to look haughty and
affronted.

'Don't pretend, Henry. You have been extorting
money from Lord Baybrook. It is immoral, illegal
and probably dangerous. His father-in-law won't

live for ever and when he dies Baybrook is going to be a very rich man.' She took a sip of tea and was proud that her hand was rock-steady. 'Rich enough to take revenge on you in any way he chooses. Legal or illegal.' Was it her imagination, or had Henry gone pale?

'What do you want?'

His immediate move to negotiation made her wary. She had expected counter-threats, or, at the least, bluster. 'For you to stop demanding money. Write to Baybrook, tell him that no more will be asked.'

'Is that all?'

Of course it was not *all*. He was still being too accommodating, too calm. 'And you will return all the money you extorted.' Henry's jaw dropped. 'Just how much did you receive, Henry? How much did you demand from Baybrook every month?'

'Two hundred,' he snapped.

'Two hundred pounds? Two thousand four hundred a year. My goodness, that was ambitious, Henry.'

'He can afford it. And it is guineas, not pounds.' He smirked, obviously counting the golden treasure in his mind.

'Two thousand five hundred and twenty pounds,'

she amended. 'A mistake to gloat about the guineas. That's an additional one hundred and twenty you are going to give me.' Could she convince him his only hope was to give her the money, or would he call her bluff?

'Give you the money? Are you insane? Why should I do a damn fool thing like that?'

'Because I'll see you in gaol if you don't, brother dear. My child, my fear and danger, my near disgrace. I think I have earned it, don't you?'

# Chapter Twenty-Two

Grant held the hired hack to a controlled canter as he entered the village of Hawkwell. He had made good time, leaving London by post-chaise for Rayleigh as soon as Martin's assistant returned. Kate might have had a fast passage by the steamer, but he would be close on her heels.

'I couldn't do as much as I'd like, sir,' the man had explained, passing the notes across. 'But there's the address. In Rayleigh he's run up a fair amount of debt and they say he's a spendthrift on his own pleasures. His wife doesn't spend much at the local dressmaker or milliner, though. They think he keeps her on a pretty tight string and there are rumours he's not above knocking her around when he's in his cups. He also has a bit of a reputation for gambling—cock fights, the local card school, that sort of thing. The merchants I spoke to didn't have much of an opinion of him as a land-owner. They say he leaves it all to his bailiff and he doesn't pay enough to get a man of the right calibre to do that wisely. I've made a note of the major debtors, sir.'

Now Grant drew rein in front of the church lych-gate as a thin man in a clerical collar and bands came out and closed it with care behind him.

'Good day, Reverend.'

'Good day, sir.' He smiled up at Grant. 'Have to take care or we get straying sheep in the church-yard and the silly creatures poison themselves on the yew. One could wish the Good Lord had given such useful animals more intelligence, but one cannot question His ways. May I assist you in any way, sir?'

'I am looking for Sir Henry Harding's house. Bel-champs Hall, I believe.'

'Yes, indeed.' Was it his imagination or did the vicar's smile become less genuine? 'You have the right road. Just continue through past the green, take the second on the left and it is rather under a mile.'

'Thank you.' Grant touched his whip to his hat brim and urged the hack into a trot. So, debts, a reputation for gambling and not the vicar's favourite member of his flock. If Sir Henry was a churchgoer at all.

The clergyman's directions were accurate. Grant came alongside a high brick wall at about three-quarters of a mile from the village and then slowed as he saw a hired vehicle standing on the driveway. A postilion was perched on a low wall smoking a clay pipe and, clearly visible through the window of the vehicle, was the face of his own footman.

'Giles.'

'My lord!' The footman threw the carriage door open.

'Is her ladyship inside?'

'Yes, my lord. She went in three-quarters of an hour ago. My lord—'

Grant swung down from the horse, tossed Giles the reins and strode up to the front door, leaving the footman mid-sentence. He had his hand raised to the knocker when instinct stopped him. Better to scout the ground before blundering in. Something strange was going on with Kate and her brother and he would rather discover what it was without it being filtered through whatever barriers they chose to erect.

The house was very quiet. Grant glanced into windows as he trod softly around the moss-covered path that skirted the walls. In one room a lady sat, head bent over some sewing, but she was no one he recognised. He rounded the corner to find himself on a flagstone terrace overlooking a bleak, level garden. Halfway along a glazed door stood ajar and, feeling a touch melodramatic, he walked cautiously up to it. Voices came clearly from the room inside.

'Just how much did you receive, Henry?' That was Kate's voice. Grant edged closer. She sounded very calm, very cool and strangely dangerous. He was grappling with that when she added, 'How much did you demand from Baybrook every month?'

*Blackmail?* That had to be what they were discussing.

'Two hundred,' a man snapped. And that must be her brother, Henry.

'Two hundred pounds? Two thousand four hundred a year. My goodness, that was ambitious, Henry.'

Kate sounded not at all shocked. In fact, from her question, she had obviously expected to hear that money was being extorted. A faint hope that she was talking about money for the support of her child faded. That sum was way in excess of what might be expected to provide for a by-blow. Not that he'd ever had to do the sums himself… Grant jerked his attention back to the voices in the room.

'And it is guineas, not pounds.'

'Two thousand five hundred and twenty pounds. A mistake to gloat about the guineas. That's an additional one hundred and twenty you are going to give me.'

Nausea gripped his gut. Kate wanted the black-mail money, was demanding it in a hard, cold voice that belonged to another woman, not the one he'd married. Not his Kate.

'Give you the money?' her brother protested. 'Are you insane? Why should I do a damn fool thing like that?'

'Because I'll see you in gaol if you don't, brother dear. My child, my fear and danger, my near disgrace. I think I have earned it, don't you?'

Grant reached for the door handle, his vision blurred by a haze of anger and betrayal. Kate, his Kate. He would never have believed that the woman he trusted with his life and his honour would turn into this hard-voiced, grasping witch.

*Never have believed it.* He jerked his hand back so hard his knuckles hit the rough surface of the brick, the pain like a dash of icy water in the face. *Trust.* If he abandoned her at this first test of his feelings, what did that make of their marriage but a hollow sham? This was Kate. Yes, she had not told him that Baybrook was Anna's father. Yes, she had not told him why she had come to Essex. But there could well be reasons as painful and as difficult to talk about as his feelings about Madeleine had been. He owed Kate his faith and, if things really were bad, his understanding and forgiveness. He had to get her to trust him to give her that and he could begin by not leaving her to fight this dragon alone.

Henry was spluttering now. 'Where the devil do you think I am going to get that money from? I have spent most of it.'

'Well, unspend it, Henry. Sell things, borrow, pawn. I want a banker's draft for every shilling.'

'Or what? All right, I agree that I'll write to Baybrook, tell him his debt's paid. But you can't get the money out of me, and if you utter any more threats, I'll just have to keep you here until you see reason.'

So, she had been right to leave Giles with instructions. 'My man is outside in the carriage. He knows what to do if I do not come out, or if I send him a note without a certain code word in it. I really am not as foolish as you always thought me, Henry. And as for how I intend to extract that money from you, why, I will simply confess all to my husband. Grant Rivers is a law-abiding, honest man and—'

The door behind her opened. 'I am flattered that you think so, my dear,' said a deep, calm voice.

'Grant.' Kate found she was on her feet, facing the door where her husband stood surveying the room with a chilly hauteur that sent a dangerous wave of sheer desire through her. Behind the broad shoulders in the caped greatcoat she could glimpse the butler, bobbing about in agitation.

'Sir? My lord?'

Grant half turned and handed Claridge his hat and gloves. He kept hold of his riding crop. 'Thank you. That will be all.' He shut the door in the butler's face. 'Sir Henry Harding, I assume? My brother-in-law.' He stayed on his feet, looming over the seated man at the desk. 'I wish I could say it is a pleasure, but I doubt it will be, for either of us.'

'Grant, please sit down.' He might be intimidating Henry, which was a good thing, but he was terrifying her.

'If you wish, my dear.' He picked up one of the heavy carved chairs that sat against the wall and spun it across, one-handed, to thud in front of the desk next to Kate, then he sat down, crossed one booted leg across the other and began, very softly, to tap the riding crop against the polished leather. 'So, allow me to summarise the situation as I see it, Harding. Your sister is with child by Baybrook. You send her away where he cannot marry her even if he wishes to, and then you extort money from him under threat of informing his immensely wealthy and very, very moral prospective father-in-law. Am I correct so far?'

Henry stared like a mesmerised rabbit in front of a stoat until Grant slapped the crop harder against his boot and Henry twitched. 'Yes, well…'

'And you put her in the way of a confirmed rake in the first place? Yes, I assume so. And not content with ensuring that he pays a suitable sum to your sister to raise her child decently you decide to keep it all yourself—and to ask for as much money as you think you can possibly extract. Yes?' There was another slap of whip on leather.

'Yes. But now she wants it all! She threatened me!'

'With me. Very wisely. I am trying to recall what

the judicial penalty for blackmail is.' Grant rocked the heavy chair back and studied the ceiling, deep in thought. 'So few people come forward with a complaint, that is the problem. Most seem to deal with it by other methods. Direct methods.' He brought all four chair legs back to the floor with a thud and Henry cringed back in his own seat.

'You mean *murder*? Catherine said you were an honourable man!'

'And she is correct, I hope. Let me think now. The navy is always short of men. That would give you a healthy outdoor life with plenty of fresh air and exercise, and we are not at war at the moment, so there are only falls from the mainmast, shipwreck and over-amorous shipmates to worry about. Oh, and the food, of course. Or there's the East India Company—always on the lookout for men, I understand. A pity India is such an unhealthy country, but we can't have everything. I am making new acquaintances all the time these days. Men of influence in the navy and the East India Company for example.'

'You wouldn't.' Henry was pale now—in fact, Kate thought he might vomit on his shiny new desk. 'I'm a married man.'

'From what I hear Lady Harding would be quite

relieved by your absence. Of course, your loving sister would support her in remaining here, make sure she had a good bailiff and not the useless one you inflict on your tenants now.'

'I'll pay! I'll find the money somehow, although I don't know how…'

'We'll work it out, never fear, Harding.' Grant stood up and nodded to Kate. 'Ready, Lady Allundale? I'll be back tomorrow, Harding. Oh, and don't try to make a run for it. I know far too much about you.'

Kate was confused, anxious and deeply relieved to have Grant there, all at the same time. The mixed emotions might be uncomfortable, but at least he now knew the truth about her. But how did he feel? There was no way of telling, not when she could not ask him, could not take his hand and look into his eyes. He was in control of himself, of Henry and of the situation, but whether he was furiously angry, disgusted or merely resigned to her betrayal she had no idea, and a chaise containing a lady's maid and a footman was not the place to find out.

She thanked Giles for his attentiveness and Wilson for her patience and then sat, hands folded in her lap, her mind utterly blank of any kind of meaningless small talk while Grant surveyed the flat farmland on either side of the road back to South-end. He had tied the hired hack on behind the carriage, so she had not even had the time to sit and think without looking at him and having that steady green gaze look straight back at her.

Perhaps this was how a prisoner in the dock felt as she watched the faces of the jurors. Guilty or not guilty? Condemned or pardoned?

Somehow she kept control of herself on the interminable drive back. Kept her chin up, her back straight, her expression composed. One did not show weakness in front of the servants. Besides, pride would not let her give way.

When they reached the Ship Inn and Grant issued orders for the hired horse's return she dismissed Wilson and Giles and climbed the stairs to the large suite of rooms she had taken. Jeannie and Anna were bright-eyed and pink-faced from a chilly walk along the beach. Charlie and Mr Gough were still out there, swathed in scarves, skimming pebbles, prodding driftwood and doing whatever men and boys did by the seaside.

'His lordship has returned with me. Please let everyone know that we are not to be disturbed until dinner time. His lordship has a great deal of business to attend to.' *Such as dealing with his deceitful wife.*

'Which is our room, my lady?' Grant had come up the stairs while she stood on the landing, steeling herself.

'Through here. I took virtually the entire floor.' He was addressing her formally and the chill of it was like the touch of a cold finger on the nape of her neck, unpleasant yet bracing. She walked in through the door he opened for her and took the chair by the window, let the light fall on her face. There was no hiding anything now.

Grant sat down facing her and leaned forward, his forearms on his knees. 'Are you all right, Kate?'

It was the last thing she expected him to say, this expression of concern for her, and it almost undid her.

'Don't cry,' he said, firmly and without reaching for her. *The prosecuting counsel...*

'I am not and I will not.' Easier to promise than to keep, she suspected. 'You seem to know a great deal, but I expect you would like me to tell you myself why I have lied to you.'

Grant moved, an involuntary gesture that she read as acknowledgment of her betrayal. So be it. 'Henry likes to gamble and he met Jonathan in some hell or another and invited him to stay. I think he had made up a plan on the spur of the moment when he realised that Baybrook needed to escape his creditors and get out of London for a while before news of his debts reached Lord Harlington, his future father-in-law. I did wonder whether it was some deep-laid plot or whether Henry simply had a flash of inspiration, but it was probably the latter. He brought him home, made much of him, invited all his cronies round for card play, let him shoot our coverts. And did nothing when Jonathan began to flirt with me. I thought Jonathan was serious, that Henry's unconcern meant approval. I was inexperienced, lonely—ripe for the plucking, I suppose.

'I told myself I was in love, that he was an honourable man who intended marriage. I was not the first naive girl to fall for it and I will not be the last. When Jonathan had gone, his pockets lined with enough winnings from the local squirearchy to keep his tailors happy, I realised he had made me no promises, not even to write. And then I found I was expecting and Jane told Henry and he went off to London.'

'To tell Baybrook he must marry you.' Grant leaned back in his chair and steepled his fingers.

*The judge listening to the evidence, weighing it up...*

'That's what he told me, but I realise now he knew perfectly well that Jonathan was in no position to do that. He was contracted to the daughter of a powerful and wealthy man and he could not afford to risk that alliance. Henry told me about it when he got home. *He'll pay,* he promised. And like an idiot I asked if that meant there would be enough for me to have a little cottage somewhere, raise the child in modest respectability. He laughed and said that we did not need money for that, he would find a home for the baby easily enough. And then he explained it all, how he could extort money from Baybrook for years, how he needed to get me out of the way so Jonathan could not find me, how a foundlings' home would take my baby.'

'I think I would like to see your brother through the sights of a duelling pistol on the nearest common at dawn,' Grant remarked. 'What did you do then?'

'I did as I was told and I went up to the lodge in Scotland.' Now they were coming to it. The story so far had been one of her own foolish innocence in allowing Jonathan to seduce her. But what followed was not innocent. 'I should have written to

Jonathan, told him that I was not in league with Henry, promised him I would support a statement to a magistrate. But I didn't. I allowed myself to be used. And then it was too late, I was on my way north and all I could think about was how to get away, how to keep my baby.'

'You left it very late.' Grant's voice was dispassionate. She found she could not look at him, so she watched Charlie running along the road towards the inn, laughing and calling back to Mr Gough. *My son. I could lose him, too.*

'I wasn't well at first, and then I had no money. It took me a long time to get it together, stealing the odd shilling from the housekeeper's purse over weeks so no one would notice and suspect. They were all paid by Henry. I had nothing to offer them to win their loyalty.' Charlie had vanished, but she could hear his voice faintly from the hallway below, happy, laughing. She shrugged. 'You know the rest.'

'Why did you tell me that Anna's father was dead?'

'At first, just instinct to hide, to cover up. That was why I told you I came from Suffolk and didn't tell you about Henry's baronetcy. And then, later, you were so protective, so possessive. I was afraid you would confront Baybrook, call him out. If I told you about the blackmail, then that made you an accessory after the fact, didn't it? So you would have no option but to expose Henry, and I know he deserves it, but it could have ruined Jonathan if his father-in-law found out and cut him off financially.'

'You have a high opinion of my sense of honour and of how law-abiding I am,' Grant said drily. 'It did not occur to you to tell me this whole story and let me set it right?'

'Of course not. I had deceived you, allowed you to marry me, save Anna and myself, embroiled you in this. How could I turn around and dump the whole mess at your feet?'

'It was why you were so reluctant to come to London, I suppose. Kate—' He broke off. His lower lip caught between his teeth, then, as though he was making himself ask, he said, 'Did you meet Baybrook in Green Park by appointment?'

'No! When you told me how you felt about me, saw for myself that you were happy in our marriage, saw how much you trusted me, I knew I had to stop pretending everything was all right. I went looking for Jonathan to find out exactly what Henry had been demanding, promised him I would put it right somehow. I saw him in the park that day and followed him.'

'Anna has his eyes, that unusual clear green with gold flecks.'

'She got that from him?' Kate shook her head, bemused by the detail. 'I can't remember what colour his eyes are. Anyway, I knew I had to go to Henry, make him stop, get the money and pay it back.'

'All two thousand five hundred and twenty pounds,' Grant said.

'How did you know it was that much?'

'I arrived outside the window just as you were discussing it, demanding that he give it to you.'

Kate thought back on what she had said, when she had said it, when Grant had walked in the door. So that was how he knew so much. 'You must think I am as bad as he was, that I wanted the money for myself?'

# Chapter Twenty-Three

'I had a bad moment.' Grant held up his hand and she saw the raw graze across his knuckles. 'I hit the wall, which was foolish. But you are my wife, Kate. I owe you my loyalty. I owe you my trust.'

He meant it, she could tell. For a moment the happiness bubbled up, almost painful in its intensity. Then she realised that he was making himself trust by an effort of will, against the evidence. The happiness wavered and went out like a candle flame in the wind.

*He has to trust me because he is loyal to me. Not because he knows I wouldn't do such a thing, not because he loves me. Grant is honourable and Madeleine rejected him and Charlie. Now he has the courage to risk his heart and his happiness all over again on a woman who has been deceiving him since the moment we met. What if I let him down, slip up, fail to have the nerve to always be truthful?*

Grant needed to believe in her, she realised. He needed that faith that she would be true to him.

*I am on a shaky pedestal where I have no right to be.*

'Thank you.' She could feel the pedestal rock beneath her feet as she groped for balance, the right words. 'I was optimistic in thinking Henry would actually give me the money, but I had to try. I would have given it all back to Jonathan somehow.'

'Will you let me deal with this if I promise not to call Baybrook out? I will repay him, assure him of our silence, of the end of Henry's extortion, provided he forgets he ever met you.' When she opened her mouth to protest he smiled thinly. 'And Henry can repay me.'

'It may take some time.' It seemed she could breathe again. Grant believed her.

'I will put some of my own people in. That will sort him out. He may come to think longingly of a nice sea voyage to India after all, by the time I have finished with him.'

'I am glad you are on my side and not against me,' Kate ventured, daring a feeble joke. Grant's smile was still tight. 'I should not speak lightly. And

I should not expect you to deal with Baybrook. It was my fault. I will—'

'You will do no such thing.' With the suddenness of a pistol firing Grant lost his temper. He was on his feet, his fist thudding into the wall, his voice a barely contained shout. Kate stared horrified at the smear of blood from his unhealed knuckles, the mark of violence across the neatly papered wall. Grant never lost his temper, never shouted. He swung round, towering over her. 'I deal with threats to my family, my wife, my daughter. Is that clear?'

Kate nodded, unable to drag her gaze from his face. 'I am so sorry.'

He swore, crudely, harshly. 'And don't apologise!' It was a shout now. Grant slammed away across the room, turned and glared at her from ten feet away, six feet of infuriated male pride and muscle. 'Your brother, who should protect you with his life, uses you, an innocent, to bait a honey trap, makes you party to a criminal act, puts you in fear for your child. You could have died in that hovel. You probably would have done if I had not come past by the merest chance. You have the guts to fight for your daughter, take risks for her. You have given my son the mother he deserves, made my house a home, driven away my demons.'

Grant lifted his hands, scrubbed them across his face. 'Don't you dare apologise to me, Kate.' He stared at her as though he had forgotten who she was, what they were doing there. Stared as if he was having a revelation and not a very happy one at that. Then he moved. Ten long strides took him past her to the door. 'Get back to London first thing tomorrow, let me sort this out. I don't know when I will be back.'

He stopped, turned on the threshold and came back to her, pulled her into his arms and took her mouth. The kiss was hard, possessive, almost punitive. Through her confusion she could taste his anger and his desire and, beneath it all, a sort of desperation.

And then he was gone, booted heels clattering down the steps.

'Lady Allundale?'

Kate blinked and the room came back into focus. Mr Gough was standing in the doorway, regarding her warily. 'Yes?'

'His lordship has…er…left?'

'Yes,' she repeated and somehow managed to think of something other than Grant's mouth on hers, kissing with the sort of desperation a con-demned man might use if he were to be hanged the next day. 'We are going back to London tomorrow morning, first thing. Please can you arrange that, Mr Gough?'

'Certainly, Lady Allundale.'

'Was that Papa? I didn't know he was coming here. I heard him shouting.' Charlie appeared from his bedchamber door, a clean shirt half on. 'Papa never shouts like that.'

'He has had a very trying day, dear.' *Possibly almost as trying as I have had.* Kate forced back the hysterical laughter that was threatening. 'We will be going back to Grosvenor Street tomorrow, first thing.'

'Oh, good.' Charlie's anxious expression turned to a broad grin. 'It is interesting here. I like the sea. But it's not long until Christmas and we've got to get ready.'

'Yes, of course.' Kate hoped she looked less fraught than she felt. Christmas had completely slipped her mind. There was the anniversary of the old earl's death to deal with and the challenge of creating a perfect new set of Christmas memories for Charlie and presents to buy and... *And a husband who I thought I understood and now...*

'Run along and finish getting changed, Charlie.

And try not to bother Mr Gough. He has lots of things to do.'

She went back and sank down into the chair, considered indulging in hysterics and concluded, rather wildly, that they would have to wait. 'Wilson!'

'Yes, my lady?' The maid had a pile of folded underwear in her hands. Gough must have lost no time in telling her the news.

'What is the date?'

'The fifteenth, my lady.'

The old earl had died on Christmas Eve. They would travel back to London tomorrow and she must decide the best way to handle the anniversary for Charlie. Then there was Christmas to prepare for, which was also Anna's birthday. When would Grant be back—and in what mood? No, this was definitely no time to have the vapours. Kate blew her nose briskly and found some paper and a pen. Lists were what she needed now. *And my husband.*

The clock struck midnight as Kate reached for the last sheet of paper and began to wrap up the pretty dress length and ribbons she had bought for Jeannie. All the presents had been bought in exhausting expeditions around the shops in the days after they got back from Southend.

All that was left was to worry about Grant. The note had arrived this morning from, of all places, Newport Pagnell. What he was doing there she could not imagine, nor could she gauge his mood, for it had simply read:

I will be there on the twenty-fourth. G.

Something had been written beneath that scrawled initial, then crossed out. She had squinted at it, held it up to the light, to a candle flame, and all she could make out was a small circle. Or perhaps a heart.

Now it was Christmas Eve. She had not dared hope, had hardly dared think about Grant and instead had plunged into planning, shopping and endless decision-making. The staff were not used to the family spending Christmas in London and seemed incapable of making the slightest decision without her. So footmen had been dispatched to enquire when evergreens would be available in Shepherd's Market, Cook had been given guidance on two weeks' worth of menus, decisions had been made on when the staff would have their Christmas meal, which carriages would be required for what church services and when a holly wreath should be hung on the front door.

Now Kate just wanted to sleep and not be plagued by dreams about Grant vanishing into the mist. She gathered up the scissors and ribbon, brushed paper scraps off the bed and took off her robe. As she reached for the snuffer, there was a noise from Grant's bedchamber, then another. Muffled, cautious sounds. Sounds of someone who did not want to be heard.

When she snuffed the candle a thin line of light showed beneath his door. He was home.

Kate reached for the wisp of negligee that lay at the end of the bed, then, with a shake of her head, fetched the old flannel wrapper. This was no time for seduction. Either this marriage would hold because of what was in their hearts and in their minds, or it would not.

She made no effort to be quiet as she opened the connecting door. Grant was sitting on the side of the bed in the position she knew meant that he was contemplating pulling off his boots and was really too tired to bother, or to ring for Griffin. He looked up as she entered and she stopped, thinking wryly that when she had been rejecting thoughts of seduction she had not counted on the physical effect that her husband had on her. He looked saddle-weary, travel-stained and beyond tired. And he also looked magnificently male, strong and determined.

'I am so glad you are home,' she said simply. 'Let me.' And as she had once done before, when she had first come to Abbeywell, she straddled first one leg, then the other, and pulled off his boots.

'Thank you.' He waited until she turned and then reached out, put one hand on either side of her waist and drew her in to stand between his spread thighs. 'I went to see Charlie first, woke him up. I wanted him to know I kept my promise to be back.' He looked up at her, serious, watchful.

'Of course.' She resisted the urge to smooth his wind-tangled hair. Goodness knew what had happened to his hat. 'Has he gone back to sleep or did he tell you the plans for tomorrow?'

'He told me and went back to sleep. I had to promise to inspect all the decorations, right down to the very miniature yule log in the drawing room. You've done a magnificent job between the pair of you.' He put his head slightly to one side as he studied her face. 'Don't you want to know where I've been?'

'I don't care, so long as you are back here.' It was the truth. She trusted him to deal fairly with Henry and she knew he had not called Baybrook out. He would not risk killing Anna's father. She gave in to the urge then and lifted her hands to cup his face. 'I missed you.'

'I lost my temper back there in the inn.'

'I noticed.' Was that the faintest curve of his lips? 'You lose it so rarely that it is most impressive when you do.'

'I swore.' *Yes, that is most definitely the beginning of a smile.*

'But not at me.' He had her tight against him now and the old flannel wrapper seemed to be having no effect on his body's responses.

'No. At me.' The ghost of the smile flickered and was gone. 'Kate, you have a very short-sighted husband who could not see what was under his nose, nor read what his heart was telling him.'

It was suddenly very hard to breathe, let alone speak, so she leaned forward and kissed him lightly on the lips until the gentle returning pressure gave her courage. 'You can read it now?'

'Yes. And I love you, Kate. I think I have loved you for a long time and had no idea what it was. I should have realised in that moment in the receiving line at the Larminster reception that what I was feeling was something far more than happiness.' His voice was harsh, but the green eyes locked with hers were tender and vulnerable and full of promises. 'I puzzled over why I trusted you despite your deceptions, despite what I heard with my own ears, and then it hit me in the Ship Inn. And I had been cold and grudging. I made you tell me your secrets as though I was forcing a confession out of you, when I should have taken you in my arms and held you and protected you and trusted you without reservation, without you having to explain a thing.'

'Oh, my love. You aren't a saint.' She tugged at his arms and he came to his feet, held her by the shoulders as he stared down into her face. 'We could both have trusted more, risked more—if we were perfect, but we aren't. We are human and we had both learned the pain of love betrayed.'

'You called me… Kate, you can't…' How could the fact that this strong, articulate man was having trouble getting a simple question out make her so happy?

'I can. And I do. I love you, Grant. I have loved you for months and I did not dare tell you.'

'Did not dare?'

'You would have been kind to me, wouldn't you? You would have felt sorry for me. I could live with loving you without hope of that being returned, but I could not bear your pity.'

'Oh, Kate. That must be the only thing you would not dare.' Grant pulled her in close so that she was against the hard strength of him, safe and surrounded by love. By impossible, wonderful love. It didn't matter that Grant smelt of leather and sweat and horse. It simply made this moment more real, more certain that it was not a dream. 'I love you so very much.'

'Come to bed,' she said into the crumpled folds of his neckcloth. 'Show me.'

'I'm filthy,' he protested half-heartedly, his fingers already on the buttons of his waistcoat.

'Most of it is your clothes.' Her fingers were as urgent, pushing the coat back from his shoulders, tearing a ribbon on her old robe as she threw it aside. 'I don't care. I just want you. Now, always.'

There was no finesse left in either of them. They fell on to the bed in a tangle of limbs, of kisses, of desperate fingers, all impeded by Grant's breeches, which he kicked off with a final heave before he rolled Kate over, covered her with his body and slid into her in one movement.

Then he stilled, propped on his elbows, his hips cradled by her thighs, his forehead resting against her brow. 'Home. Home at last.'

His heart thudded over hers, his breathing was

ragged, his fingers, always so sure, so controlled, shook as they sifted through her hair. The lack of control touched her as no skilled caresses could ever have done and she tipped her head to capture his lips, curled her legs around the slim hips and rocked him deeper.

It became a blur, a mixture of passion and love, of relief and joy and urgent need. Kate knew she was talking, broken phrases, words, his name. 'I love you. I love you. Grant…'

He stretched up above her on his hands, tightening the junction between their bodies so she could no longer tell where his pleasure ended and hers began. She looked up and saw he was watching her, even as he lost control and let the wave crash over him. 'I love you. Kate. Now. Always. *Kate.*'

# Chapter Twenty-Four

They went to church in the morning with Charlie and sat and thought about the old earl and then came home and spent the day talking about him. Grant told them tales about his own childhood and had Charlie alternately gasping and giggling about the tricks he used to play and the trouble he would get into.

'Truly? You let all the hounds into the house while Great-Grandmama was having the Ladies' Church Social and they ate all the cakes and peed on the Chinese rug? And you climbed all the way to the top of the great oak on the front lawn?'

Kate rolled her eyes at Grant, who grinned and shrugged. 'And fell out and broke my arm and spent a month learning to write left-handed so I could do all the lines my tutor set me as punishment.'

'Tell me again about Great-Grandpapa and the bishop and the bull at the church fête.'

Kate curled up in her armchair and indulged herself by watching Grant, relaxed and happy, sprawled on the hearthrug with his son. The day that could have been so sad, the anniversary of a loss where they could not be together, was turning into a happy time and, she suspected, the beginning of a family tradition. She and Charlie had planned it together, both of them, she was certain, convinced that this time Grant would be home in time.

After luncheon Charlie announced that he was going to write down the stories in case he forgot any. 'And I'll add my stories, too,' he added, marching off to the desk by the window.

Grant put his arm around Kate and pulled her down beside him on the sofa at the other end of the room. 'I must tell you where I have been these past days.'

'I confess I am consumed with curiosity about Newport Pagnell.' She curled into the crook of his arm and played with the curling ends of hair around his ears. It was bliss to be able to touch Grant without wariness, without being afraid that her gestures would be read, quite correctly, as signs of love.

'I took your sister-in-law there. When I left you I went back to Belchamps Hall, riding a positive tidal wave of anger with your brother. She overheard our discussion and delivered a bombshell to dear Henry by announcing that if he was paying off his debt to Baybrook, he could pay her an allowance and she was going to live with her sister.'

'So Henry is going to repay the money? I would have thought that was like wringing blood out of a stone.'

'Apparently I look forbidding enough for him to believe my threats about the navy or India. One of the brightest clerks in my banker's office is going down there to do a complete audit and Henry's about to acquire a new bailiff in the form of Grimswade's nephew, who is as tough as his uncle and has been cutting his teeth as my farm manager.'

'You are brilliant, Grant.' She kissed his ear.

He broke off in an attempt to capture her lips. 'Temptress.'

'Grant! Not in front of the children.'

'Anna's fast asleep and Charlie's lost in composition. Oh, very well, I'll behave, but that gown is devilishly provoking.' When she escaped to the other end of the sofa he growled, but carried on with his story. 'I made arrangements with Henry, sent off all the necessary letters, conveyed Lady Harding, bag and baggage, to Newport Pagnell and got back to town late yesterday afternoon. Then I tracked Baybrook down—'

'You didn't hit him or call him out or anything dreadful?'

'No. I managed to convince him that I intended to give him money, not demand it, and we ended up having a very civilised dinner at his club. He's not the scoundrel I thought him to be. Or perhaps I should say that he isn't now. He seems to be genuinely fond of his little heiress and he doesn't want to hurt her, at least as much as he doesn't want her father finding out about his sins. He's more than grateful about the return of the money and he accepts that it was not your doing.' He looked at her quizzically. 'What is it?'

'Men are so strange. You were breathing fire and brimstone, you were ready to call him out just for insulting me in the park and now there you are dining with him.'

Grant shrugged. 'He gave us Anna, didn't he?'

'Yes, so he did. And Madeleine gave us Charlie.'

He pulled her close again and they sat in silence, watching the children as the winter daylight ebbed into darkness and the candlelight glowed off holly berries and swags of evergreens and the fire burned bright in the grate.

Kate had thought of the same night one year before as she'd carried Anna up to her cot and Grant and Charlie went to change for the grown-up dinner they had promised the boy so that he could make the toast to his great-grandfather's memory. A year ago she had been cold, desperate and in pain with no hope for the future, only a desperate will to make it through somehow.

*I wonder if I can be any happier than this?* she thought, watching Grant bend to kiss Anna goodnight. *Perhaps, when I tell Grant the final secret I am keeping.*

Christmas morning dawned bright and, to Charlie's huge delight, snowy. 'May we make a snowman?' he asked at breakfast. 'There's all that snow in the back garden. Or...' His eyes grew wide. 'The park! We could build dozens of snowmen, an army of snowmen!'

'This afternoon,' Grant promised. 'Presents first. Anna's birthday, then the staff, then our Christmas presents.'

Anna was predictably more enchanted by the silver paper, the flicker of candlelight and the trailing scarlet ribbons than she was by her presents, but, as Kate pointed out to Grant, he was going to get far more fun out of her presents than she was.

'I know. I want to spoil her, to make up for that first birthday, that first Christmas,' he said, smiling at the dolls, the pretty dresses, the stuffed rabbit and the little horse on wheels.

'You gave her that first Christmas,' Kate whispered in his ear and then found she had to blow her nose very inelegantly.

They lit the yule log together, played with Anna, listened to the sounds of fiddle music, singing and laughter wafting up from below stairs. It seemed the staff were having a good time getting ready for their Christmas meal. Charlie, bursting with pride, led Kate and Grant, with Anna fast asleep in Grant's arms, downstairs to deliver the family's Christmas good wishes and thanks for all their hard work during the year.

'He is growing up so fast,' Kate whispered as Cook gathered Charlie to her capacious bosom and gave him a hug that turned his ears scarlet. Then they trooped back upstairs, collecting Mr Gough as they went, and shared out Christmas presents.

*My family,* Kate thought as she watched them, the love filling her heart as softly as the snowflakes swirling down outside the window. Charlie was thrilled with a new saddle and a pair of ice skates. Grant peacocked around the room in the heavy silk robe Kate had found for him and winked at her to show he knew exactly how she imagined him wearing it, with nothing underneath. The tutor was delighted with a subscription to a circulating library and Charlie presented his parents with two pairs of handsome, and only slightly lopsided, bookends that, he confided, he had made with the assistance of the estate carpenter.

Kate was trying not to crane her neck and see if there was anything left in the litter of paper for her when Grant announced, 'We are going out for a walk.'

'We are?' Kate almost protested that it was too cold, too snowy, and that she wanted to spend as much time as possible with Anna on her first birthday. But there was something about Grant's expression that was both serious and yet happy. He had a surprise for her and she was not going to spoil it for him.

'Yes, and I have a new bonnet for you to wear.' He lifted a hatbox, white with bright red ribbons, from beside his chair.

Kate took the box and opened it. The bonnet nestled in tissue paper, a confection of white velvet with a wide brim to frame her face and a delicate pale blue gauze veil with deeper blue silk ribbons, the colour of her eyes. 'Grant, it is lovely. It is almost—' *Bridal.*

'You did not have anything pretty a year ago,' he said. 'Shall we go out now? We'll be back in time to build a small snowman, Charlie.'

Kate took Grant's arm and allowed herself to be led through the snowy streets, along narrow ways she had not known existed, up to the door of one of the little chapels of ease that had been built to serve the expanding neighbourhood north of Oxford Street. It was not one they had ever used and, when they entered, it was obvious from its plain furnishings and lack of memorials that it was not a fashionable church.

Grant had been carrying something in a straw basket, the kind that a goose would be brought home from market in, and Kate had been vastly curious to see what it held. He set it down on the porch and took out a posy. Trailing ivy, the red of holly berries, the pearl glow of mistletoe, crimson ribbons.

'It was rather a plain wedding, was it not?' Grant said and handed her the bouquet. 'One sprig of holly, if I remember rightly. I think we should do it again, don't you?'

'It made me very happy, that first ceremony,' Kate said, wondering how it was possible to want to cry, even as she smiled. 'But I would like very much to marry the man I love, all over again.'

'Shall we?' He crooked his arm for her and together they walked down the aisle. She saw a clergyman waiting in a side chapel, two chairs set before him.

'Welcome.' He came forward, shook hands, ushered them to the seats. 'I have never blessed a marriage on Christmas morning before,' he confessed. 'Weddings, yes. So many working people take advantage of the holiday. But this is rather special, is it not?'

*So special.* 'Grant, thank you,' she whispered and did not realise she was crying until he took off his gloves and gently wiped away the tears with his thumb. He was giving her the one thing their marriage lacked, the one thing she had not thought important until that moment—a romantic wedding day.

The clergyman handed them a battered prayer book to share. 'I thought we would read it through,' he said. 'And then I will do the blessing.'

They sat, following the familiar words read in the old man's steady, gentle voice. Grant slipped the ring he had given her from her finger and then, as he made his vows, slid it gently back.

'With this ring I thee wed, with my body I thee worship...'

Kate knew she was crying again, happy tears that slid down her cheeks and moistened her smiling lips and, when they rose from their knees, made their kiss salty and sweet.

She thanked the clergyman with Grant, linked her arm through his again and went out into the brilliant sunshine of the snowy noonday. 'That was the most perfect Christmas gift, thank you.' He simply squeezed her hand against his side, but she could tell from his face that he had been deeply moved by the little ceremony. 'When you came, that Christmas Eve, I thought you were my Christmas miracle. And now we have another, our love.'

'We have two very different Christmases we will never forget.' Grant's voice was husky. Neither of them spoke for a while as they crunched through the snow.

'I have a gift for you that might make this one even more memorable,' Kate confessed as they came into Berkeley Square. 'I did think I ought to wait another few weeks, just to be certain, but I can't bear to keep the secret.'

'Oh, my love.' Grant stopped dead, right outside Gunter's tea shop. 'I did wonder whether you were simply blooming because you were happy or whether there was another reason.'

'Both,' Kate said. 'I'm in love, I'm blissfully happy and I think we are going to be a family of five for next Christmas!'

\* \* \* \* \*

*This is the second story in Louise Allen's*
LORDS OF DISGRACE *quartet*
*Book One*
*HIS HOUSEKEEPER'S CHRISTMAS WISH*
*is already available*
*Look for Books Three and Four, coming soon!*

# MILLS & BOON®

## Why shop at millsandboon.co.uk?

Each year, thousands of romance readers find their perfect read at millsandboon.co.uk. That's because we're passionate about bringing you the very best romantic fiction. Here are some of the advantages of shopping at www.millsandboon.co.uk:

* **Get new books first**—you'll be able to buy your favourite books one month before they hit the shops

* **Get exclusive discounts**—you'll also be able to buy our specially created monthly collections, with up to 50% off the RRP

* **Find your favourite authors**—latest news, interviews and new releases for all your favourite authors and series on our website, plus ideas for what to try next

* **Join in**—once you've bought your favourite books, don't forget to register with us to rate, review and join in the discussions

Visit **www.millsandboon.co.uk**
for all this and more today!